THE WINDEMERE AFFAIR

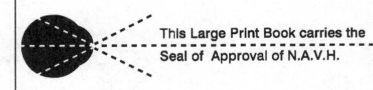

THE WINDEMERE AFFAIR

JUDITH ROLFS

THORNDIKE PRESS
A part of Gale, a Cengage Company

Farmington Hills, Mich • San Francisco • New York • Waterville, Maine
Meriden, Conn • Mason, Ohio • Chicago

LIBRARY OF CONGRESS CIP DATA ON FILE.
CATALOGUING IN PUBLICATION FOR THIS BOOK
IS AVAILABLE FROM THE LIBRARY OF CONGRESS

ISBN-13: 978-1-4328-6225-1 (hardcover)

Published in 2019 by arrangement with Pelican Ventures, LLC

Printed in the United States of America
1 2 3 4 5 6 7 23 22 21 20 19

To my sister Joy and my brother Jim —
love you
forever.

PROLOGUE

Morning mist scented with pine and wet grass coated Albert Windemere's golf cart. He tightened his grip on the wheel as he passed the green on Pine Willow Course. The pin placement on the back edge would make for a tricky putt to be sure. Funny, the things you notice at a time like this.

He inhaled deep and slow, feeling the warmth of the orange-gold sun escaping the horizon. Huge oaks, spectators to twenty seasons of golfers, stretched their shadows across the fairway. Albert patted his pocket, congratulating himself on his precise preparation.

The luminous dial of his watch read 5:40 AM. He had at least twenty minutes before the course swung into motion. By then everything would be over. Now that it was time, a sense of joy slid over him. He pressed his foot to the pedal for the cart's uphill climb and then turned off the paved path to enter the woods behind the fifth green. A squirrel, disturbed on its breakfast quest, chittered noisily and darted away.

The gunshot at five fifty, silent and precise, didn't even disturb the sparrows' morning song.

1

Most days I love being psychotherapist Dr. Jennifer Trevor, wife to my husband, Nick, who makes me laugh almost daily, and mother to three spirited and delightful children. Yes, I'm totally prejudiced.

I was forced out of my job at the Fullness of Life Center over the Directive Ninety-Nine horror. I feared I'd never work again, but the publicity actually improved my reputation instead of destroying it. Go figure. Five months later, I opened my private practice in downtown Lake Geneva, the perky resort city halfway between Milwaukee and Chicago, and I've not lacked for clients since.

Counseling individuals is like hunting, searching for what's out of sync in their lives and guiding them along a path of change. Some resist progress, which can be frustrating, but I've never had a client I didn't find fascinating.

9

Lately, however, listening to the chaos of dysfunctional lives has been draining my own serenity. By bedtime I'm a shriveled balloon and even seven hours of sleep isn't enough to inflate me again.

Last night I awoke from a 2:00 AM nightmare with clenched fists and admitted I needed a vacation. Plus, the "togetherness tank" with my equally busy lawyer husband needed a refill.

Europeans take a six-week summer holiday. Surely, I could manage seven days in August with my husband to keep sweet peace in my psyche. I teach clients the value of playtime. Now I'd model it.

Fortunately, Nick was between cases at his legal firm and could disappear with me for a week.

Our teens, Collin and Tara; and our eight-year-old, Jenny, squealed with joy when we proposed an extended visit without us to Nick's parents in Arizona. So much for missing mama! I was OK with their excitement because vacation memories with sixty-something grandparents riding horses and hiking mountain paths would be priceless.

I'd have preferred a week in Hawaii or Mexico, but it wasn't in the budget. Plus, I feared Nick and I would succumb to our usual travel mania, which has happened more times than I care to recount. I'm a sightseeing addict. Out west with the children last summer, we didn't miss a single tourist attraction and returned home more exhausted than we'd been on our day of departure.

The arrangements fell into place with amazing speed. God is in this, I reassured myself.

Nick did a quick online search and read me the description of Pine Willow Resort in Wisconsin Dells: "A secluded four-hundred-acre retreat, twenty-seven-hole championship golf course, tennis, two pools, stables, and a four-star restaurant."

I clapped my hands. "Best of all it's only two-and-a-half hours away. Why waste a day on each end of our week in planes and airports when we can ride straight to our destination in our temperature-controlled box on wheels?"

Nick grinned. "Not to mention arriving on the golf course before noon." Four days later, Nick drove the children to Mitchell Airport in Milwaukee while I took our sad-eyed chocolate lab to the vet and returned home to pack.

I braced myself for Nick's usual moans while he loaded clothes, snacks, and sports equipment into the car. He didn't disappoint me.

"All this for a short trip? We're not moving, you know."

I squeezed the muscle in his forearm. "Packing light has never been my forte. Besides I'm keeping your heart healthy with weightlifting."

"Or setting off the big one prematurely."

"Hey, the golf clubs and tennis rackets are essential."

He grimaced and finished loading.

I set my reading book bag on the floor of the passenger seat next to my purse and hopped in.

Nick prayed as we pulled out. "God send angels to guard our children and home during our absence."

"Amen." I rested my hand on his shoulder. "Pine Willow here we come. A week of bliss and rest."

2

The first few days of our getaway were delightful. Our next-to-last afternoon, I noticed a sudden buzz of whispering among the restaurant staff.

I turned to see our sweet, talkative waitress who wore a large gold "LINDA" pin above her heart, nose-to-nose in animated conversation with another server whose black ponytail bobbed from side to side as she repeated, "No way."

I leaned closer, straining my ears, and overheard the words *gun* and *man's been shot.*

Noticing my stare, Linda picked up a coffeepot from the warming stand and headed toward me. I waited all of two seconds to quiz her.

She spewed her commentary like a news report in fragments. "Yep, you heard right. Man's been found dead on Pine Willow Golf Course. Shot." She paused to take a breath. "In the woods behind the fifth hole. Police shut down nine holes for now. Somebody named Al Wind, Windman, no Windemere. That's it."

I pressed my hand across my mouth.

"Yeah, ain't it awful?" Linda lowered her voice, eyes bulging. "He and his wife rented a villa at the resort . . . maybe I shouldn't be telling you this. Sure don't want people getting scared and leaving." She looked around.

The manager was nowhere in sight.

"Something else."

"What?" Nick and I asked in unison.

"Rumor is the bullet was self-whatchamacallit." Linda turned up her nose.

"Self-inflicted?"

"Yeah, that's it. No one heard the shot. Musta been a silencer on the gun. I seen these on TV shows a lot." She looked toward the kitchen. "Excuse me. I got an order up."

Nick reached for my hand "Honey, you're white. Are you OK?"

"This is awful."

"You knew him?"

I took a sip of water to stem sudden nausea and drew a deep breath. "I . . . I can't say."

"OK. You don't have to. It's written on your face. I assume he was a client, or you'd tell. I'm so sorry." Nick covered my hand with his.

My man reads me well.

"Actually," Nick continued, "I've heard of Albert Windemere by name and reputation. We were never formally introduced."

Linda returned a few minutes later to collect our plates. Before she could whip off I asked, "Are you certain you heard Mr. Windemere shot himself?"

"I think so. Did himself in. Not as horrid as a murder at least. But dead is dead. That's what counts."

I sat speechless, watching Linda sweep up our plates and stack them on her left arm. She turned and race-walked to the kitchen.

I met Nick's gaze. "You bet how someone dies matters. Guilt from suicide can torment family and friends. I've worked with enough clients through the painful self-examination that follows. They assume somehow they had the power to stop the event but failed."

Nick ran his palm across his forehead. "How sad to believe you have nothing to live for. I can only imagine what total despair he experienced to kill himself."

"I refuse to believe it. Al was thrilled with

15

his life," I whispered to Nick. "These rumors make me angry. He wouldn't kill himself. Never."

Nick squeezed my hand before pouring more cream in his coffee. "Sweetheart, nobody can be sure about suicide."

I flinched and set my cup down with a clatter. "Subtle life stressors that a psycho-therapist observe are often a signal. With Al it was quite the opposite. He radiated emotional and spiritual health."

"If you're so sure he wouldn't kill himself, who'd want him dead?"

I shrugged. "It's true he had some problems. Privacy issues prevent me from discussing them. His life wasn't perfect by a stretch, but with his new attitude he could cope with ups and downs. Anxiety rose in my voice, and I bit my lip. "He had plenty of enemies."

"Windemere co-owned American Realty, a huge firm in the industry." Nick stroked his chin. "With a reputation for being on the shaky side ethically. I've had two clients suffer major losses from bad investments. Rumor is he was an unsavory character, a bit on the wild side."

Linda appeared with our bill, cutting off my reply. "No hurry, I'll take this when you're ready." She refilled our waters and trotted off to dispense warm-ups and gossip to adjoining tables.

I opened my makeup bag and applied gloss to my dry lips, debating my next words. I'd never breach confidentiality. Common knowledge I could reveal. "Al was rebuilding his reputation."

"Good for him." Nick raised his eyebrows. "Was he married?"

No harm saying, it would be in the newspaper obit. "His wife, Rose, is a sweetheart. Before her health problem, she used to do amateur theater and some playwriting — a talented gal."

Nick glanced at his watch. "We tee off in less than an hour even if it is only going to be nine holes. You're obviously upset. Would you prefer I cancel?"

I forced a smile. "Al's death is disturbing for sure, but there's nothing I can do now. This is still our vacation after all. I'll catch up with you on the practice range in half an hour. I left my cell phone in our room and want to check messages." I grimaced. "I need assurance the rest of our world is intact."

Nick stood and gave me a hug. "OK, meet me on the putting green."

I strolled back to our room past burgeoning flowerbeds, unable to shake the image of a bullet exploding in Al's body. I'd spoken to him by phone only a week ago. Now I'd never hear his voice again on earth. A tear slid down my cheek. I prayed silently for the soul of this dear man and paused to stroke the petal of a sunflower.

How brief, beautiful, and fragile life is.

3

The Pine Willow lobby resembled an indoor forest. A stone-rimmed pool collected water from a continuous, fifteen-foot waterfall. Lacy ferns, ivy, and other greenery accented plump beige sofas.

I whisked past the two clerks chatting at the empty reception counter. A strong scent of chlorine wafted from the indoor swimming pool and made me wince. No shiny silver elevator for me. I took the stairs to the third floor to release my pent-up energy.

Sticking my key card in the slot, I waited impatiently for the green flash to enter. The maid had already been to our room, freshened the towels, and made the bed; but otherwise, everything was exactly as I'd left it, which seemed impossible. When someone you know dies, shouldn't the world look different?

The light blue walls held gilt-framed pictures of sailboats on peaceful seas. Peace?

19

Mine had evaporated. The yellow and white floral bedspreads brightened my spirit a bit. Beauty, order, and harmony do this for me.

I grabbed my phone from the charger and pressed messages. A solid knock sounded on the door, followed by the word "Police."

My blood pressure raced as I opened to a man holding a police ID in his outstretched hand.

"Dr. Jennifer Trevor? Inspector Jarston." Elegantly, he drew out each syllable of his name.

My heart thumped. Were our children OK?

"I've come to question you regarding a shooting at the resort. I understand you knew a Mr. Windemere?"

I pressed my back against the wall for support. "Yes, I do, did. My husband and I are here for a getaway. We just heard. How horrible!" I jabbered, struggling to grasp why he'd want to talk to me.

"May I come in? I have a few questions."

I took a deep breath and opened the door wider. I wasn't accustomed to entertaining a male guest alone in my hotel room, but who says no to a badge?

"I understand you were Mr. Windemere's counselor."

"How did you know — ?"

"From my conversation with Mr. Windemere's wife . . . oh you meant know that you're here?" Inspector Jarston answered my unfinished question as he strode past me. "When I called your office, your assistant, I believe Ellen was her name, informed me."

I gulped. Ellen would only have revealed my whereabouts if Jarston used his police credentials. Poor thing. She'd be wild with concern and curiosity. I made a mental note to call her later.

"I'm here to discuss Mr. Windemere's emotional state to help clarify if his death was suicide or murder. This will take a few minutes. Mind if I sit?" Jarston lowered himself onto the stuffed armchair near the sliding door leading to the balcony without awaiting my answer.

I sputtered, "Will you excuse me? I'll be right back." I whipped into the washroom, closed the door and splashed cool water on my face. This couldn't be happening. Ever since my first speeding ticket I'd been intimidated by anyone in law enforcement. I patted my face dry, ordered my legs to stop shaking, and willed my nerves to settle.

When I returned, Jarston's head was bent over his notepad. He reminded me of my junior year high school English teacher. A navy linen blazer covered broad shoulders atop a stocky frame. Perhaps a football player at one time? A thick, brown crew cut topped his serious face. I guessed his age at around sixty.

Keeping as much distance as possible, I perched on the edge of the king-size bed about ten feet away.

Jarston cleared his throat. "You said you knew about Mr. Windemere? How?"

I summarized the waitress' report. "I don't understand why there's confusion about the cause of death?"

Inspector Jarston straightened. "A scrap of paper was in Windemere's pocket with the words, '. . . can't go on like this' signed Al Windemere. We'll authenticate the signature on the note. Mr. Windemere's wife believes it to be her husband's writing but refuses to believe he'd kill himself. In situations like this, denial is not uncommon."

A shiver crawled up my spine. Inspector Jarston was impersonally discussing the death of a man I cared about. "For the record, we initially investigate every apparent suicide as a homicide."

"Oh." I exhaled the sound softly. I had no idea.

"Mind you, I'm not saying Al Windemere was murdered. The weapon was a forty caliber Glock registered to him. His finger-prints are the only ones on it. Murderers don't normally leave weapons behind; suicide victims do."

"But to go out on a golf course to kill yourself? That doesn't make sense."

Jarston raised his shoulders. "Why not? This protects his wife from the burden of finding his bloody body. You may imagine it's not a pretty sight."

"Were there other clues, footprints, what-ever?"

His stare bored into me. "Inquisitive, aren't you? Shall I chalk up your questions to too much TV–CSI? I don't mind oblig-ing with an answer. No prints could be traced in the crushed leaves around the trees where his corpse was found. However, the body was in an unusual position for a suicide. A silencer on the handgun elimi-nated sound. I will admit this seem curious. Why bother deadening the sound if com-mitting suicide?"

I blinked at the picture of the horrific scene forming in my mind. Every inch of me didn't want to imagine it, but I couldn't stop. I focused on the wall behind Jarston where a framed picture depicted a farmyard with two hefty cows grazing. Oh, for the sweet simplicity of a quiet day in the country.

"I can see it's puzzling. How did he get on the course that early?" My detective instincts went into full gear, and I lost my discomfort in his presence. "I mean, if he was shot, where had the murderer come from? The pro shop probably wasn't open yet."

"Rental of private homes bordering the course often includes golf carts. Jarston's voice droned on. "Anyone entering the course before dawn probably wouldn't have been observed at the pro shop until 6:00 AM when staff arrived.

"So, no witnesses?"

He shook his head.

"Who reported the body?" Asking questions would be better than answering his. To my surprise he humored me.

"A golfer hunting for a ball he hit over the green. He entered the woods, came upon the scene, and reported it at 7:40 AM. Using the number on the golf cart, it was traced back to the Windemere rental villa he and his wife occupied. She was still in bed when we notified her. The unit backed up to hole three on the course. You seem overtly interested in these details? Why?"

"Because suicide seems implausible based

on our counseling history."

"By the way, did you, by any chance, see Mr. Windemere at the resort before his death?"

"I had no idea he was here."

Jarston made a note on his pad.

I gulped, suddenly realizing why Jarston readily answered my questions. He was sizing me up as a suspect, studying me.

"Enough. Now your turn. "Jarston pulled a folded paper from the inside pocket of his jacket and extended it to me. "Ms. Windemere signed this release. You may speak freely to me about their counseling."

I reached for the form.

"According to Rose, she attended two sessions for joint marriage counseling. You also had multiple individual appointments with her husband. She's certain his death was homicide not suicide, and the poor woman is frantic she'll be the next victim. Your immediate cooperation is essential."

"Of course. Where's Rose now?"

"Under police protection at her villa where the family was supposed to celebrate her birthday. Some present sadly." He whipped out a handkerchief and mopped his forehead.

Client-counselor ethics flashed through my brain. Rose may have signed a release form, but Albert Windemere hadn't. I quickly reviewed client confidentiality boundaries. Information could be revealed in cases of obvious danger to self or others. Rose could be the next victim, she was at risk, because no way did Albert Windemere commit suicide. I had to do all I could to protect her.

My phone beeped. I jumped. Nick would be wondering where I was. I texted him that I'd skip hitting practice balls and meet him on the tee.

"Let's speed this along." Inspector Jarston's tone, quiet but firm, grated on my nerves. "Allow me to make something clear, Dr. Trevor. Your client's right to privacy becomes secondary when there's a question of a life in jeopardy."

I folded the paper he'd given me and handed it back. "Legally correct. Certainly, I can be cooperative without revealing any unnecessary personal information."

"His wife said Mr. Windemere was in treatment about six months total. Is this correct?"

I took a deep breath. "Closer to eight months. I wrote up his discharge last month."

"How frequently did you see him?"

"Weekly visits the first three months then

tapered off to every other week, finally becoming monthly, supplemented with phone calls as needed."

"Isn't that a rather short period for major counseling? I thought the process went on for years." The fingers of Jarston's left hand steadily tapped the chair arm.

"Clients know in advance that my specialty is intense, short-term, solution-based therapy — usually six months is sufficient. Additional sessions can be added if needed."

Jarston's phone dinged. He whipped it from the inside pocket of his suit coat, read the message, wrote a response, and tucked it away.

His stoic face reminded me of a talking robot. I pegged him as an introverted, melancholic personality with minimal social skills. Given an intricate problem to solve, I'd expect he'd be content alone indefinitely. The inspector settled back in his chair, obviously staying longer than the few minutes he'd requested.

"Dr. Trevor, please consider carefully before you answer. I'd like your professional opinion regarding Mr. Windemere's emotional state."

The air in the room seemed to still, and I rubbed my hands together. Finally, the crux of our conversation. I searched my brain for the best words. I had to say this right.

"Shall I repeat the question?" Jarston asked.

"No, Inspector. Please understand I'm still dealing with shock over this horror. Counselors often develop emotional concern for clients. I know I do, but I'll do my best to be analytical. I've mentally reviewed our sessions and particularly his demeanor. My answer is no. Al Windemere was not suicidal. He was very engaged and hopeful about his future at this point."

Jarston jotted a note on his pad. "What was his presenting problem during your initial counseling session?"

I closed my eyes to help me think. "When he first came to see me, Al was mildly depressed — which is why he made the appointment."

Jarston sat up straighter and bristled visibly. "Yet you claim he wasn't suicidal? Interesting. Then the cause of this mild depression was?"

"Painful relationships. Areas of earlier dysfunction and immoral behavior in his personal and professional life created a lingering negative impact on his present. He experienced what we commonly called guilt. I drew up a treatment plan requiring individual sessions for him and joint work with his wife Rose on these issues. From the start, Al threw himself into the counseling process."

"Please be more specific."

"Mr. Windemere's wife was diagnosed with cancer over a year ago. She's in remission now, but her illness had distressed him greatly. It forced him to re-examine repeated, unfaithful behavior toward her as well as his own attitude toward death."

"Typical reaction I suppose when a family member develops a potentially terminal disease?"

How to answer? My arms formed a triangle, elbows digging into my sides. If only I'd had time to process my thoughts for this interrogation. "Sometimes, but not always. Mr. Windemere struggled because during most of their marriage he was extremely self-focused, money-driven, and neglectful of his wife and children."

I turned my hands over in my lap. I had to honor who this amazing man had become. "I was impressed by his sincere repentance and determination to make it up to Rose. I wish all my clients were as motivated. He made a rapid turn-around."

"Maybe you're a miracle-worker?"

"By no means. He'd recently become a Christian — a huge factor in his changed priorities. He'd also begun making restitution in his professional relationships. Integrity suddenly became very important to him."

The Inspector scribbled a note. "You mentioned his relationship with his children?"

"Yes. Al's former workaholic tendencies had interfered with his fathering. In counseling we worked on strategies to make amends for years of neglect."

"Was this successful?"

"Unfortunately, his teenage son, Ken, left home ten years ago at age seventeen, joined a cult and disappeared. Al tried unsuccessfully to locate him. His grown daughter, Crystal, lives nearby but remains alienated. However, in terms of making business amends, Al made progress, which pleased him tremendously. I urged him to be patient. We formulated long-term goals." I smiled recalling his enthusiasm. "Mr. Windemere was an ideal client to work with."

"If this dysfunctional family dynamic was the primary cause for Mr. Windemere's depression, wouldn't it be natural for him to remain discouraged by his failure to restore connection with his son and daughter?"

The inspector impressed me. He used

counseling jargon well, perhaps an armchair psychologist or a former therapist.

"Well-put, but the answer is no because Albert had come to view life in a healthy perspective. I'm not sure you'll understand, but basically, he underwent a spiritual change through connection with Christ. One comes to understand how to deal with discouragement when trusting God to help right past wrongs."

Jarston stared as if I'd just spoken Greek. "Moving on. Any other family problems?"

"I recall that his earlier intense antagonism toward his brother, Aaron, had changed to genuine concern on Al's part. I'm not sure what Aaron's response was."

"Do you know if Aaron was also at the resort for Rose's birthday celebration?"

"Sorry, you'll have to ask Rose."

Jarston stroked his chin. "Back to his initial counseling visit. Describe the appointment in detail please."

I stared at the fleur-de-lis wallpaper and began "He strode into my office boldly carrying a black briefcase with gold initials. Some people will pay $500 for thick leather to carry their files. I wondered why he'd bothered to bring it, but then I understood his work went with him everywhere. It had become his identity."

"Isn't this rather common among highly successful men?"

"Definitely."

"Go on."

"He shook my hand firmly. Not limp-fish style like men who don't have frequent contact with professional women."

Jarston's eyes riveted on mine, feeding my nervousness. I cleared my throat. "Some men grow more handsome with age. Al's six-foot height made him seem invincible, like a stately Robert E. Lee without the beard. His thick, gray hair was carefully combed and his attire was impeccable down to his polished black wingtips."

"Nicely groomed, yet depressed? Isn't this unusual?"

"His wasn't clinical, but situational. Clinically depressed people let their appearance go and aren't goal-oriented like Al." I shifted on my chair. "He was very warm and likable with a nice blend of humor and forthrightness. Not to say he wasn't uncomfortable initially. Most clients are. His first words were something like, 'I've never been to a shrink before. Excuse the terminology if that's offensive.' "

My gaze shifted to the weave of the hotel carpet as I considered what else was appropriate to share. My mind was back in my office with Al. "I answered, 'I don't shrink brains, but I can help if you're willing to be open and honest.' Tension stretched like a net around him when he talked about his past lifestyle. I saw the stress in his hands pressed together tightly." I glanced down. Like mine were now, clasped palm against palm.

Relax Jennifer.

"Stressed? Yet not suicidal?"

Sensing Jarston leading me toward his theory, I picked my next words with great care. "Al expressed anger and frustration. Mild, not acute, depression."

Jarston jerked his head in denial. "How can you tell the difference?"

"Sleep patterns for one. He reported falling asleep fine but waking during the night and being up for a couple of hours. I saw no need for an anti-depressant — I believed we could work through his issues with cognitive therapy, and we did."

"I see." Jarston took more notes as he listened.

Did he? "Al was dealing with a healthy kind of self-disgust, the kind that motivated change. As a new Christian, he'd seen for the first time the emptiness of life driven by selfish, materialistic motives. We discussed physical, emotional, and spiritual nurturing, as I do with each client. He needed to balance his life in each area." I swished the back of my hand across my eyes to wipe away the sudden wetness. He'd made such a valiant effort.

Jarston raised the horizontal bushes above his eyes. "Rose Windemere claims he had enemies with strong motives for murder. Did he mention any during the course of counseling?"

I stiffened. "I know he'd given some clients self-serving advice bordering on illegal and was making amends."

Jarston leaned forward. "Why did you stop counseling if Albert Windemere still had this restitution work to do?"

"I knew he was capable of completing the process on his own."

Jarston sighed. "Any contact since your formal sessions ended?"

"A bit and always by phone. The first time he asked me to give him a reading list of inspirational books."

"Did you?"

"Yes. St. Augustine's Confessions, some of Chesterton and C.S. Lewis. Al was fascinated by the Christian faith. He also consulted me about some generous contributions he was considering to several charities. He wanted my opinion about their

34

integrity."

The inspector's hand shot up in a stop gesture. "I'm not interested in that. You mentioned other calls?"

"He wanted me to see his daughter for counseling. Unfortunately, he had trouble convincing her to come. He made several appointments for family members, which were either cancelled by them or no-shows. I also tried to put together a family group therapy session without success."

"For what issues?"

"I can't answer without violating their privacy." I smiled hoping to soften my refusal.

Jarston harrumphed. "That's all." He glared at me. "For now." He stood.

I grimaced at the last two words but stood also like he'd pulled my string.

"Please review your records and notify me if anything else might have bearing on our investigation. When will you be back in your office?"

"Monday," I stammered. "I hope I've persuaded you against the possibility of suicide?"

"A lot can change in a man's life in a day, let alone a month. Whatever the truth is, I'll find it."

Inspector Jarston exited without another

word. No "thank you," no "good-bye." Yet an aura of competence. I hoped and prayed I'd communicated in a way respectful of the dignity of the new Albert Windemere.

I checked my watch. If I hurried, I could still make our tee time. I patted my hair, grabbed my golf shoes and hurried to the clubhouse.

Our vacation had lost its aura of delight. How can the death of a vibrant man be anything but sad? Yet, Albert Windemere was truly in a better place. I could be confident and joyful about that. I prayed that his killer would be found before killing again.

At this moment, my time with my husband seemed even more sacred.

4

I approached the practice green where Nick was bending over a dimpled white ball, ready to stroke a ten-footer. In his purple logoed shirt and gray pants skimming Dexter golf shoes he looked the part of a professional golfer, and much younger than his forty-three years.

"Hi, handsome, haven't I seen you on the Golf Channel?"

"I wish. If only I struck the ball like a pro."

I jabbed his shoulder. "Some day."

"All checked in. Hey I like your wild Annie look today."

"Thanks." Ever since I got a semi-curly perm, my hair required little effort. The style of my hair is not sophisticated or elegant, which I admire but will never be.

Nick is my imagined version of Rhett Butler from *Gone with the Wind.* His incessant teasing can be annoying, but other than his wisecracks, and a few extra pounds around his middle, he's my definition of perfect.

I look younger than my age, too, which is a miracle of genetics with the high-stress schedule I keep. Six days in the sun had deepened both our tans.

Nick lined up his next putt, speaking without looking up. "I was starting to wonder if you'd changed your mind."

"Of course not."

Nick ambled over and dug his putter into his golf bag behind the cart. "I'll give you two strokes a hole."

"Three!" I pulled on my golf glove and joined him on the golf cart. It whined and we were off.

"How are the kids? You talked a long time."

"I didn't call them yet. I had a visit from the law."

Nick slowed the cart and stared at me. "What's up?"

"A police investigator, Inspector Jarston, questioned me about Al Windemere."

Nick widened his eyes. "He found out about your connection already?"

"Al's wife is still here. She told him about our counseling relationship. I tried to persuade Jarston that Al's committing suicide was out of the question. I'm not sure

I succeeded."

Nick shot me a quick, piercing look. "Jen, I share your sympathy for the Windemere family, but let the police draw their own conclusions."

I shook my head. "I'm sure the poor man was murdered."

We reached the first tee, and Nick hopped out and grabbed his driver. "You can't know for sure, although rumor is he had a playboy lifestyle. He could have any number of disgruntled husbands upset with him." Nick whipped the club back and forth through the plush grass waiting for the foursome ahead to clear the fairway. "Nine times out of ten a murderer knows his victim and has a grievance against him. Sad to say your client may have had a ton of enemies."

I held my club parallel to the ground for a long stretch and changed the subject. "To think I rushed here. What's holding up those golfers in front of us?"

"It's slow because nine holes were closed earlier for the investigation. Sweetheart, you have the patience of a flea."

"Less. Waiting is not my strong point." My neck muscles tightened. "Here we are in the midst of a sunny eighty-degree day discussing murder. Rose adored her husband. I hope she's all right. What a shock.

Maybe I should contact her . . ."

"Whoa! It's great you care, but this isn't your personal crisis. Seems to lead to burnout and isn't that why we're here?" Nick stuck his golf ball inside the ball washer and pumped the handle vigorously.

I caught my breath to silence a defensive retort — my normal mode.

Nick strode to the tee box. You can't help every person."

I grimaced. "You're one to lecture — always involved in a pro bono case. If I can comfort Rose in any way, I should. OK?"

"If God's leading go for it."

Nick placed a Pinnacle golf ball on a tee and cranked a drive 250 yards, splitting the middle of the fairway.

Pungent marigolds and purple pansies in various shades filled the railroad tie flower boxes around the tee and reminded me that life, this moment, was real and sweet, even if we were standing on the property where Al had met his death. "Until we die, Nick, I want to cram all the kindness, generosity, and fun I can into every day."

"Atta girl. Now hit the ball."

I drove my ball a hundred and forty yards to the right edge of the woods.

"Nice."

I relished the sound of approval in his

voice. An adult child of an alcoholic thrives on praise. "If this is what we have to look forward to in retirement, I'm going to love it." I snuggled closer to Nick on the cart.

"Yeah, for about two weeks." He laughed. "I know you, Ms. Go-and-Do."

The smell of leaves and freshly cut grass mingled as we sped down the lush fairway. My brain whirred over Al's tragedy.

What could I do to help his widow?

5

I unlocked our door and basked in the coolness of our room while Nick tested out a new putter at the pro shop. The bed looked inviting. I drew the thick blue curtains shut and then flopped atop the comforter in my clothes and shoes. The air conditioner fan made the humming white noise I love. I stretched my legs and arms catlike, curled up on my side, and reached for the paperback on the bedside table.

Reading usually helped me nod off. The image of Rose, Al Windemere's sweet wife, planted itself in my mind. I sat up, reached for the phone, and punched zero.

"Front desk," the clerk enunciated the words.

"May I have the phone number of the Windemere villa, please?"

The tone switched to a lower pitch. "For security reasons, we're not allowed to give out this information, ma'am." I thanked her and set down the phone with a *thump.*

I hunted through the check-in packet beside the TV and found a map with the villa layout. "Where are you, Rose?" I spoke aloud, a carryover from years of talking to babies and toddlers.

Two of our three babies were big now — Collin, fourteen; Tara, twelve; and six-year-old Jenny. I missed them all more than I'd expected. Nick and I had never vacationed longer than a weekend without our children since Jenny's birth.

I pictured strong-willed Tara giving her grandparents orders. She delighted in being bossy in my absence. Nick's Dad wouldn't let her get away with much. Collin, easygoing like his papa, wouldn't object. Jenny lived in a world of perpetual joy. The kids were fine. Now to focus on poor Rose.

Only twenty villas on the property. Surely, I could find Rose — her police protection should be obvious.

Decision made, I undressed and whipped into the shower. The warm steam reactivated my energy. I patted myself dry with a thick towel then slipped on a T-shirt and a skirt of miracle rayon that could be crunched into a ball and still look great. I strapped on two flimsy sandals advertised as Shoosies. I'd purchased them for a ridiculously low price while resale shopping.

Ten minutes later, I tightened my grip on the wheel of my Chrysler minivan, as I waited for the lady in the car ahead of me to decide whether to turn toward the pool or the recreation building. The inner voice I've come to recognize as the Holy Spirit coached. *Say a prayer for drivers who annoy you. You may be the only one ever praying for them. Yes, Lord.*

Past the golf course and tennis courts, I followed a winding road with ten MPH posted every fifteen yards. Who would want to speed past this gorgeous scenery anyway?

Squirrel and bird feeders dotted the landscape, reminding me of the continual feast Nick provides for the wildlife in our yard. As soon as I found Rose, I'd text him in case he returned before me.

Should I have run off? I'd be gone only an hour in place of taking a nap. Nick knows I want to track down Rose. I swear he often anticipates my plans before I know them.

This murder had jolted my equilibrium. Who would want to kill Al? Someone connected to his family, perhaps a person comforting Rose even now?

I hit my brake in time to avoid bumping a white SUV backing out of a driveway. The urge to blast my horn surged into my brain.

The anger subsided as quickly as it came. Where was the driver going in such a hurry?

On the map, the villa area hadn't looked far, but the winding roads and low speed lengthened the drive. Finally, I spotted a rustic cedar sign declaring "The Woods." I drove past streets with woodsy names: Windwood, Pepperwood, Birchwood. The villas, two-unit buildings constructed to resemble log cabins in the North Woods, were irregularly spaced, perhaps to save as many trees as possible.

Police protection shouldn't be hard to spot unless they used an unmarked car. I turned down Oakwood. A squad was parked outside Building 720.

Standing on the villa's covered porch, a model-thin, attractive woman engaged in animated conversation with a police officer. Blonde spiral curls fell on her shoulders. I recognized her as Windemere's daughter, Crystal, from a wallet picture he'd shown me.

I parked and walked up. The chitchat stopped cold.

The policeman had his back toward me. "Excuse me for interrupting. I'm Dr. Jennifer Trevor." I held out my hand. "You must be Crystal. Please accept my deep sympathy over your father's death."

Crystal glared at me. Icy green eyes beneath thin arched brows. She'd be beautiful except for her turned-down lips creating a sullen image.

"Trevor. I recognize the name. You're the counselor he tried to get me to see."

"Yes, you refused." Why had I reminded her? "May I see your mother briefly to express my condolences? Is she inside?"

The policeman stepped forward asking to see my identification. My hands tensed. I dug in my purse, withdrew two business cards, handed one to him and the other to Crystal.

Crystal handed it back and apparently had a change of attitude toward me. "We'll be leaving shortly. Our chauffeur's an hour away. In the meantime, your visit might do Mother good. Wait here."

I made small talk with the policeman about the temperature — always a safe topic — until Crystal reappeared and gestured me in. "Mother's in the living room." Turning sideways, she let me pass and returned to her conversation, better known as flirting.

I entered the darkened interior. My sandals slip-slapped across the dark wood foyer floor. A vase of gladioli rested on a pine sideboard with two red suitcases next to it.

I called out Rose's name.

"To the right," a tiny voice answered. "In the living room."

Diminutive and frail, Rose sat on a sofa the color of sand. She clutched a box of tissues. Her gray hair, long and lovely when I first met her before chemotherapy, was now a half-inch stubble. With a spiked, sporty style, she looked chic in her pink linen shorts outfit.

"Is it really you, Jennifer?"

I approached and hugged her gently. From years of working with clients who experience the loss of a spouse or a child, I know how important physical touch is during grief. If only I could do more. "My husband and I are vacationing at the resort. Inspector Jarston came to my room to question me about Al's death. I'm so sorry."

"His murder." Rose shook her head. "I hope you set him straight. Al didn't kill himself. Someone shot him." Her small manicured hands rubbed up and down her arms as if the motion could hold her together. She patted the cushion at her side. "Please sit."

"Thank you. I'll only stay a few minutes. I wanted to express my condolences and be sure you're OK. I can only imagine how hard this must be. Please know I'm available if I can help."

"Thank you. I know Al respected you."

"He was a wonderful man."

Rose's smile held sadness. "Few people thought so. In fact, many said just the opposite."

I didn't know how to respond. I said nothing.

"I'm glad you knew Al at his best, after he'd changed. These last months we were closer than ever. I have you to thank."

"Not me. Christ changed his heart. He was determined to work at being a better husband and father."

A sob escaped Rose's throat. She dabbed at her nose. "Today's my birthday. Al insisted on making a big fuss over it. We were to have a family brunch at the resort to celebrate. Now I want to permanently remove this date from the calendar forever."

"I can't tell you how sorry I am."

"Join me for tea? I was about to pour a cup. My driver won't be here for at least an hour."

I checked my watch. I didn't want to upset Nick by being gone too long, but how could I refuse a few moments with this poor woman? I was a link to her husband's emotional recovery and the last months of his life. "I'd love tea."

Rose stood unsteadily. I took her arm and guided her to the dining area. I pulled out her chair at the square, oak table where a white china teapot nested on a trivet surrounded by cups and saucers and a matching creamer and sugar bowl. Butter cookies on a small crystal dish sparkled with sugar.

"I'm shaky. Please pour, Jennifer."

"Of course." I filled our cups.

She directed my attention to two small pictures on the side table of a blond boy and girl. "I always bring photos of Crystal's children when I travel. Darrin's in first grade; Jessica's in third. My only grandchildren, as far as I know. A shadow crossed Rose's face. "Our son, Ken . . . I don't even know if he's still alive. He left home at seventeen. Ten years ago, Al must have told you." She shook her head as if to clear pain.

"Yes. He felt badly about the estrangement."

"For a long time after Ken left, Al refused to even speak his name. He finally came around and made an effort to find Ken, to no avail. I've had more than my share of heartache."

I nodded, wondering if during this difficult time Rose had the solace of faith in God. "This past year when Al found comfort in God, he shared his new life in Christ with you?"

Rose looked down. "Yes, but it's hard to trust a God who allows so much sorrow."

"I understand. Human choices can lead to great pain —"

At that moment, to my dismay, Crystal strolled in and scowled before taking a seat across from me and pouring tea for herself. "I thought you were only staying a few moments, Dr. Trevor?"

"I invited her to stay," Rose said.

The back of my neck tingled. I looked away.

"Since you counseled my father, you must have seen his suicide coming. It would have been nice to be spared this final humiliation and all the publicity. I, for one, won't miss the man. Mom, you know what a lousy father and husband he was."

Rose gasped. "Crystal! Don't say that."

"Mother, everybody knows."

"He changed." Rose defended.

"You'd like to think that, but did he?" Crystal lashed back.

Rose's gaze sought mine for confirmation.

Before I could speak, more words whipped back and forth between mother and daughter.

"Then why did he kill himself?" Crystal glared at me as if daring me to contradict her opinion of her father.

"Be still, Crystal," Rose admonished. "I can't bear to think your father would leave me by choice."

The pain in Rose's voice pierced my heart.

"Daddy dear, always melodramatic. Suicide or murder? Now we have to submit to a police investigation." Crystal twisted her legs in her chair. "Who knows and who cares how he died. He's dead — finally." Her last words slurred. She must have drunk something other than tea before.

I've witnessed intense emotion but never heard a daughter speak with such hatred of her father. Not for a second did I believe she didn't care about her dad. Her emotions were way too raw for a disinterested daughter.

I took another sip of tea and searched my mind for words to placate her, finding none.

Rose ignored Crystal and turned toward me. "You know Al became a Christian almost a year ago, after my cancer diagnosis. God became more than just a word to him. He prayed for me every day through my treatment. Probably why it was successful . . ."

"The driver will be here any minute. Drink your tea," Crystal interrupted.

Rose obediently lifted her cup.

"Prayer is powerful to be sure," I said.

"Al's relationship with God had become hugely important to him." Rose gazed expectantly at me. "He couldn't have committed suicide, could he? That would be against his faith." Her voice trembled but she went on. "He'd made arrangements for us to do the things we'd always dreamed of. We were planning a trip around the world." She was crying now. "If he left me by his own hand, I couldn't bear it . . . ."

"Mom, I can't stand it when you cry."

"Where did I leave my tissue?" Rose fumbled through her pockets, finding nothing.

I slipped into the living room, grabbed a box, and set it on the table in front of Rose.

I couldn't believe what I was seeing. How sad. Crystal, selfish daughter, life-is-all-about-me, said nothing to soothe Rose.

I patted Rose's arm. "Being a Christian doesn't prevent someone from committing suicide in a moment of weakness or chemical imbalance, but in Al's case I don't believe he did."

Rose's eyes clouded with tears again. "I know he didn't, no matter what anyone says." She drew in a deep breath. "It could have been one of any number of people. Al didn't always endear himself to others, but I understood his ways."

Crystal patted her lips with a napkin. "Except remember he left a suicide note."

" 'Can't go on like this' it said! What kind of message is that? A few words on a torn piece of paper. I'm fearful the police would rather close the case than complete a thorough investigation." Rose turned pleading eyes on me. "You know small town police budgets are limited. Al was murdered, plain and simple." Her voice took on energy.

"Mother, give up your denial."

Why was Crystal so adamant about her father's death being suicide? To feed her hate?

I knew she wanted me gone. Instead I asked, "Rose, was Al in some kind of trouble? Can you think of any acquaintance or business associate with a motive to kill him?"

"Quite a few." Rose sighed. Suddenly her eyes brightened. "Will you do me a favor? Contact Al's executive assistant, Angela Thursted. She'd know if someone from work had a motive. I'd ask her myself, only she and I aren't on the best of terms. Angela used to cover for Al's err . . . previous indiscretions."

"My father's affairs." Crystal spit out the word and glared at me with eyes hard as concrete. "Mother, what's the point?"

The chill in Crystal's voice when she said "Father" made me wince. Why had she chosen now to bring up this painful subject of infidelity to Rose?

Rose ignored her daughter and dabbed at her eyes. "You see why Crystal can't help me."

Crystal stood and stomped her foot like a little child. "Mom, I know it's hard for you to believe Father would take his life, but in light of his past behavior, suicide is no shock. The police are handling the investigation. You don't need to involve Dr. Trevor. And if we need further assistance, a private investigator would be more appropriate than a counselor."

"As long as Jennifer turned up like an angel, she can make some discreet inquiries for me." Rose turned toward her. "I'm in no position, nor you, Crystal, with this attitude." Her voice trembled.

"I'm not a detective, but I'll do anything I can." I didn't want to get involved, but how could I not offer?

Rose waved her hand. "Counseling and investigating both examine people's motives, right?"

"Rose, if you like, I'll stop by Al's office

when I return and make inquiries of Angela."

Crystal appeared ready to explode. Before either could say another word the chauffeur appeared at the door. "Shall I load the bags, ma'am?"

Rose reached over and squeezed my hand. Was it my imagination or had her color improved slightly? "Jennifer, you're a dear. Bill me for your time or I won't have you do this."

Crystal opened her mouth to protest again.

Rose got to her feet. "I need to use the bathroom. Excuse me."

Crystal watched Rose leave the room. "Your assistance won't be needed," she barked at me. "Mother's simply overwrought."

"I understand, but I will respect your mother's wishes." I tried to sound gracious despite Crystal's rudeness. My legs were numb as Crystal showed me to the door. Her intense anger toward her dad saddened me.

I made a mental note to check the newspaper obit over the next few days.

A tremor went through me as I started the car. I shivered and turned down the air conditioning. If Al's murderer was a business associate would the killer attend the funeral?

6

I slid open the door to our balcony and joined Nick who was reading the newspaper. The sweet scent of hydrangea seeped from the gardens beneath.

His eyes blazed. "Where have you been?"

"I'm sorry. I meant to send a text and forgot." I bent over and kissed him. "Are you starving?" I asked.

He pulled back. Hungry and bored is never a good combination for my husband.

"I figured it out, but a message would have been nice."

"I'm sorry. I hoped I'd make it back before you returned. Let's not bicker, OK?" I filled him in on my excursion, which placated him a little.

"I wanted to swim before dinner." Nick wore his bathing suit.

"We still can. I'll be ready in a minute." I slipped into the bathroom and put on the new black and white polka dot one-piece

I'd purchased in the resort shop the day before and quickly tore off its tag. Some things are best not discussed when a man is grouchy. I draped a white eyelet cover-up over my suit.

We strolled to the steamy indoor pool enclosure with a view of the outdoors through a wall of glass. I jumped in and issued my usual water challenge, "OK, Sharkie, you're on. Catch me."

Who says only kids can have fun in the water? So what if we get occasional stares from adults who think we're crazy?

I finally got a smile out of Sharkie and grumpy disappeared.

We did several laps in the eighty-two-degree water before returning to our room to dress for dinner.

The resort's main dining room, The Willows, shimmered with candlelight from small, crystal bowls at each table.

I squeezed Nick's arm. "My type of place. Ambiance and good food."

Following the host to our table, I caught sight of Crystal. She was seated near the rear with a man whose back was toward me. I couldn't tell if it was her policeman friend out of uniform or someone else. I guessed the latter from the cut and expensive fabric of the casual clothes he wore. Evidently, she hadn't gone back with Rose.

I ordered the pecan-crusted mahi-mahi our waiter recommended and sides of wild rice and broccoli drizzled with Hollandaise sauce. Nick chose prime rib, baked potato, and vegetable medley.

"Don't expect to eat like this next week when I'm your chef again," I joked.

"I know better." Nick covered my hand with his. "Hard to believe we actually got this special time away. Except for today, it's been great," he said.

We were silent several seconds soaking in the atmosphere. "This proves it's possible Nick."

"What?"

"Having fun without the munchkins like the days BC."

"BC?"

"Before Children. How can I enjoy myself this much without them? A little remorse please. Am I a horrible parent?"

Nick squeezed my hand. "You're a great mom and wife, just not typical."

"I hope so. Every so often I pull out my imaginary measurement tool to assess how they're doing spiritually, socially, academically. I get that there's no guarantee how they'll turn out. I just want to know I did my best."

Nick sipped his water and smiled. "I miss them, but I'm savoring you now, sweetheart. We never really had much time alone. The babies came so quickly, Collin in a year and Tara after two."

"Because I couldn't wait to see if we could have children! What a delight they are, even if they do stretch us."

As we chatted I sneaked an occasional glance at the table where Crystal sat. She and her date seemed to be arguing about something. I longed to catch a glimpse of his face. She was absorbed and never even looked in our direction. From the rigid expression on Crystal's face, her anger was becoming more intense, although her voice remained low.

We lingered over our main course. Finally, our waiter ambled over to ask if we saved room for dessert.

"Of course." Nick smiled. "Only question is which? Tempt us."

Crystal and her dinner companion stood to leave.

"On second thought, I'm too full," I said. "Thanks anyway."

I hoped they'd walk past our table so I could see him, but they exited by a side door leading to the lakefront.

I gripped the table to keep from jumping up and following. Nick took his time finishing his coffee. I hid my impatience with a semblance of calm.

Finally, Nick paid our bill, and I took his arm. "It's too early to go to our room. How about a stroll along the lake?" A tinge of guilt nudged me as I made the suggestion. I knew Nick would enjoy it. Truth was I hoped to see Crystal again.

"You know I never turn down a lake walk, Mrs. Trevor."

We joined other couples meandering along the lakefront. I scanned the area, but Crystal and her companion seemed to have disappeared. Disappointment mingled with relief. I had no reason to be checking on her.

I focused on my husband who deserved all my attention and refused to admit these pleasant days were marred by murder.

By ten-thirty we were in bed.

"Hmm, another day older. Let's see if you improved with age," Nick whispered, rolling toward me in the king size bed.

I moaned and surrendered to his touch.

Later, I pressed my pillow into a comfortable base for my head and pulled a cotton blanket over my legs. A soft midnight rain marched like tiny tin men on the roof. I fell asleep wondering if it rains in heaven.

Nick and I headed back to Lake Geneva Sunday night. "Ready to return to our world of purpose and responsibility?" he joked.

"Only because I must. I sometimes suspect our adult personas are an illusion. I'm really me when I'm sun-soaked and playing outdoors carefree as a child."

"OK by me — if I get to be your playmate."

I poked his shoulder playfully.

My current clients popped into my mind one by one — the lives for which I feel responsible during counseling and sometimes even after termination. This week, I added my first murder victim to the group. I was lost in thought staring out the van window.

Ten minutes past the Dells, Nick turned off the radio. "Can't get this Windemere situation out of your head, can you?"

"No. Poor Rose is so confused. I believe she fears deep down Al might have killed himself but can't bring herself to vocalize it. Consciously, though, she claims to be convinced he's the victim of a murderer, which makes her afraid for her life. Either way, she can't win. She wants me to ask his personal assistant if he had any enemies. The police will already be all over that by now, but she'll feel better if I check."

"Jennifer, don't get too intense about this. You know how you obsess about people's problems."

"Because I don't deal with legalities like you, I work with hearts and souls. That makes objectivity harder." I sighed.

"I don't like to see you push yourself. With the kids at camp in Arizona and visiting your parents, we can still enjoy an extended honeymoon." He smirked. "At least in the evenings when we don't have work."

I reached for the hand Nick extended between us and turned my head to enjoy the fleeing Dells scenery for the last time. "I'm sad these delightful days are about to end."

"I have an overnight trip later this week to Indiana to take a deposition. Come with?"

"It'd be impossible for me to take off again. Don't worry, sweetheart. Your trip will free me up to check into the Windemere murder." I smiled and jabbed his shoulder playfully.

"Oh great! Be careful."

7

Ellen, my office manager, at my request, had scheduled a light client load my first morning back to simplify my work re-entry. I'm trying to be smarter about pushing myself.

Bless her heart, she also checked our house every day and watered our houseplants. This prevented my nightmares over a spontaneous pipe burst or the like. At almost sixty-five, my efficient Ellen has no plans to retire, thank God. We're her adopted family because her children are grown and live out of state.

Our house — Stonewood we call it — deep in the woods, is like nature's womb. I don't take the privilege of living there for granted. From any window, I see God's creation daily, and my spirit soars. Nick and I custom-designed it ten years ago with a den wing and separate entrance for me to counsel clients who require extreme privacy.

Usually I keep home as a refuge and work from my office in Lake Geneva.

Phone messages needed tackling first. Ellen had labeled one a priority. Paul Jacobsen of Jacobsen, Shearson & Reingold Law Firm. Contact him on an urgent business matter regarding his client — my eyes did a double take — Mr. Windemere. What would Al's lawyer want with me?

I reached the lawyer's secretary immediately. Jacobsen was in a meeting, so she put me through to voicemail. Jacobsen's recorded voice flowed resonant and full-bodied, perfect for a lawyer. Seconds later, the man himself came on.

"Thanks for returning my call. I'm representing the estate of Al Windemere and need to discuss provisions in Mr. Windemere's will that involve you."

"Me?" I gulped.

"Yes, Mr. Windemere requested your counseling services in a somewhat bizarre fashion. The will states that family members — his son Ken, should we be able to locate him; his daughter, Crystal Windemere Vandley; and Al's brother, Aaron — are beneficiaries of his trust provided each first has three counseling sessions with you to address breaches in their relationships with Mr. Windemere. If they refuse, they may name a charity to receive their trust fund instead."

I squeezed my phone to keep from dropping it. "That's an incredible stipulation. Can they be required to do that?"

"Absolutely. His wife receives the bulk of his estate, but separate trust funds have been established for each of his children and brother. You must know since you counseled Mr. Windemere, Al felt extremely guilty about the emotional wounds his family suffered from his previous lifestyle. He told me he tried without success to get them into counseling sessions with you while he was alive, but they refused. Now it will be mandatory."

Numb, I forced my brain to process Jacobsen's words. "Go over this once more please."

"Al didn't want to be eternally hated by his family members. He knew he failed them. He saw this as a last chance to accomplish what he couldn't do while alive. Your counseling skills impressed him and he had total confidence you could help free his family from bitterness over past hurts as well as help his wife deal with her grief should he die before her. Of course, his wife's decision to seek counseling with you is optional and doesn't affect her inheritance."

A request for my services from a deceased client? Too bizarre. I bit my lip to keep from saying what I was thinking: *now I've heard everything.*

"You'll be well compensated, of course," he immediately added. "Mr. Windemere was quite generous."

I gasped, astounded at the figure he mentioned.

"Isn't that sufficient?"

"More than enough. It's just . . . this is so . . . unusual. I hate to say, let alone think this, but perhaps Mr. Windemere committed suicide. Everything is so . . . planned."

"Not true. Mr. Windemere required counseling be a condition no matter how old he or his family members were. He believed this would be a final attempt to right wrongs. When he added the provision to his will several months ago, I assure you neither he nor I expected his death would be this soon."

I released my pent-up breath. "Al Windemere must have known, as should you, that counseling is rarely effective if forced."

"We discussed this. He understood under duress this may not be helpful, but it's still a last chance to make things better. He wanted to try."

I was speechless.

"There are a few other conditions, plus some business restitution situations, I'll need to meet with you to explain and to get your signature on some legal documents, including a liability release for you. I assume your husband will represent you?"

"Of course."

"Are you both available to join me this Wednesday for lunch at noon?"

I opened up my calendar. "Later would work, about one thirty?"

"Fine." He suggested a diner in downtown Lake Geneva."

"I'll call back later if it's not good for my husband, otherwise count on it." I hung up and stared at the phone while pondering this unique request.

Life is full of surprises. From the grave yet.

8

At three, I had a free hour. Mindful of my promise to Rose, I drove to Al Windemere's former office building. It wasn't difficult to locate. The white-and-gray etched sign in front of the steel and glass six-story building read American Realty Investment in three-foot letters. The structure took up most of a square block.

I smiled at the comfy, patriotic word, *American,* sort of like apple pie, welcoming investment dollars. Safe and sound. From what Paul Jacobsen had said, reality was anything but.

I hadn't called first, fearing a brush off. Showing up, I might have a chance to see the woman Rose believed could have answers about Al's presumed murder.

Ivy plants overflowed two black wrought iron pedestals in the marble-tiled reception area. A stiff-postured receptionist with black hair bundled atop her head and held by a tortoise clip smiled a welcome. I pulled out my business card, like a high school hall pass I hoped. "I need to see Angela Thursted, Mr. Windemere's executive assistant."

The receptionist consulted a clipboard. "Is she expecting you?"

"No." The syllable fell like a bowling ball between us. "I only need a few minutes. It's very important."

She looked surprised I'd even ask to see her without prior scheduling, as well she should. "Ms. Thursted is very busy. Would you like to make an appointment? Perhaps next week?"

"I believe she'll see me briefly if you tell her it's about Mr. Windemere. I spoke with an air of supreme confidence praying it seemed real, because I was faking it.

Being pushy isn't my style. As the child of alcoholics, I grew up trying to hide in the background, seldom making requests of anyone or speaking up for myself. Obscurity seemed safer. As a professional, I'd trained myself to use every ounce of human authority I possess.

Angela and I had never met. I'd talked to her by phone several times when she scheduled Al's appointments, and I knew she'd recognize my name.

The efficient Ms. Straight Back whose posture I admired hugely, sent me a cold look before disappearing. Moments later, she returned shaking her head and escorted me — apparently against her better judgment — down a hallway carpeted in olive Berber. We entered a room about 20 by 24 that housed at least seven computers, possibly the lifeline of American Realty's national holdings. I quickly surveyed the avant-garde equipment, technology eons beyond my limited ability.

"Ms. Thursted is in the rear office. You may go in."

"Thank you."

Angela wasn't alone to my disappointment. Two men and one woman sat before monitors. They didn't look up. The person I assumed to be Angela rose from a desk facing the window. "This is a surprise. How do you do, Dr. Trevor?"

Her welcome was as gracious as a society hostess with an unexpected visitor. I appreciated her kindness. The hand stretched toward me felt like velour on a stuffed bear seldom touched. Small, square, gold-rimmed glasses partially hid her swollen brown eyes. It didn't take brilliant deducting to guess she'd been crying recently.

"Thanks for seeing me," I murmured.

A well-sprayed, tightly twisted French braid, ornamented with a mauve bow, constrained her thick, brown hair. The ribbon matched her silk blouse. I admire perfection in hair, makeup, and matching accessories, although personally, I'm more casual — probably because it's easier, and I have three children to get out the door every morning.

Angela turned to the olive-skinned woman next to her, and like a drill sergeant, issued orders then nodded in my direction. "Come this way." She called over her shoulder, "I'll be right back."

I followed Angela into an adjacent conference room and took the chair opposite her "You're obviously busy. I won't take much time. First of all, I'm very sorry about Mr. Windemere's death. It must have been a terrible shock." I hoped my voice conveyed my sincere sympathy.

"Overwhelming."

Professionally or personally or both? I was curious and wanted to ask but didn't — too blunt and rude.

She leaned forward and appeared curious to hear me out.

"I'm trying to piece together a picture of Mr. Windemere's last days. The police, as you may know, haven't yet ruled his demise a suicide. Suicide is the hardest type of death for a family to accept. Mr. Windemere's widow believes he was murdered and asked me to explore if anyone to your knowledge might have had a business grudge or a personal motive to harm Albert Windemere."

I noted the nod of reverence by Angela when I said her boss's name. Hero worship or simply because the dead are often accorded more homage in the grave than in life?

"The police were here." Angela's tone was abrupt. "I told them everything I know. You can get a copy of the police report to save time." Her face was as impassive as a bank teller's.

"Just a few questions. Was there, I mean were you aware of any animosity between Mr. Windemere and his business partner?"

Her eyes grew wary while I groped for words. "Ms. Trevor, why would I discuss anything with you assuming I knew?" Angela bristled.

"Because you care about justice for your former employee." I pulled my linen blazer closer. The air conditioning and her attitude created a distinct chill. "Mr. Windemere had tremendous confidence in you. A woman in your position at his right hand knows about everything going on."

Angela sat immobile, studying me.

"Executive assistants make the business world function," I added, hoping to encourage her with truthful comments.

"And we know when not to get involved."

"If there's been foul play, Mr. Windemere would want you to help expose it. Also, the rest of his family may be in danger."

Angela slid her bracelet up and down her wrist as if it were her most important task at the moment.

I waited giving her space.

Finally, she spoke. "Maybe I should talk to you. I have nothing to hide."

I breathed a silent *Thank You, Lord.*

Angela pulled her chair closer and stared at the wall behind me before speaking. "I also believe Mr. Windemere was killed."

"Any idea by whom?"

"Several possibilities come to mind. If this happened a year ago, I could list more than a dozen people with motivation, but since his recent religious conversion, Mr. Windemere has been trying to smooth over hard feelings among clients and colleagues. Several people, one especially, objected to the change in him." She shot a furtive glance at the closed door.

"This person you're referring to was his

partner?"

"Yes." She looked down at her shoes.

I'd guessed as much from comments Al had made during counseling. "Describe their relationship please."

Angela crossed her legs. "Mr. Halston and Mr. Windemere had intense differences, not unusual, between two talented men. Lately, their conflicts intensified."

"What did they typically disagree about?"

"For years, Mr. Halston complained Al didn't pull his weight. He closed deals but created unreasonable expectations and time frames. Mr. Halston frequently expressed his anger, claimed he was always left holding the bag."

"How did Mr. Windemere respond?"

"He ignored Mr. Halston, which made him furious. I could hear their shouting matches in my office located between theirs. Several times, Mr. Halston threatened to dissolve their partnership but always thought better of it." Her eyes widened. "To my amazement, a few months back, things started improving between them. At least apparently."

"What caused the change?"

"Mr. Windemere became more reliable. Commitments were met on time."

"You mentioned several people with

beefs." I pulled a small pad from my purse. Angela took one look and froze. "If you don't mind, a few notes will help me remember details. I won't let anyone know where I got this information. Please go on."

"Put it away. I want everything I say kept confidential." Angela squirmed.

"As you wish." She seemed to be wiggling about how much more to tell. I hoped I hadn't scared her into changing her mind.

I exhaled deeply.

To my relief she continued.

"This past year after his counseling sessions began with you, Mr. Windemere became easier to get along with and more sensitive to others around him and their problems."

She paused.

I held my breath afraid she was through. "Mr. Halston wasn't comfortable with the change in Mr. Windemere. Things came to a head when tension developed about the previous clients Al wanted to reimburse."

I raised my eyebrows. "And?"

"We always have some disgruntled investors who blame us when they lose more than they should have invested in the first place. We're careful to inform clients in all our contracts, verbal and written, that our investments are uninsured and high risk

76

while having tremendous return potential."

"I imagine clients focus on the idea of 'tremendous return' and ignore the risk."

"Exactly. When Mr. Windemere suggested reimbursements for a failed deal, Mr. Halston feared it would damage the company's reputation.

I filed mentally a possible motive for murder.

"We had a block of ten dissatisfied clients involved in a questionable land investment deal that went bad last year. Mr. Windemere regretted the advice he'd given them and the negative impact. He insisted on righting the situation and did for all but two, who were out of the country at the time. Their lawyers are still clobbering us with complaints and lawsuits."

"Which clients?"

"They're back in the States. Robert Debold owns AAA Excavating. Joanna Tuler of Creative Clothing, Inc. Mr. Debold is on the verge of bankruptcy and holds Mr. Windemere personally responsible. He called again today ranting as usual. Halston refuses to follow through with the restitution."

I made another mental note. Two individuals and a partner with a motive to murder. "Did you observe anything unusual in Mr. Windemere's behavior during the week prior to his death?"

Angela's eyes started to fill. "I've asked myself over and over since hearing the horrible news this past Friday."

"I'm truly sorry, Angela." My heart hurt for her. The professional wall of Angela Thursted, shored up with sand, was breaking. She worked to compose herself.

"Ms. Trevor, that's all the time I can spare." She stood and patted the sides of her head to flatten any stray hairs, as if the motion could put her emotions back in place, too.

"Thank you. Can you make an appointment for me with Mr. Halston before I leave?"

"He's out of town, and I don't know when he'll be back."

Interesting timing. I kept the thought to myself.

"Please keep my card and call me if you think of anything else."

9

We stayed in vacation mode our first night back attending a dinner theater presentation of *Guys and Dolls* in Williams Bay. Nick insisted we enjoy every minute of our time sans children. My focus kept shifting to Albert Windemere's will. Afterward, we stopped at the Abbey Resort for their famous Deadly Chocolate Torte, a local phenomenon.

Two couples were dancing to Frank Sinatra's "I Did It My Way" when Nick whirled me onto the floor. I spun around to the music and prayed, *Lord, not my way but Your way in all things. How involved should I become in Albert's affairs? Guide me.*

Nick put his lips next to my ear. "We should come here more often. I love the subdued atmosphere, dim lights, and Frankie crooning in the background."

"I don't think they'd enjoy having our three kids dancing with us most nights."

"You're right." He laughed.

We returned to our table and inhaled the scent of chocolate. I poked my fork into the dessert with vigor. Nick savored a mouthful of cake. "Dr. Trevor, aren't you feeling guilty about these calories?"

"Very little since we're splitting it. How well we counselors can rationalize!" I swiped my napkin at a dribble of chocolate escaping my mouth.

"Guess what?" I'd waited for the right moment to tell Nick about Al Windemere's will stipulations. "Weird, your counseling services being engaged by a dead client?" I can never shock my unflappable husband.

He reacted as I expected. "You do get into the strangest situations, Ms. Trevor." Nick leaned forward. "Jennifer, doesn't this elaborate advance preparation make you wonder if Al Windemere committed suicide after all?"

"Or perhaps he sensed his life was in danger."

Nick pushed his chair back. "In all my years of practicing law, I've never heard of making amends after death. I wish it were more common. Windemere's assuming moral responsibility for cheating people and trying to make it right is solid and biblical. I'm impressed." Nick got a twinkle in his eye. "How did you answer Jacobsen? Shall I guess?"

I sighed. "You already know."

"Might you be putting yourself in danger?"

I shook my head. "I'll simply be acting in a professional capacity."

"Did you pray about it?"

"Yes. Besides how could God not want me to do this?"

"We both know there are plenty of good things needing doing that should be done by others. What about your time? Can you fit these clients in along with your current ones without undue stress? I'm sorry if I sound negative, but have you forgotten why we went away?"

"My schedule will be tight, but I can manage."

"OK. Under the circumstances, I understand why it would be hard to turn this down, but stick to the counseling and the paper trail only? I want you safe."

"Absolutely." Relief surged through me. I wanted Nick's approval, not only as my husband, but I might need his help down the road.

"Promise if it becomes too much, you'll refer these clients to somebody else?"

I nodded and rested my hand on his arm.

"Thanks. Then it's settled." I sucked in my breath. This was way out of my comfort zone.

10

I pulled up five minutes late for our meeting with Paul Jacobsen. Nick stood at the door of the restaurant, flicking through his cellphone. I fished some quarters from my purse, paid the parking fee, and then hurried over and pecked his cheek. "Cut my time too close again."

"What else is new?" I smiled as he held the door open for me. On time in my husband's dictionary meant fifteen minutes early. For me, it meant one minute 'til, give or take, or five after. It's a wonder our marriage has survived.

The sign on a metal stand in the restaurant entranceway invited us to seat ourselves.

I slipped my arm through Nick's and eyed the setting as we walked. Enormous pottery held hanging plants on half-walls that set off the dining area and created a patio effect — a contemporary contrast to the frequent Victorian and French Country decor of the Geneva Lake area.

Less than a quarter of the tables were occupied. It was too late for the business-lunch crowd. A man sitting alone toward the back of the room waved.

When we approached, he stood and stuck out his right hand. "Paul Jacobsen. Nice to meet you both."

"Likewise."

He had a stocky build topped by a jovial face with a white beard matching his thick head of hair — classic Santa Claus. Come to think of it wasn't gift-giving his work at the moment, distributing Al Windemere's fortune? I repressed the urge to state my observation.

I settled into a seat directly across from Paul and took a sip of the water already poured at my place.

"Thanks for joining me." Nick made small talk about the weather as we waited for our waitress to come take our order. I chose the day's special: bean soup and taco salad, as did Nick and Paul.

I was eager to get on to business. "Paul, I've told Nick about our previous conversation."

"Yes," Nick interjected. "I've never heard of a requirement for counseling sessions and a business restitution process after death."

Jacobsen opened his napkin and placed it in his lap. "I expected this would be of interest. To say the least, it's hardly conventional."

"I have a question. What happens after the sessions if the clients want to go on?"

"Continued counseling will be at family members' discretion and expense. I'll disburse their individual trust funds after you notify me that three sessions are completed."

"Will this hold up in court if any family member fights it?" Nick asked.

"They can try, but it would be foolish on their part. Everything is legal. You'd be surprised at the conditions people require for their progeny to honor. Will your schedule allow you to fulfill these stipulations?"

"Yes, I'll make time." I heard the tremor in my voice. *Al, your creative brain worked overtime to design this. Manipulative, yes, but immensely caring.* "I . . . I'd be honored to do this on his behalf," I stammered.

"In addition to the financial compensation you'll receive, Jennifer, Mr. Windemere also bequeathed you several pieces of furniture from his private collection. I understand you shared his fondness for antiques."

"How sweet of him to remember." A surge of warmth mingled with sadness flowed through me.

"The pieces are currently in storage. Rich Nichols, owner of the storage facility, will contact you after the family has made their personal selections."

"How very kind," Nick said.

"That he was. Al was an easy guy to like. We'd become close friends. In the early years we used to butt heads about happiness in the midst of misfortune and argue philosophical stuff. I'm a Christian, not by birth, but by choice after years of agnosticism and in-depth study of the Christian faith. I'm also the parent of a Down's Syndrome kid. Al followed my intellectual journey and eventually did his own exploring."

"Interesting. This would have been before he started counseling with me."

"Yes. All these God talks eventually led to Al's becoming a believer and a church goer." Jacobsen munched a cracker before continuing. "As a new Christian, he applied biblical principles to everything in his life."

Jacobsen transferred his briefcase to the empty chair as the waitress deftly set bowls of soup and salad in front of each of us.

"I can identify with Al's faith journey." Nick stuck his spoon into the soup and stirred it. "A few years ago, I quit being a fence-sitter after studying different faiths. Christianity made sense when I researched the basis for belief. I used to think I had to give up reason. How wrong I was."

Paul chuckled. "Quite the opposite. Reason validates the authenticity of Scripture and the existence of Christ. Let's bless this food."

"Go ahead," Nick and I said in unison.

"Thanks for this provision, Lord. Guide our discussion. May You be honored in all we think, say, and do now and forever. Amen."

I liked his simple prayer. "Paul, Al probably told you, I use biblical principles in my counseling because they're the most effective way to help people solve problems."

"And Al applied them to his life. He read Proverbs like 'Don't lie, don't cheat others even if you can get away with it.' 'Forgive and love your enemy,' the exact words of Jesus, 'If somebody takes advantage of you, allow yourself to be defrauded.' This verse from Corinthians really intrigued Al." Jacobsen pointed in my direction. "Al said he worked on forgiveness principles with you."

"Not just forgiveness intellectually but getting out the root of bitterness deep inside. That's so vital for mental and physical health. So many illnesses spring from roots of bitterness or guilt. Forgiveness is sound psychology and theology. So is loving others as yourself."

"You can imagine the huge impact this made on Al. He went into business believing whatever he could get his hands on was his, even if the ethics were wrong and others got hurt. He wouldn't mind me sharing because in recent months he told everyone he met, as you already know, as his counselor, Jennifer."

I set down my glass and stared past Paul, remembering many similar discussions with Al.

"Al stopped blaming people who mistreated him and refrained from manipulating others," Paul continued. "He experimented with concepts like returning good when treated shabbily, performing unknown acts of kindness."

The waitress returned with three huge taco salads and slid them off her tray with silent efficiency.

"Al had a guy he'd hated for years, sent him anonymous gifts like box seat tickets to the Brewers game, later a box of steaks," Paul resumed. "I don't know if the guy changed his ways, but Al claimed he felt freer, no longer harbored any bitterness. Another guy who Al hadn't spoken to in a year called me wanting to know what was up. Next thing we knew the guy joined our men's Bible study group at church. Al loved to tell that story."

Nick whistled softly as he plopped sour cream atop his salad. "Without blame and bitterness, there'd be no personal injury suits, just tax and estate work."

Paul laughed. "And a lot of lawyers out of work."

"But it's the right way to live," Nick added.

Paul sipped his iced tea. "Back to wills, Al recently was making amends to individuals he'd wronged by manipulating them into a get-rich-quick, dishonest land deal. He'd almost finished before his death. Two investors have been on extended trips out of the country. That's where you come in, Jennifer. As his executor I have authority to arrange monetary reimbursements, but I need you to personally explain to them Al's motivation for this. You can do a better job than I can."

I smiled. "I'll enjoy that."

"Joanna Tuler is still out of town. I'll e-mail you when she returns. You can see Mr. Debold now. He just returned this week from overseas — the sooner the better."

"I have a light work schedule this week. I

can fit him in tomorrow."

"So it's a go, Jennifer? Your lawyer approves?" Paul glanced at Nick.

Nick pressed his arms on his chair leaning back. "I see no problem as long as Jennifer's not in danger. Can we assume these clients and family members won't be hostile?"

"They should be happy," I inserted.

"One thing doesn't make sense." Nick bent forward. "Why would someone want to kill Albert Windemere when he was being nice to everyone?"

"I wish I knew." Paul cleared his throat. "Jennifer, these restitutions should be simple. Working with Al's family may not be. Al said his daughter and brother weren't willing to forgive him, despite his repeated overtures before we drew up this will. I believe he would have told me if that changed. As for his wife, Al said things were OK between them, but grief counseling will be helpful."

"This is a huge act of manipulation on his part. How sad if somebody in his immediate family hated the poor man enough to want him dead." Nick gestured the waitress for more water. "Unless, maybe his death was a suicide after all."

"Which I don't believe. Al never would have killed himself," Paul insisted.

I shot Nick an annoyed look. "I second that."

"You should have seen the plans he had for using his money. Al even started a lunch ministry for executives. He said, 'Somebody's got to get through to guys like us, Paul. We're fools!' "

I silently filed Jacobsen's words as further argument against Al committing suicide.

Nick flipped through the papers in front of him. "I would have liked to know him these last months. I've reviewed the documents you faxed to Jennifer, Paul." Nick leaned forward. "We're good if you can attest to Al Windemere's mental state at the time he changed his will?"

"Good point. Of course that's significant. When he executed this will" — Paul focused on Nick — "rest assured, Al knew exactly what he was doing. I will vouch for that.

"Al figured he'd never get his brother and daughter to accept professional help any other way. They may not like it but will do what's required to get the money." Jacobsen squared the papers in front of him. "His divorced daughter's clothing and gift business has never been profitable, and his brother is too wise a business person to reject a financial gift of this magnitude."

"Positive force — money," Nick agreed.

I listened quietly. "What about his son?"

"We're still trying to locate him. I'm hoping he'll resurface with the publicity if he's alive."

My detective brain went into high gear. "With this much money at stake, a family member's financial need could have been a motive for wanting Al dead because they'd assume they'd be beneficiaries."

"True," Paul said, "which is why each family member will sign an exception to the nonconfidentiality release prior to their first counseling session. If something pertinent about Al's death turns up during your appointments, you may pass it on to me and to the police." Paul turned to me. "It's a big commitment, Jennifer. Are you ready to sign on?"

"And possibly dangerous," Nick interjected. "Are you absolutely sure?" Apprehension tinged Nick's voice.

I patted Nick's arm and met his gaze without wavering. "It's the right thing to do. I want to try for Al's sake. I know I can't guarantee results. Some people find bitterness a likeable companion and remain highly resistant to counseling."

"Jennifer, if anyone can turn these family members around, Al believed you could."

"I appreciate the vote of confidence. I'd

like to tell the family members myself about the counseling arrangement. Hopefully, it'll take some of the sting out, and we can start with a positive relationship."

"As you wish. Here's where you sign." Paul pointed.

My fingers trembled as I picked up the pen to finalize the agreement. From the corner of my eye, I saw Nick look away. I knew he feared one of Albert's relatives was his murderer. *Lord, give Nick peace and protect me, please.*

11

I called Robert Debold, owner of AAA Excavating, at his office first thing in the morning.

Debold's assistant informed me, in a nasally tone, that her boss was out for the day. "May I have his home number?" I asked, not expecting her to comply.

To my surprise she rattled off his phone number and address. At least his financial problems weren't so bad that he was in hiding.

Debold picked up on the third ring.

"Mr. Debold, Dr. Jennifer Trevor. I have information for you regarding a financial settlement from American Realty that I believe will please you."

"Yeah? Whadda the crooks do? Win the lottery? Is this a joke?"

"I assure you it's authentic."

"So shoot. What is it?"

"I'd like to discuss the details in person.

Are you available at three?"

"Sure. Come on over." The skepticism in his voice was unmistakable.

Visiting a man at his home during the middle of the day was not among my usual habits. I repressed the thought that the golf course murder occurred in the light of day and made sure Ellen knew where I was going. I resolved to be careful. Nick tells me that I'm naïve and over-confident, and he's probably right.

The residential area where Debold lives, a secluded semi-wooded subdivision of Williams Bay, resembled a section of New England transported to Wisconsin. His house, two-story brick with a steeply pitched, cedar-shingled roof, had a white wooden porch stretched across the front. Nice, although I'd expected something more ostentatious from such a reportedly big investor. Then again, I reminded myself, the wealthiest among us often live modestly.

Debold, a hefty man with thinning black hair, olive complexion, and thick side burns, answered the door wearing a gray sweatshirt and navy Bermudas spotted with white flour. "C'mon this way," he ordered, leading me back to a kitchen painted yellow with an array of stainless steel appliances.

"Excuse the mess." Debold waved his arm

at the charcoal granite counters that ringed the walls. Food items covered almost every inch. "It's my night to cook. I make dinner three times a week since my wife went back to work full time. She makes more money than me these days, so I get the dirty work. Not that I mind cooking. I'm making a great marinara for tonight. We just got back from visiting my kid at school in Italy, and I picked up a century-old recipe. Want to taste the sauce?"

"No, thanks, but it's kind of you to offer."

Debold looked insulted that I'd declined. My mistake.

"Have a seat. What's up?"

I pulled out a kitchen barstool. To my dismay, Debold stood a foot from my face, uncomfortably close. I could smell his coffee-tinged breath, and I stiffened. I'm used to conversing with clients who don't occupy my facial space. "As I explained on the phone, I represent Mr. Windemere . . ." When I said the name. Debold's face reddened. Hastily, I added, "I know you had some unprofitable business investments with his company and —"

"You bet I did!" Debold let loose a tornado of swearing. "Don't mention his name again in this house. I don't understand the mumbo-jumbo of investments. I'm an excavator. Do you know what I do? I move earth. Just a hard-working guy who built a business out of nothin' but a lot of sweat. I figured a man like Windemere, who never even gets his hands dirty, must know somethin' about making money or he wouldn't survive in the financial industry."

Any notion of hospitality or my trying his cooking evaporated. He seemed pleased to have an audience for his tirade. Perhaps his wife tired long ago of hearing his complaints.

"How did your paths cross originally?" I tried to get him calm and refocused.

"I met the guy at a charity golf outing. Some charity. He was working his own bottom line, that's all. We had a couple drinks after golf. A fun guy, good storyteller, so I thought. We played golf a couple more times, and pretty soon I figure I can trust the guy. I seen him around women and knew he was a player, but, heck, I'm not going to hold that against him."

The gleam in his eye left nothing to imagine about Debold's view of fidelity in marriage.

"He spoke the language of finance like he'd been born to it. He made ya believe he'd deliver on every word. The jerk. What made me angry besides losing the money was being snared by his lies. I trusted in his big deal, got in on the ground floor. My radar's usually good, but this time it went haywire. You better believe I reinforced my shield. Chances of anybody getting close to me again are slim."

Sadness shot through me. Losing trust in human beings is a huge loss. "Please know Mr. Wi— he — was sincerely sorry for the misfortune he caused. He assumed full responsibility and wanted to make things right."

"Since when?" Debold had returned to the stove, shook spaghetti sticks from a package, cracked them in two, and dropped them into a pot of boiling water. "I never seen that jerk do nothin' but talk and serve himself. The guy drives a fancy car and lives in a lakefront mansion, so I give him control over my company pension package. I say design somethin' real nice, real safe."

"It's true. Your trust was violated . . ." I didn't want to be rude, but Debold's volatility made it hard to complete a sentence.

"And now I got nothin'. I coulda done what he did for me at the track and had more fun. And all he says is tough luck and walks away. What does he care? He made his money." Debold painstakingly adjusted the heat under the spaghetti and then picked up a stainless steel timer and set it.

"Mr. Debold, that why I'm here, if you'll let me explain —"

"I know. I read the paper. Now the spineless slimeball has gone and killed himself. And I'm a suspect."

"There's no reason to think —"

"Yeah? The police were here yesterday. They wanna know if he killed himself or somebody got to him and where was I at the time of his shooting. I told them I didn't shed tears however he died."

Debold stood inches from my face, eyeball to eyeball. I backed up, feeling a chill race up my spine. His rage was like a matchstick waiting for flint. It wasn't directed at me. He needed hearing out. I'd wait. Venting anger in an appropriate manner to a safe person helps the healing process. He could rant all he needed. I wasn't going to leave until I'd had my say.

Debold listed in painstaking detail his investment losses, occasionally running to the stove to stir his sauce. All the while, he watched me warily, as if I'd come to steal his last dollar.

I tried to interrupt again several times to no avail.

Finally, Debold ran out of steam. I jumped in, using the calmest voice I could muster.

"Mr. Debold, I've been hired to assist in settling Mr. Windemere's estate. When he died he was involved in making amends for certain clients' financial losses. One of those reimbursements concerns you."

"Go on," he ordered. I grimaced at his breath. How I wished he wouldn't stand so close.

"You'll receive total reimbursement from Al Windemere's estate for the financial losses in your personal portfolio and in your company's pension plan, plus interest for the time your money was tied up. Mr. Windemere hoped there'd be no hard feelings on your part afterward."

Debold squinted, as if it might help him understand. "The man couldn't deal with his guilt? Was he crazy?"

"No. His motive was to do the right thing because he hadn't always done so in the past. Hopefully, you won't harbor bitterness over his previous actions or financial strain because of problems he caused."

Debold flinched but remained speechless.

Now that I had his attention, I charged on. "Mr. Windemere's legal firm needs you to sign this release." I reached into my briefcase and pulled out the form. "If you want your lawyer to review the document first, fine. Send it back to the address on the letterhead. However, the sooner the better so you get your money back, with interest, of course."

He reached for the paper in a daze. "That's it?" he stammered.

I nodded. "One more thing."

He eyed me warily. "Here comes the catch."

"I'm a licensed therapist. If you continue to have unresolved anger issues, we can meet for several counseling sessions to work through them at no expense to you. Think it over, you can decide later. Your emotions may change drastically after the settlement. The choice is yours. I just want you to know it's an option."

Debold plopped onto a kitchen chair and stared at me as if I were demented. "Windemere's dead, and now he's gonna pay me back?" His posture suddenly stiffened. "Gimme a break! This must be some kind of trick."

"No. Mr. Windemere began this process when you were out of the country. He was aware the property you invested in had exceptional risk, more than he'd disclosed. You'll recall I told you he was in the process of restoring clients' losses such as yours when he died. Most investors already received their settlements. His lawyer is completing his wishes using my services."

"What interest is he paying? One cent on the dollar?"

"Full restitution with interest three points over prime."

Behind Debold's glazed eyes, I sensed his emotional struggle. The impossible was about to happen. He couldn't have dreamed a better solution to his financial dilemma. After months of badmouthing Windemere, it wasn't easy for Debold to believe his enemy could be capable of an altruistic action on his behalf.

"I understand this is highly irregular and may take some time to sink in." I began to gather my things.

Debold sucked in his breath. "Lady, I'll believe this when I see it. If what you're saying is true, instead of hard feelings, I'll even buy flowers for the . . ." He must have thought better of the word because he amended with "for Windemere."

Debold agreed to send the required paperwork to Paul Jacobsen. His handshake was strong, but his facial features had softened. "Thanks, lady. Don't worry about me. I don't need counseling. I'm Catholic. I know what confession is for. He did me wrong. Now he's making it right. What's not to forgive?"

When I strode down the walkway, I heard Debold through the open door. "Wait'll I tell my wife! She's gonna fall over."

Inside my car I took a moment to lower my head. "Lord, what a privilege to be the bearer of good news to this man and see joy replace anger before my eyes. The fun should have been Al's."

At a stoplight on my return trip to my office, I prayed again that Al's murderer would be caught and thought again about Al's partner, Halston. He had to view these repayments as admission of American Realty Investment's incompetence or at best, poor financial judgment. Other investors might file lawsuits in the future whenever the company made an error in judgment, or even if a good investment soured, they might want reimbursement, a very legitimate concern on Halston's part. Debold's restitution was appropriate, because Al had acted unethically but many losses could be attributed to client's greed and inappropriate risk-taking. I understood Halston's anger.

The light turned green, and the car behind me revved up with thunderous noise to make sure I knew I was two seconds late pulling forward. I caught up with the flow of traffic. My thoughts stayed elsewhere.

If Halston couldn't talk Windemere out of this restitution policy, would the man murder Al to protect the company?

Questions swirled until my head hurt. One thing was clear. I wanted to interview Halston. I called Ellen on my cell. "Make an appointment with Harold Halston at his earliest convenience."

Minutes later she buzzed me. "He's still out of town. No word when he'll be back."

"Make a note to keep trying."

My suspicion mounted. Was Halston hiding out somewhere because he sensed his life was in jeopardy also or because he was a murderer?

I braced myself for my encounter with Crystal. I didn't expect this to be easy.

12

Crystal lived four miles from downtown Lake Geneva, in a subdivision of 4000-square-foot homes with five-acre yards, a little tough on neighborliness, I surmised.

Ellen had arranged with Crystal Windemere Vandley for me to stop by. I wanted to observe her reaction to the provisions of her father's will in person. As a counselor, I'm trained to assess what goes on in people's heads by studying body language and visible emotions. These skills were what I counted on now. Crystal's attitude the other day made it impossible to rule her out as a murder suspect.

I strolled up to the ornate carved front door and prayed before ringing the bell. *Lord, make this stipulation in her father's will positive for her, please.* Angry people, I well knew, could be ugly. I'd had enough with Debold.

My finger on the doorbell signaled a black

Doberman with haunches like the Loch Ness monster to bound to a barking and attack position behind the half-glass front door.

I froze. Large dogs have frightened me ever since a German shepherd attached himself to my thigh at age thirteen.

Crystal grabbed the dog's collar. I assumed to keep him from going through the door. She opened a foot. "What's so important that you needed to see me again?" Her voice sounded like gravel. I was too busy watching the dog to be annoyed by anything she said.

"Provisions of your father's estate, which affect you."

That got her attention.

"All right, come in. Be quiet, Milton." She yanked the dog to a sitting position, his body heaving and mucus dripping lavishly from his mouth. Crystal pointed toward a sitting room furnished with contemporary leather and chrome furniture.

I picked my way cautiously around Milton. To my relief, Crystal closeted the beast in what appeared to be a utility room before coming to sit across from me. The dog had unnerved me. My voice shook slightly as I explained the stipulation of her father's bequest. Her eyes were wide when I finished.

"What bizarre thing has the man done now? Even after his death, I'm not free." She spluttered rather than spoke. "He'd become totally unglued this past year. Honestly, I don't believe you helped him a bit. Based on his new craziness, he was worse after you counseled him!"

Ouch! I took a deep breath. "I'm sorry you feel that way, because in order to receive your personal inheritance you must have these three counseling sessions with me."

"An ultimatum, how typical of father! Leaving me some money is the least he could do. I deserve every penny for what he put me through."

"We can discuss that during our sessions." I withdrew a folder from my bag. "I need you to sign this form." I extended the paper.

Crystal snatched it from my hand.

"It appears I have no choice. If I weren't so time-challenged right now, I'd contest this ridiculous clause. My looney father!" Crystal scratched her signature on the page. "Mother may have ruled out suicide, but I certainly haven't. This manipulation further indicates he was demented. I knew several months ago when he started spouting all that religious mumbo-jumbo."

107

Genuine sympathy flowed through my veins. Nobody likes being backed into a corner. Al's bequest was manipulative, no doubt, even if the motive was honorable. Not that bribery is always bad. I often urge parents to use healthy incentives for motivating kids' behavior.

As Crystal leaned against her chair, crossing her arms stiffly over her chest, I recalled what Al had said during our sessions: Crystal had never been properly disciplined as a child.

"I'll co-operate, but don't expect this to change my feelings toward him." She tossed the signed paper at me.

"I understand." I thought of Victor Frankl in a World War II concentration camp resolving that he'd do what they wanted, but no one would control his mind.

"My office assistant will send you a copy for your records. She'll call you tomorrow to set up the appointments."

"I can't wait." Crystal glared and marched me to the door.

How many children had killed their dads in a fit of rage? I made a note to check those statistics.

Nick and I lingered over after-dinner coffee following one of our favorite non-home-cooked meals — boxed lasagna with salad and garlic bread. Being with Robert Debold had given me a taste for Italian food. The scent of oregano filled the kitchen. Evening news filtered from the TV in the family room and into the dining alcove, cozy and warm in contrast to the chill outside. I poured vanilla-flavored cream into my mug of steaming decaf.

Nick stirred his coffee. "Why do you suppose Al believed forced counseling might work? You can't remake his family relationships."

I gazed at the antique gaslight fixture spearing the darkness outside our French doors as I sought words to help me explain. "Al Windemere was a changed man, a walking miracle. He wanted to make his family aware of God's love and have them realize he sincerely loved them. If they'll give counseling a chance it could work." I sighed. "I feel the weight of this."

"Just don't get too intense about the outcome."

Nick knew my pattern. "I both love and hate the fact that you know me so well."

Nick pushed his chair back. "Sure do. 'Come to Trevor & Associates Counseling Services. Find new pathways to process past hurts and strength to move forward while I exhaust myself.' How's that for a public relations blurb to get more clients, as if you needed more. The problem is you obsess about each one."

"Only the tougher ones." I grinned, ignoring the edge in his voice and then headed into the kitchen area to unload the dishwasher. A draft of steam shot out. "New subject: I miss the children. Wonder what they're doing tonight."

Nick chuckled. "You're thinking of them because you're doing kitchen duty, and your helpers are gone."

I threw a dishtowel at him. "No problem as long as I have you."

He sauntered over to help. "I have a light day tomorrow. Can you meet me for a picnic lunch at the lake?"

I winced. "Sorry. Al's memorial."

Nick frowned. "I'm beginning to wish you never got involved in this."

"While honoring Al's memory, I intend to give the guests a once-over. The murderer might be present."

13

Al Windemere's lengthy obituary in the *Journal* listed his membership in numerous local civic, social, and business organizations. No doubt an influential man in the community, even if not always well liked. Mourners streamed into the mega-church, Creekside, that Al had attended these past months. Two hundred plus gray chairs formed a huge semi-circle around the platform stage where the closed coffin was positioned.

I glanced at the ceiling, high and dome-shaped remembering architects built ancient European cathedral ceilings high so people could feel close to God as possible. Not a bad idea. The sky does that for me.

Visitation took place before the service began. People waited silently in line to make their way to the closed casket draped with a white linen cloth. Several dozen red roses and a framed picture of Al rested atop it.

Some people walked right on by, others stopped to touch the outside of this large bronze rectangle holding Al's remains. On their way through the line they viewed picture boards of Al on tables that flanked the metal coffin.

Rose stood to the left greeting mourners. Aaron and his wife were on Rose's right. Crystal flitted back and forth bringing her mother water and occasionally urging Rose to sit on the chair behind her.

The aqua blue carpet emitted a strong chemical odor, recent glue-down installation, I suspected. I forced myself to endure it. No one else seemed bothered.

I wove my way through the receiving line up to Aaron, his wife, Lorraine, and Rich, introduced as Aaron's business associate and friend. The funeral director kept the line of mourners moving expeditiously.

Organ music signaled the service was about to begin. I took my seat.

The Windemere family filled the first row. Crystal's ex-husband and Aaron's faces were unreadable masks. The children must have been kept away, which saddened me. I believe that children benefit from being included in funeral services. Plus, I'd hoped they might hear positive things about their grandfather. I doubted Crystal had praised

112

him in any way.

After the solemn singing, a short gray-haired man introduced himself as Pastor Forester. He delivered an impassioned oration and praised Al's civic accomplishments. "Al is now in the presence of God. Can you be assured of joining him some day?"

He explained salvation in detail. "God has a plan for each of your lives. Someday you'll stand before Him to give an account."

I no longer wondered if I'd ever get a passport to heaven based on my sinlessness and good deeds, not that doing them isn't great. The sacrifice of Jesus' life on the cross and His amazing resurrection assures me entrance.

From my seat midway in the church, I discreetly scanned the room for any distraught or tearful women other than Rose. Angela Thursted, who sat several rows back, dabbed at her eyes. A nicely dressed woman sitting three rows ahead and to my right caught my eye. She seemed very moved by the pastor's message. From time to time, she pulled a handkerchief from her handbag and blew her nose. I guessed her age to be in the mid-forties. She wore a black and camel print dress in a soft fabric, perhaps silk. Her shoulders were enfolded in a black shawl with Navajo bead embroidery. Three-inch black patent heels with a matching handbag completed her elegant couture. Friend? Business associate?

Two men rose to give short eulogies: Paul Jacobsen and another man from Al's Bible study. Both spoke of the peace and security Al had found in his life and elaborated on his joy being in the presence of God.

As we filed out, rows emptied front to rear. I tried to get close enough to chat with the woman wearing the shawl. She remained about six feet ahead as she exited the building.

By the time my eyes adjusted outside in the bright sunshine, she'd reached the end of the sidewalk.

Weaving in and out among the guests, I came within three feet of her at the curb. "Excuse me, please, may I speak with you?"

She ignored me. She had to have heard. She folded her legs into a Lexus and drove off. Apparently, this mourner wasn't staying for lunch. Who was she?

Nor was I. I'd done enough time damage to my day. Next break I had I hoped to find a chance to speak to Aaron alone to tell him about the counseling stipulation in Albert's will. I noticed Aaron had acted as though he'd been in a daze during the service. The brothers, Cain and Abel, came to mind.

Jealousy drove Cain to kill. Had history repeated itself? Was Aaron Al's killer?

14

Clients filed non-stop through my afternoon. I finished progress notes, stacked my
folders, and called Ellen in.

"Here. All set to file."

Her organizational habits were outstanding. Even the pantry shelf in my break room
had labels. I joke that my brain organizes
concepts efficiently, a great plus as a counselor, but my hands scatter papers with
abandon. I need Ellen's skills. She and I
enjoy our professional friendship, and I can
trust Ellen to be discreet.

"You look exhausted."

"I am. And I miss the children. Now that
we're home from the Dells, our house seems
strange without them and their friends running in and out. I'll admit, though, their
extended visit with Grandma and Grandpa
Trevor allows me time to handle extra work
involving Albert Windemere, for which I'm

grateful. I have a session tonight at eight-thirty."

"Do you want me to stay?" Ellen asked.

"No, but thanks. My comfy couch is beckoning me, but I need food more than rest. Having a chicken parmigiana dinner at the Café Italia with Nick takes precedence. I have to be fully alert for my clients, and a nap could leave me groggy.

Now and again when I counsel, remnants of my unhappy childhood surface. If my counseling can help relieve someone's pain, I feel as if I add a little piece of redemption to my own ugly past.

My cell phone buzzed. Nick's name appeared.

"Sorry, darling. I can't join you for dinner. I have to prepare for an emergency pretrial hearing. I'll be tied up for the next several hours at least. Don't skip dinner." Nick worried I'd turn into a feather if he didn't encourage my regular mealtime. It's true I do sometimes forget meals.

"No problem. I'll grab something at the deli. See you later."

I made notes in preparation for my next client, slipped into my cardigan, and hurried down the doublewide staircase onto the quiet street.

Small businesses surrounding mine had

already closed for the night, an eye doctor on the right, and two accountants on the other side. Lights went out in the lawyer's office as I passed. Everybody except me ends their business day at 5:00 PM except for tax season when the accountants stay later.

The evening was shrouded in dusk as I headed for Gina's Deli three blocks away. My low heels crunched over the sidewalk. A carryout from the Italia would be tastier, but farther. After sitting all day, walking in the night air felt good — at least at first.

Tonight, I wished my office were downtown on Main Street in the hub of activity rather than having to walk these semi-deserted streets alone at night. A gentleman had been murdered six months ago in a nearby alley. I found myself looking over my shoulder, tensing at every sound.

Was it my imagination or were eyes poring over me? I believe it's possible to sense someone staring. I'd swear I had an observer. I passed cars parked along the sidewalk and scanned each to see if someone were inside. The vehicles appeared empty, but were they?

A block ahead, a couple hurried along arm-in-arm and disappeared into a building. Out of nowhere, a man appeared on the other side of the street, walking directly across from me. I hadn't seen him come out of a business. He wore a blue baseball cap and a jacket. Shadows from surrounding buildings wove around his body as he walked. My blood froze in my veins.

Stop being hyper. Still, I reached inside my purse for my pocket-sized pepper spray, the half-ounce size. If I ever needed to use it, my plan, which I'd rehearsed numerous times, was to make a direct hit, then run fast. I wished I'd purchased the two-ounce size with a stronger, pressurized punch that perhaps could throw somebody off balance. Truth was, though, that I doubted I could act fast enough with either one.

Why couldn't I talk myself out of this creepy fright? If only I'd grabbed my cell phone before rushing out of the office. I kept glancing across the street. The man kept pace with me. A four-inch branch cracked to the ground a few feet in front of me. The sound iced my heart. I stopped dead.

Stopping is not a smart move. Keep going, Jennifer. *Jumpy aren't you?*

Subconsciously, Albert Windemere's murder had me spooked. I could be a target if someone feared what I might find out. I forced myself to concentrate, to slow my throbbing heart. Who would gain from Al's death? Ms. Windemere had access to all the money she could spend. Crystal had her own business. Even if it wasn't hugely successful, she seemed to manage. Her ex-husband, John, did all right. What about Al's brother and sister-in-law or Aaron's business manager, Rich? Did their business have financial problems? I made a mental note to check.

Windemere's killer might dislike my knowing family secrets. If I uncovered something incriminating during counseling would I have the same knowledge that led to Al's murder? Reason enough to stay off lonely streets at night.

Clip clop, the man's pace never changed. Three long blocks had never seemed so far.

An image of Rose came to mind. Rose knew about the extramarital affairs. Al had confided this to me during counseling. Had that spurred her to infidelity? Perhaps a sexual entanglement of hers became the motive for Windemere's murder. I pushed away the thought. Sweet, loyal Rose? Who else might stand to gain from Al's death? For that matter, who had something to lose if Al didn't die?

The figure in the dark cap kept nearly perfect step with me.

My conjectures got me nowhere and only increased my fear. I tried my formula for dealing with anxiety. Pray. Replace the troublesome thought with a good, noble, pure and true one. It usually worked, but not always fast enough.

Out of the corner of my eye, I observed the man with the baseball cap start across the street toward me. A van zoomed around the corner forcing him to jump momentarily back to the curb. I quickened my steps to a run.

Ahead, the lights of Gina's Deli twinkled in the dusky night and beckoned me like a Christmas tree. With every foot nearer, I pushed my pace faster.

I plunged inside the bright shop, panting. A brass bell on the door announced my entrance. I inhaled the comforting, pungent smells of sauerkraut and cheese.

The clerk looked fourteen but may have been twenty, I'm rarely a good judge of age. She sauntered over to slice, scoop, or pour for me. "What can I get you, ma'am?"

"One second." I looked out the storefront window. The man I'd assumed was following me had disappeared from view. Was he still out there?

The clerk put on latex gloves, yawned, and waited for me to make up my mind.

I jabbered. "How quiet the shop is tonight. I usually come for lunch." Maybe small talk would settle my heart if I could slow its beating enough for conversation.

She shrugged. "We close soon. Most of our regular customers have already been in. It's a sorta slow night."

Not for me! Every nerve and muscle in my body vibrated in super speed. I chose dill chicken salad on homemade rye with a side of coleslaw. "Decaf also, please. Everything to go." The deli coffee was always better than what I brewed in the office.

The girl gave me an empty cup and pointed me toward the coffee bar. I added cream and sugar and sipped some of the warm liquid before I covered it. The familiar taste relaxed me. I chided myself for being silly then forced myself to smile. Still I wasn't eager to go back outside. I must stop reading mysteries.

When I'm scared, I make myself do what I dread. It annoys me to be frightened. I reasoned I hadn't been accosted or even approached. Too much imagination going on.

The clerk handed me my white bag, which reeked deliciously of dill. I wanted to get back as quickly as possible. Outside, I shivered despite the warmth and quickened my steps. At least, on the way back, I had my bag of deli for a weapon or a peace offering for any monster of the night.

I walked fast, not breathing normally, until I was back at my desk with my doors locked. No baseball-capped figure had shown up.

I ate quickly and finished my last appointment of the evening, leaving without writing up progress notes, which could wait until tomorrow.

"Thank You Lord," I said aloud when I pulled into our garage.

Half an hour later, Nick found me in the laundry room off our bedroom sorting laundry. Taking tension out in vigorous housekeeping works for me. Vacuuming is the best therapeutic salve for my nerves. Unfortunately for my house, I'm not stressed often enough.

Nick brushed my cheek with a kiss. "You look tired, hon. How was your evening?"

"Don't ask."

"That bad?"

"Yes. I do want to tell you, but give me a few minutes to put this load in."

Nick went into the bedroom, stripped, threw on his terry velour robe and returned carrying more dirty clothes. With one swift motion he dumped the laundry into the washing machine. I like that he often pitches in with household chores so we avoid the expense and scheduling issues of weekly help. A cleaning service comes once a month to deep clean. I never notice dirt until spiders leave me pretty weavings.

Once the machine started gurgling, we settled on the over-sized tapestry loveseat in our bedroom. I told him about my walk and feeling like I was being watched. "I know it sounds silly, but I'd swear I was."

Nick stiffened. "Did you get a look at the person?"

"No. If this murderer isn't discovered soon, I might need counseling myself." I tried to laugh, but the sound came out hollow. "To think a perfect stranger could shake me up like this!"

"I never wanted you to take this on."

"You didn't say no."

Nick pulled me closer. "If I thought you were in real danger, I'd insist you stop."

He lifted my chin and stared into my eyes. "Jen, counseling the Windemere family is one thing. I wish you weren't involved, but I understand. But back off about searching for evidence leading to Al Windemere's killer, OK? That could put you into a dangerous position. Let the police handle that, not you."

I turned away. "I'm already involved on both fronts."

"What's logical about getting into danger?"

"I'm feeling better now. I'll be fine. You know I have an overactive imagination. Still, I promise to not go anywhere without my cell phone." Had I said that to reassure him or me?

"Then there's nothing more to discuss. You are so stubborn." He scowled and stomped off to bed.

Within minutes, Nick was snoring. I went to sit in the dark family room and pray. *Lord, help us be unified. I made a commitment. I want to follow through, but I don't want my husband angry, and I surely don't want to die.*

15

The next morning, the sunlight glowed brightly as I drove to American Realty Corporation for my appointment with Harold Halston. Finally, he'd returned, and I would meet Al Windemere's partner.

Sunshine's always a spirit-lifter for me. I smiled, determined to keep smiling no matter what the next hour brought.

Angela escorted me to Halston's office door and retreated. I observed her cautious look and sensed she'd like to stay and listen. Not a chance.

Halston was on the phone but waved me in. I was taken aback by his resemblance to Al Windemere. Same height and build, except Halston's hair was still black and his eyes appeared less warm, his demeanor less outgoing than Al's.

"I'll be with you in a minute." Halston swiveled in his chair, finished his conversation, and spoke into his inter-office speaker.

"Hold my calls." He snapped out specific instructions if certain clients called.

Halston's office was six times the size of mine. Dark walnut furniture, well-polished and obviously expensive, dominated the room. An expansive picture window formed a decorative border for the ever-changing, gorgeous lake views. Outside two water skiers glided along the water. Off to the right, rooftops of Lake Geneva homes and businesses spanned the distance to the lake.

Halston flicked his gaze in my direction without making eye contact. "Before you tell me what this visit is about, allow me to compliment you." His tone was brusque. "You helped Al end an ugly habit. I never thought he'd quit drinking. I'd been working on him to join AA for years. Can't say I was ever a great example. Liquor didn't affect me the same way though. Al got crazy. You accomplished a miracle in that man in a few months." Halston laughed, a light throaty sound. "And nobody needed it more. Take my word for it."

"Thanks for the kind praise, but whatever changes occurred, God deserves the credit, not me. Incidentally, I'm surprised Mr. Windemere told you about his work with me."

"He not only told me, he'd rave to anybody who'd listen about his changed life and his religious experience. Now what can I do for you?"

"I hope you don't mind my asking a few personal questions."

Halston's eyebrows lifted, but he didn't refuse.

"For starters, how would you describe your working relationship with Mr. Windemere?"

"Simple." He twirled a pen between his hands. "Lousy." Fury ringed the word.

"As Al's former counselor, through an unusual stipulation in his will, he's asked me to try to resolve ill feelings in the business relationships in his life."

"Bad feelings between us? You bet there were. But talking to you would never make me change my opinion of him. Not his death either." Halston snarled.

"What were the issues?"

Halston looked away. "Where do I start? Did you ever read Dickens' Tale of Two Cities?"

I nodded.

"Remember the opening line, 'It was the best of times and the worst of times'? With Al and me it was the best in each of us and the worst of us at all times. We were at one another non-stop."

"Yet you remained partners?"

"What can I say? Our chemistry worked." Halston shrugged. "We each had business skills the other lacked. That's what originally drew us together and what kept us partners. Neither Al nor I went to college. A couple of the last of the breed of self-made men, we earned our degrees the hard way, right in the marketplace, and built all this." He waved his arm. "Proud of it, too."

"With good reason, I'm sure. I checked American Realty on the web and, frankly, I'm impressed."

Halston stuck his chest out. "A multi-million-dollar company with branches in three states. To keep going we tolerated a lot from each other. It's common knowledge that Al worked odd hours, socialized too freely, if you know what I mean." Halston looked slyly at me. "His work habits were, to say the least, unorthodox and drove me wild. The man rarely missed an actual deadline, yet he raised my blood pressure plenty, wondering if he'd make it."

"I'm sorry to hear he caused you such distress."

Halston straightened in his chair. "Darn right, but don't go where you're heading. Not enough to kill him. What Al lacked in organization, he more than made up for in creative deals. He could analyze financial reports like a ten-year-old reads cartoons. His conclusions were nearly always right, and no one was better at sales."

"A mutually beneficial partnership."

"Darn right." Halston pounded his desk. "We were a dynamic, if tortured, duo."

Halston followed my gaze to his desk covered with clearly labeled files and papers neatly stacked and arranged in rows.

"True, I'm the drudge." He shrugged. "So what? I drove Al crazy, too. We respected our differences even if we did fight like mad. As I said, the financial balance sheet made it worthwhile."

I didn't need to encourage Halston to talk. He reminded me of a drain with the plug pulled.

"Al rarely completed a project more than ten minutes before it was due. Talk about stress; he drove me crazy." Halston halted for breath. Pulling out a folded handkerchief he dabbed at wet spots on his brow and upper lip. How many others had Harold Halston ranted to about Al? Obviously, a lot of emotion swirled through their relationship. "Heard enough?"

"Thanks. You're helping me understand what's been going on. I can see why losing Al is a hardship for you, for the firm. Regarding Al's death? Do you believe he was murdered, or do you accept the suicide theory?"

"Haven't given it any thought. He's dead. I'm moving on."

My face must have shown my reaction. "Your quick dismissal seems strange."

"If you're wondering, did I kill him," Halston added quickly, "not unless I did it as a sleepwalker. God knows, I dreamed it more than once and would have liked to at least a hundred times. In the business world, we didn't have to be best buddies to operate together." Halston ambled over to the window. "Al was a capable man in his own way. I don't begrudge him that, but I'm glad I don't have to deal with him anymore. Now if you're through with your questions . . ."

"Just a few more. Do you know any business associate who might have a motive to kill him?"

"Probably at least twenty people were seriously shafted by Al's unethical behavior, but nobody could prove it. He'd been making amends with his own money. I told him no way the company's going on the line for a payback that implies our liability. Bad enough for the industry he was doing what he did."

"How well did you know his family?"

"I met Aaron, his brother. They were

always at odds. There's a possible murderer for you."

"Was Al involved in Aaron's business?"

"We handled real estate investments for Aaron and his manager, Rich Nichols. Aaron did well with his floral business, and Rich had a small account. Both had cash to invest."

"I didn't know the floral business was that lucrative."

Halston chuckled. "It didn't hurt that Aaron owns the shopping center anchored by his Floral World. He and Rich were co-investors in several condo developments we handled. Rich has a sideline in antiques, too — a furniture warehouse on Sand Mount Road in the industrial park. He co-owned it, and Al bought and restored antiques. A nice extra business to have."

I pondered what else to ask. "American Realty Investment will go on as before?"

"As soon as I hire some young, hungry guy to replace Al in sales, I won't miss him. I'd have done this sooner, but he wouldn't let me."

The phone on Halston's desk rang and was answered in another office. He looked at his watch. "I'm outta time. Listen, too bad Al's dead. He was a pain in the you-know-what, but see me in a couple weeks. I may just miss the aggravation now and then although I'm a guy who goes forward. No grudges. No regrets."

"A smart way to live." I wondered if it were true.

Halston's intercom buzzed. "You're due at your board meeting, sir," his assistant announced through the speakerphone.

Halston extended his hand. "It was a pleasure meeting you."

"Here's my card, please keep it in case you think of anything else that might be helpful. Thanks for your time."

Halston's attention was already back on his paper-laden desk, selecting files for his meeting. I had to admire his sense of order; the controlled flow of a CEO who likes to micromanage. I had one last question that I wasn't going to ask. Could I believe what he told me?

I hurried to my lunch with Nick.

"Table for two," I told the hostess at the Geneva Inn. She seated me at my favorite lakeside table.

Nick and I meet weekly for lunch on Wednesday for a special sharing time. Years ago, when we'd been feeling disconnected because of our busy schedules, I devised this plan. As a young married woman, I'd been shocked that you could sleep, eat, and even have frequent sex with your spouse but become emotionally distant. Above all, I didn't want to lose our emotionally intimate relationship.

The waitress approached.

I ordered water with lemon, no ice, and a straw. Minutes later Nick slipped in across from me. "Surprising me again. Hon, you're early. First time this month."

I smiled. "That's right. Been waiting an hour."

"Yeah, sure. And I shot a sixty on the golf course with eight birdies." He chuckled as he opened his menu.

The waitress appeared at his side, introduced herself as Hannah, and read off the specials from a list. An older waitress hovered beside her. Training day, I surmised.

Nick glanced at me. "Have you decided what you're having?"

"Beef barley soup and garden salad with ranch on the side, please."

"Sounds good. Make that two and add a hamburger to my order. I'm famished."

Hannah collected our menus and left. Nick folded his arms and leaned back. "Let's hear your Windemere update."

"Pretty much the same. I'm still putting together a picture of Al's last month and looking for a murder motive."

"He never mentioned being in jeopardy during any of your counseling sessions?"

"No." Between bites of raw carrot from the relish tray, I reviewed my interview with Halston. "What do you think of their relationship, Nick?"

"Sounds like a fairly typical business partnership. One guy with strong sales ability and one with good organizational, bookkeeping, and follow-up skills. I get the impression Al Windemere probably promised clients a lot to clinch deals and let Halston worry about delivering. Halston knows organizational men are more dispensable than a great people person who can sell, so he wouldn't rock the boat."

The waitress delivered our orders.

Nick bit into his juicy burger.

"Despite the obvious frustration for him as the detail person. Still the operation apparently worked well for years. I can't imagine Halston wanting to end a successful arrangement by eliminating his business partner," I said.

"He wouldn't have been dumb enough to believe he didn't need Windemere if what Halston said was on the level," Nick noted.

"How about their company? What did you find out about American Realty's finances?"

I picked the green onions out of my garden salad. The red ones are my favorite.

"Solid as a rock. No major outstanding debts, judgments against them, liens, etc.," Nick stated.

I finished my soup, patted my lips with a napkin. "A murderer needs a motive."

"Have the police released their final report?"

"Not yet. I checked. Enough of this murder topic. Time for our Intimacy Reviver."

We took turns discussing our closest moment to each other this past week, the nicest thing we did for each other, and when we were proudest of one another. As usual, I basked in Nick's words from this simple sharing.

We'd barely finished when Nick looked at his watch. "Time's up. Sweetie, I've got to run."

"No problem. If you're in a rush, I'll get the bill."

He bent over and gave me a peck on my cheek. "I owe you. I'll pay you back later tonight."

I grinned. "Yeah, sure."

I sat a few minutes doodling murderer and motive on the paper napkin then crushed it. No need to scare the waitress.

16

After my next counseling appointment, I had two free hours. I skimmed Al Windemere's two-inch-thick client file. With all the record keeping required these days, it doesn't take much to build a stack of sheets in a client's folder.

I hunted for a cell phone number for Aaron Windemere. A man intoned in a deep voice, "Aaron's Flower and Gift World, Rich speaking."

"Aaron Windemere, please."

"I'm sorry. He's not available." Rich introduced himself as the shop manager. "May I be of service?"

"When will he be back?"

Rich explained that Aaron was giving a 2:30 PM presentation at the Community Garden Club's Open Meeting. "It's not too late to attend if you're interested."

I combed my brain for an image of Rich. Store manager and friend of Aaron I'd met at the funeral luncheon. I doubted he'd remember me. From memory, I drew a picture. Pleasant guy in his late forties, very tall, and he'd been gracious during our brief introduction.

I checked my watch. If I hurried I could make the program and be back fifteen minutes ahead of my next appointment at four.

"Yes, I'd like to attend."

His directions were simple enough. I hung up, gave Ellen instructions during my absence, and headed for my van.

The meeting room in the Community Church Social Center held about fifty women. At the door, I paid a five-dollar entrance fee to a cordial lady wearing a silky floral dress camouflaging her precious bony, bent-over skeleton.

She announced loudly to the eightyish overseer guarding the moneybox, "We've a new girl, Sarah. What's your name again, honey?"

"Jennifer." I smiled and wrote my name on a stick-on nametag. No one had called me "girl" in a long while. I adore older ladies; they're so sweet. It won't be long before I'm one.

A gray-haired woman, stooped so much

she appeared to have lost at least eight inches of height, bustled over. "Emily Thorsen here, and you're . . . ?"

"Jennifer Trevor."

"Welcome. We're delighted you came. Perfect timing. We're just about to start."

"Thank you." I intended to slither toward a seat in the back, but one of the matronly buxom ladies at the speaker's table noticed me and waved me to a front chair. So much for blending in without being noticed. I estimated not more than five people under sixty-five in the room with me.

Aaron stood behind three long tables pushed together end to end across the front of the room. Vases, baskets, and buckets packed with flower stocks filled the tops of two tables. On the floor under the tables, greenery, ferns, baby's breath and other fillers I didn't recognize draped profusely from buckets. One tabletop remained empty, probably for his hands-on demonstration.

A silver-haired woman in a floral polyester pants suit stood next to Aaron and introduced him with an impressive verbal recital of his training and experience.

From my close vantage point, Aaron was an unremarkable man. Sandy-colored hair blended with his pale skin tones creating a subdued appearance. A substantial roll of flesh rimmed his waist. Apart from his specialized knowledge, which would invite conversation, I wondered whether anyone at a social gathering would approach him. He didn't project friendliness.

"Thank you for inviting me ladies. I enjoy getting out into the community and meeting our customers, always a pleasure."

I listened carefully.

"I'm humbled that Ms. Bickleworth suggested I talk about the arrangements I've created for some famous people — not as illustrious as you ladies, of course." A tiny line of white saliva languished between his lips as he spoke. A mild titter went through the group.

Aaron proceeded to entertain the women with the details of a recent Vanderbilt wedding. "Pink flowers covered dozens of animated robotic forms. We created floral lambs in deep shades of pink and burgundy to hold hors d'oeuvres."

The ladies hung on every word, oohing and aahing approval. Aaron's enthusiasm for his work was contagious.

I love flowers, and his stories were interesting, but a nasty idea gnawed at me. A man could be gentle and artistic and still be full of hatred. Paul Jacobsen had described a long-standing animosity between Al and

Aaron. Was Aaron the killer of his brother?

What if these sweet ladies knew they were in the presence of a possible murderer? The place would be abuzz within minutes.

Next, Aaron adroitly dipped his hand into the buckets of fresh flowers. He made quick selections, explaining his design process in detail as he snipped, pinched, and poked angled stems into molded green sponge-like forms he called oases.

He seemed mild-mannered, handling the flowers almost with reverence as he introduced them. "Here you have the columbine, next I'll add carnations, considered common and scorned for their simplicity, but oh so beautiful." He pressed them tenderly into the spongy base. "Line flowers, like snapdragons and gladioli, are essential for color and height."

I inhaled as the mixture of blooms created an intoxicating, seductive fragrance.

If one could make music with flowers, it could be said Aaron composed a symphony with these extravagant arrangements, each unique. A waif-like female apprentice about eighteen stood by his side, anticipating his needs and cleaning up after every step.

The elderly ladies' voices, subdued by time, peppered him with questions steadily, if haltingly. Aaron answered each woman with infinite patience. I had no doubt his customers loved him and his work.

After the formal presentation, the lady who'd welcomed me arose on wobbly legs supported by thick stretch stockings. "Tea is served."

I sauntered with the other ladies to the linen-covered tables in the back of the room. Two-inch, precision-cut pieces of spice cake and brownies, homemade beyond a doubt, sat on lace doilies atop paper plates. I could have eaten two of each but restrained myself. Aaron refused refreshments and said his good-byes, explaining that his assistant would sell the arrangements he'd made.

I jumped up to intercept Aaron at the door. Together we walked to the parking lot. "I enjoyed your demonstration immensely."

Aaron turned to thank me, but then paused and looked at me quizzically. "Haven't we met somewhere?" He snapped his fingers. "I know. At my brother's funeral service. Your name escapes me."

"I'm Jennifer Trevor, his former psychotherapist."

We were in front of his car now, a Honda Accord with a St. Christopher medal hanging from the rearview mirror. I explained I'd come to the event to see him and tell him about the legal requirement for his counseling sessions. He listened attentively, a kind but puzzled expression on his face.

"Well I don't have to think twice about my answer. Under the circumstances, I'm willing to give three sessions a go, but I must warn you, I like me as I am. I'll arrange for my manager, Rich, to cover a wedding appointment for me, and we can start tomorrow afternoon. I'd like to get this over as soon as possible. I'm a bit overextended with a new investment; frankly, the inheritance couldn't come at a better time."

My ears perked up. A murder motive? If so, why would he tell me so openly?

"Four o'clock?" I'd checked my schedule for openings before I came.

"Fine."

I gave him my business card with my address.

"Does my wife need to come?"

My recollection of his wife at the funeral brought up an image of a plain, sweet woman. "Only you."

We chatted a few more minutes before parting.

Aaron surprised me, wanting to start our counseling quickly, but the sooner I fit in these extra sessions while the kids were gone, the better. I intended to find out what caused the long-term antagonism and if the reason was strong enough to prompt murder.

17

A fragrance of cinnamon and roses wafted from the potpourri bowl on my bookcase. Streaks of morning sun slathered the beige walls and blue-gray furniture. My quiet office setting stirred peace within me. This room held as many secrets as a confessional and had provided a haven for my clients and me for years.

Ellen sat at her desk in the outer reception room processing clients' records and payments that had arrived in preprinted return envelopes. I handled all other correspondence and my stack was high today.

What might my children be doing right now? I smiled at the thought of them as I slipped the letter-opener into the next envelope. A three-by-five note card slid out. "Stay away from the Windemeres or you'll wish you had." My heart pounded. I re-read the words written in bold, black capital letters.

My comfortable coziness shattered. I dropped the note card as if it were a cockroach darting into my hand. I perused the room. How could my office still look serene after this violation of my private space?

I took a deep breath and forced myself to pick up the envelope and examine it. Addressed to me all right. No mistake. The font was familiar — Times New Roman, twelve point, printed with an inkjet or laser printer on a cheap white Number 10 envelope. I'd narrowed the hunt to how many millions?

Analyzing these features took my mind off the words, even as my subconscious registered them over and over. I'd received my first-ever anonymous threat. This stuff belonged in movies, not my life.

No specific consequences were stated in the note. Cliché type content. Was that good or bad? What past experience did I have for evaluating a threatening letter?

Who would send it? Was this a harmless ruse by a less-than-eager client, most likely Crystal? A dramatic, emotionally overwrought person? Did she think she could scare me away from my counseling commitment and avoid attending her sessions with me? Or might it have been sent by Aaron? Outwardly compliant, inwardly seething?

Hadn't he seemed almost too willing to proceed with counseling? Did he expect I'd cancel after getting this threat?

Al's former business partner or clients might see me as meddling. The person most annoyed with my poking around looking for clues would be Al's murderer.

Any of the Windemere clients could be trying to weasel out of what they perceived to be an unpleasant, perhaps emotionally painful experience.

Who, other than the family, would know or even care that I was involved? Moments ticked by during which I became more annoyed than scared. This note was ridiculous.

Still I needed to call Nick. Wait. I had a decision to make. Should I share this with him? Maybe not, at least not right away. Usually, I disclose everything, but if he knew, he'd insist I stop working with the Windemeres. Why should I let Crystal or whoever sent this stop me?

I squared my shoulders. It would take more than a silly note to dissuade me from hunting for Al's killer and helping his family. I picked up my steaming coffee, held it to my nose for a warming fire, breathed the vapors, and then gulped it like a drug to settle my inner turmoil.

By staying in sweet denial, I managed to

function in a fairly normal state the rest of the day.

Aaron Windemere arrived on the dot at 4:00 PM fidgety as a cricket in contrast to yesterday's smooth, poised behavior. "What exactly is this counseling about? I should have gotten more details from you." Had he been talking to someone who'd raised his concern?

Who isn't nervous today, Aaron? You should have seen my mail!

His attitude and appearance of vulnerability stirred my sympathy. He wore a dark green jogging suit with white tennis shoes. I scanned the standard intake form he'd completed in my outer office. No previous counseling experience. College-educated. Princeton. Summa cum laude.

Months ago, Al had wanted Aaron to see me for counseling. Should I be direct and ask immediately why Al considered that necessary? *Go slow, Jennifer. Don't scare him. Remember counseling 101, establish relationship first.*

I noted a reminder on the intake form. "Usually, I'd start with the presenting problem that brings you in, but this session is different since you didn't initiate counseling. It would help if you would tell me in your own words a bit about your background."

"Where should I begin?"

"What are the strongest memories that stand out as you look back on your childhood?"

Aaron pondered a minute. "In high school I hit the books hard, especially science which earned me a scholarship. After graduation, I worked in medical research a couple of years before starting my floral business."

"Why did you switch?"

He twisted his face into a grimace. "You sound like my dad. He thought I was weird."

"I didn't mean to imply that it wasn't a wise choice. I just asked."

"Frankly, I found research boring. I'd been employed part-time on weekends and every summer by a florist to help pay my school expenses, and I enjoyed that."

Aaron went into detail about the flower business and his love for the design possibilities nature presented. "Hands-on science, first hand interaction, that's what I like, not laboratory research," he concluded.

I'd expected he might be closed up, and I'd have to drag things out of him. No problem so far.

"Makes sense. You demonstrated your creative talent the other day. I was impressed, Aaron."

He shrugged. "My father disapproved when I left what he called the world of intelligentsia. He said I was nuts, that only some pansy plays with flowers. Nice pun, huh?" His slumped shoulders and mumbling revealed this was no joking matter to Aaron. "Al, of course, joined in the mockery."

Aaron's face turned red. His transformation was amazing.

"I'm sorry. That must have been painful."

"I remember Dad's exact words. 'Go waste your IQ! Pussyfoot around with your darn flowers. Ruin your life. I don't want to watch.' I can still see the sawdust in the garage where he stood." Aaron winced. "Funny how a parent's words stay with you, isn't it?"

I nodded. "Sometimes for better; sometimes for worse."

"Mine were the latter. I was twenty-five at the time and still living at home. My father actually kicked me out. I didn't mind. I was old enough to give up the free board, but his words stung."

"How did he respond later to your success in business?"

"Never knew. He died several months before I opened my first store. Now I have four locations and a booming Internet business and real estate besides."

"You're obviously pleased with your career?"

Aaron nodded. "I'm very content in floral work, although maybe my drive to succeed initially was to make a statement to my father." Aaron fidgeted and tapped his fingers lightly on the chair arm. "I always regretted that my dad and I weren't closer."

I made a note to pursue this and gave Aaron a moment to collect himself. "Feeling inadequate because you can't please a parent is painful, also very common. Many think their experience of distress is totally unique. Perhaps knowing you're not alone is a comfort."

Aaron rubbed his hands together. "My inability to please him started way before college."

"Tell me about the relationship between you and Al."

"We didn't have much of one, but I hate to think my brother would kill himself. The idea of Al's being murdered upsets me but not as much as suicide."

"Understandable."

"Death came at the worst time for Al. He was always a go-getter in search of something more. After Rose's illness, during it maybe, I'm not sure of the time sequence, he got religious and seemed to view the purpose of his life and death differently. He'd been telling me he finally knew what life was about, and his attitude changed."

"How?"

"Hard to describe. He seemed more at peace. Funny, I'd never known him to be content before. I still didn't agree with him about everything, but I could understand him better. He started acting like a buddy — we were never close before."

"Forming a better relationship with you was important to Al. He told me he cared about you very much."

"He waited long enough to show it." A shadow crossed Aaron's face, and for a moment, I heard a tone of bitterness. "We weren't the best of friends as kids."

"Why not?"

He shrugged. "Family stuff. I'd rather not go into that. It doesn't matter. I finally got past it."

I looked at my notes. "Al wanted you to come see me for counseling months ago. What was that about?"

"I don't know."

"Might it have been regarding your marriage?"

"Lorraine and I pretty much go our separate ways. She seems to be a little

152

touchy lately, maybe going through the change. I understand women can be pretty miserable during it." Aaron worked his lips into a half-smile.

He was being co-operative, answering my questions mechanically, like a contestant on a quiz show, wanting to give the right answer and move on. Aaron couldn't offer any other reason why Al had suggested he get counseling. I didn't buy that. My instincts told me he knew something.

This first session would focus only on assessment and general background issues. I wrapped it up.

After Aaron left, I wrote counseling goals in his folder. Check underlying anger. Examine family/friend relationship issues in depth — mom, dad, wife, brother.

He seemed fragile and strong at the same time. Why did I have the feeling I was missing something?

18

"I need to see you ASAP, Ms. Trevor." Angela Thursted's tone, as well as her words, sounded ominous.

I flipped through my appointment book. "I don't have an opening until the day after tomorrow other than lunch today at twelve. You could come then if it's really important."

"Yes, please."

"I have forty-five minutes. Come to my office? I'll order in sandwiches."

I gave her my address and had Ellen send out for two tuna subs on wheat with fruit cups.

At twelve o' five, Angela sat in my client chair with a napkin in her lap. White hose again, this time no sag, complemented her ivory lace blouse.

"Thanks for fitting me in."

"Sure." I slipped papers back into a client's folder to clear my desk and handed her a wrapped sandwich. I observed her left hand, void of a wedding ring. Had she had a crush on Al Windemere? I wondered if there had ever been a romance between them. I doubted she'd be his type.

Angela pushed a misplaced strand of hair from off her forehead and twisted her can of soda.

"Hope you like tuna," I said opening my waxed paper.

"It's fine." She centered the sandwich on the napkin in her lap. An aura of competence always emanated from Angela. I surmised she could run American Investment Realty without Windemere or Halston's overt management, but she'd be bright enough not to let on. She seemed the kind of woman who likes to excel and keep life in compartments. An affair with the boss might be complicated.

"Angela, you're an attractive woman. Were you ever married?" Bold question, but she didn't flinch.

"Once, for six months. Big mistake. Why do you ask?"

I stuck a straw in my iced tea. "Just wondered. Now what did you want to see me about?"

Her eyes widened. "The police were going through Mr. Windemere's file cabinet with me, and we found a business buy-out agreement. Mr. Windemere had penciled in figures. I think he was planning to sell his shares." She rattled on with details, stopping only once to sip her drink.

"I understood the partners were super-dependent upon one another and the business would suffer if they split?"

"Lately, Mr. Windemere didn't seem to care as much about the company's success. I think he wanted more time for his family and other interests. He'd gotten into antique furniture investments also."

"Did Halston know about this proposed buy-out?"

"I have no idea if Mr. Windemere had given copies of the papers to him yet. If so, he'd be upset. I heard him deny knowledge of it to the police. But the timing is amazing." Angela slid to the edge of her chair.

"What do you mean?"

"The two argued often, but Mr. Windemere always said Halston was stuck with him. He'd never leave. Mr. Halston would get annoyed about the way Mr. Windemere handled a transaction or the unrealistic time frame he'd promise for a closing that had us all scrambling. I heard Halston threaten several times to break the partnership, but when he'd cool off, he'd regret it and apologize."

"How did Mr. Windemere generally react to Halston's anger?"

"He didn't seem to care. I think each knew he could have found another partner easily or could have been a success on his own with good administrative help." She blushed. "Yet he had appeared content with things the way they were."

Perhaps this was only Angela's biased opinion.

I crushed my napkin and tossed it into the deli bag.

"Something else," Angela added. "When I assembled papers requested by the police, I found among them a company insurance policy. At the start of the partnership each man took out insurance that specifies in the event of the death of one, insurance proceeds would buy out the living person's stock. The business would revert 100 percent to the surviving partner with no financial outlay. This means Mr. Halston now owns all of American Realty Investment and didn't have to pay a penny." Angela sounded as if the man had stolen the crown jewels.

My mind cried out murder motive. I leaned back against my chair and chose my next words with care. "How nice to own all of American Realty and run it without buy-out cost. Angela, you're raising a serious accusation about Mr. Halston. You don't like him, do you?"

Angela squeezed her sandwich wrap tightly into a ball and dropped it into the garbage can next to my desk. "He's rude and unfeeling." She tossed her head back. "And often bad-mouthed Mr. Windemere behind his back."

"Which must have upset you." I eyed her sharply. "You're telling me because this could be an incentive for murder. However, such an insurance arrangement is not unusual. Your loyalty to Al Windemere is highly commendable. May I ask you a personal question?"

Angela looked at me warily but didn't say no.

I tucked a loose strand of hair behind my ear and waited a moment. "Were you romantically involved with Mr. Windemere?"

Angela straightened, her shoulders raised. "Of course not!"

"Please don't be offended. I want to be sure I view this data correctly. Forget I asked. I appreciate your bringing it to my attention. If Mr. Jacobsen knew, he never mentioned it. I'll check it out." I stood. "I have a client due any minute, so I need to excuse myself. Let me know if you learn anything more. Stay in touch."

Angela gathered her things and departed with less enthusiasm than when she'd come. I knew I hadn't reacted as strongly as she'd expected to the insurance information. I sensed an emotional switch in her had been pulled by this knowledge.

I organized my files for the afternoon. Was Angela a vindictive, scorned woman? Had she hired someone to kill Windemere? Perhaps the police were getting close to her, and was she throwing suspicion on Halston as a decoy? Human motivation is perhaps the most complex force on earth.

19

On my way home from work, I stopped at Aaron's Floral Shop to select a gift for my in-laws. I usually order floral arrangements online to save time. My modus operandi is to zealously guard every spare moment for my children, but they were away and the shop was only three blocks off my regular route, and I was curious.

The one-story, green wooden building accented with brownstone had extensions protruding in three directions. Behind the longest, a large attached greenhouse could be seen with its steamy windows.

I instantly liked the fragrance inside. Vanilla, apple, and cinnamon drifted from candles burning in glass jars on the counters. Fresh flowers in vases and hundreds of silk arrangements adorned tabletops and hung from arches of wood and metal. Hanging plants were suspended tastefully throughout.

The containers ranged from simple to ornate with a profusion of shiny brass, sculpted materials, and glazed ceramics. I'd need an hour browsing to do the place justice. Reluctantly, I turned my back on the artistic splendor and strolled to the counter to place my order.

Rich appeared from the rear room wearing casual tan slacks and a blue work jacket over a perfectly pressed blue oxford cloth shirt. Only regular exercise could create the physique of this good-looking man. His youthful features seemed contradicted by wizened eyes. He greeted me warmly, although I doubted he remembered meeting me.

I dug up memories of Rich from the funeral. He hadn't sat with the family but had assisted mourners, moving through the receiving line. Afterwards, he'd milled among the lingerers.

"May I help you?" he inquired.

"Is Aaron in?"

"I'm sorry, he's out at the moment. I'm the store manager. May I help?" I gave Rich a ten on my Competent Employee chart.

"Yes. I stopped in to select an arrangement to send to my in-laws to thank them for watching my children. Do you have something a bit out of the ordinary? My mother-in-law is very creative and artsy — she'd appreciate uniqueness."

"We can certainly manage that." Rich reached under the counter for a catalog. "Let me show you pictures of what's available. Of course, we can do a special order as well, but I think you'll find something suitable here."

He flipped through the laminated pages, showing me options and offering to call the local florist on the other end to make sure the required flowers were in stock and there'd be no change from the picture. He explained the pros and cons of various greenery and the expected longevity of different flowers.

I admired his attentiveness to detail and the way he made me feel like the only customer in the store even though two people were waiting behind me at the counter, making me want to hurry.

Rich called a girl from the back to assist the other customers and guided me to the privacy of the bridal planning counter.

"Take your time," he said. "We want your mother-in-law to be thrilled with the result. It should express her."

I made my choice and then gave him my name, address, and credit card for billing.

He looked at the name, then at me more

closely. "You're Dr. Trevor?"

"Yes."

"I understand you're helping Al Windemere's family."

I smiled before I responded to sound less rude. "I'm sorry. I can't comment." Did the whole world know?

"Al and I were on close terms. He helped me with some real estate transactions, and he used space in my furniture warehouse for his expanding antique business. If I can assist in any way, please call. My contact with the family goes back several years. Suicide is horrible," he added.

"Thank you, Rich. How very kind. Give my regards to Aaron when he comes in. By the way, did you know Mr. Windemere's death was very possibly a murder, not suicide?"

His eyes widened. "I hadn't heard." He started to speak then perhaps thought better of it.

I would have given twenty dollars, maybe more, to know what he'd left unsaid.

20

I lowered my fork speared with chicken cor-
don bleu — my yummy freezer-to-
microwave masterpiece of the evening. Nick
and I sat in our quiet kitchen alcove ex-
changing news of our day before he went to
his men's group meeting.

Nick's eyes twinkled. "I've got big news. I
expect a huge reward. I asked around, and I
think I found your mystery woman."

My attention riveted on his face. "Great!
Who is she?"

"Ann Tylore. A broker who moves in the
same investment circles and works for a
competitor of American Realty. Rumor is,
before Windemere began his major life
transformation, she and Al had a lengthy affair."

"I wonder if Rose knew she came. She
doesn't need more pain added to her memories of her husband."

Nick tipped his chair back. "As I see it,

this gives a motive to both Rose and Ann Tylore. A jealous wife or a rejected ex-lover."

"Right." I buttered my roll, thoughtful.

"Ann may have expected Ms. Windemere to die from cancer. She only had to wait for Al to be free. But by the time she found out Rose was pulling through, Al had cleaned up his act and didn't want to leave Rose, which potentially created a lot of emotional pain, maybe even murderous rage."

"I agree about Ann Tylore's motive but doubt Al Windemere's murderer could be his frail wife."

Nick shrugged. "She could have planned it and hired a killer. She seems sweet and innocent, but maybe that's an act. Didn't you say Rose acted in amateur theater?"

"Yes, and Al truly loved her. I can't imagine she could do such a thing."

"Ann, then. The mistress?"

"If she arranged for Al's murder, why come to the funeral? To gloat?"

"It's certainly been done by killers, some even attend out of remorse."

"I suppose." I sensed the skin between my eyebrows tightening. Relationships become so confusing when infidelity enters the picture.

"Well, think about it. I'm off." Nick

shoved a sugar cookie in his mouth, pulled a V-neck sweater over his head, and grabbed a canned iced tea from the refrigerator. "I'll be back around nine. What do you have planned for tonight?"

"Catching up on professional reading. When the kids return, I want to be ready to spend every possible minute with them."

His lips brushed mine. "See you later."

I settled down in front of the TV but didn't turn it on. Instead I sloughed off my slippers, stretched out my legs on the coffee table, and attacked my pile of mail, a stack of flyers, bills, magazines, and professional journals.

Halfway through, I opened a nine-by-twelve manila envelope. The address was scribbled in sloppy writing on the front. I reached in. At first it seemed as if nothing were inside. Then I felt a tiny piece of paper, pulled it out, scanned the printing, and jumped to my feet. The papers and magazines on my lap dive-bombed to the floor.

Since the first threatening note last Saturday, I'd analyzed every number ten envelope before opening it, but this big manila one caught me off guard. The element of surprise irritated me as much as the content. *Stay away from the Windemeres. Don't be foolish, or you and your family will pay.*

166

A chill surged through me, followed by anger. How melodramatic. I wanted to laugh it off but couldn't. My fingers trembled as I slipped the note back into the envelope. It needed to go back to wherever it came from.

The postmark, same as before, routed through Milwaukee. All mail from the small towns in our area cleared there.

I ran to the kitchen and grabbed my cell phone off the counter to call Nick's parents. I needed to make sure the children were OK. My hand shook. I forced my voice to sound calm. I wanted to hug Collin, Tara, and Jenny at this very moment.

Nick's mother answered on the third ring. I hurried through the 'how are you' formalities. "Please put the children on, Mom."

"Sure. Here's Jenny."

"Are you feeding my fish?" my sweet youngest daughter demanded.

"They're doing fine. Mommy misses you. Daddy too."

"Same here, Mom, but we're having fun with Grandma and Grandpa." She rattled on about their trip to the zoo and her favorite animals. After she finished, I asked to speak to her big sister, Tara.

I heard a shuffling and then Tara came on. "How are you, Mom?"

"Fine now that I'm hearing your voice. We chatted briefly. "Put your brother on next, sweetheart."

"I can't. He's not here."

My grip tightened on the receiver. "Grandma said everyone was home. Where's Collin?"

Tara laughed. "Relax, Mom. He and Grandpa are outside working in the garden, and he's covered with mud."

"Oh." I tried to mask my relief. "Give him my love." I hung up and collapsed on the sofa. If anything happened to my children, I'd never forgive myself. No more denial. Nick had to know. I dreaded his response to my correspondence.

At nine-fifteen, Nick bounded in and pecked my cheek. He dropped onto the sofa next to me.

I wasted no time. "Guess what the post-man brought?" I tried to make light of it — my defense mechanism for dealing with overwhelming situations.

"A letter from the kids?" Nick showed mild interest, clicking on the TV.

"I wish. Could you leave that off a minute, hon. I got er . . . a threatening note."

He clicked off the TV.

"What?" Nick's tone expressed the shock etched on his face.

Despite my surface composure, my hands were icy. Had all color left my face? "It could have been a bomb. I guess I should be relieved."

"Jennifer, that's not funny. What's going on?"

Prickles ran down my back. "You're making this seem like I've done something I shouldn't have." I twisted the envelope nervously. "This isn't my fault."

"Let me see it." Nick became all business. I opened the envelope in my lap and pushed the note toward him as if it carried plague germs.

As he examined it, I added, "This is, er, the second note." My voice quivered saying the words. Speaking quietly made it seem less ominous. "The first one came to my office."

"What?" Nick shouted.

"I'll get it. Be right back." I rose shakily to my feet and went into the bedroom to retrieve the note from my drawer. I didn't look at him as I handed him the paper.

"Why didn't you tell me right away?" Hurt laced his words. I couldn't bear to hear him like this.

"I figured the first was written by Crystal or a harmless busybody who knew I was working with the family and hoped to dissuade me. I didn't take it seriously."

"Obviously not," Nick mocked. "Why is that?" He glared.

"I worried you'd try to make me quit my work with the family and the investigation."

Nick folded both notes carefully and returned them to their envelopes. He looked at me with mingled anger and concern in his eyes.

"We'll contact the local police first thing tomorrow, and I'll call Inspector Jarston." I wrapped my arms around Nick's neck and kissed him. "Please don't worry."

He gently pushed my arms down. "The most important thing either of us can do is pray."

"Yes." I bowed my head. "I'm so sorry. I'll never keep anything from you again. I promise."

He took my hand. "Lord, protect my wife and children and bring this Windemere situation to a speedy end. Mend their family relationships and expose the killer."

"Yes, Lord," I added, "and heal the hurts of all those Al cared about. Thank You, Lord for Your love and protection."

We ended with an Our Father, my favorite prayer. I clung to the words, "deliver us from evil" saying them in my mind over and over.

21

I pressed the number of the Wisconsin Dells Police Department on my office phone. I wasn't thrilled about another contact with Inspector Jarston.

To my surprise, the receptionist put me through immediately.

"Hello, Inspector. This is Dr. Jennifer Trevor . . ."

I noted the nervous catch in my voice. If I got to know this man better, maybe I'd become more relaxed. He wasn't the TV type investigator depicted as a bumbling dingbat. No sane person would use such a description for Inspector Jarston.

"How's everything?" What a dumb thing to ask. He investigates crime. Everything's never fine.

"Ah, Dr. Trevor. You've called because you found additional information in your records? Tell me. What is it?"

I caught the underlying tone in his

brusqueness — don't waste my time.

I underlined the note I'd written on my pad, *Get right to it.* "I wanted to confirm that you've definitely ruled out suicide?" Even as I said the words they sounded arrogant . . . have you come around to my way of thinking?

"I'd hoped the pathology report would settle the issue, but the findings are ambiguous enough to be interpreted either way. This lack of clarity is not uncommon, but under the circumstances, it's most unfortunate."

"Yes, indeed."

"You'll be happy to know we came up with a witness, Dr. Trevor. A paperboy saw someone jogging not far from the site of the shooting, a man in a baseball cap wearing a jogging suit. Possibly no connection," Jarston stressed in the next breath, "but we put out a media alert for him to come forward. So far no one has."

I rubbed my right arm suddenly remembering the scary guy during my walk to the deli. "Interesting." I swallowed hard and told Jarston about my threatening notes.

"Obviously, someone doesn't want you meddling."

"You asked me to review Al's file. I'm afraid it didn't reveal any information that could help the investigation, but it does confirm my original conclusion. It's highly unlikely Mr. Windemere was suicidal."

"Really? Would your adamant denial of his suicide be a desire to illustrate the effectiveness of your counseling? Wouldn't a suicide reflect poorly on your ability?"

The back of my neck tingled. "To imply such a thing is insulting. I'm more concerned about giving the false impression that people like Al Windemere can't truly change. I know better."

"Remember, we have a suicide note, however suspect it may be. Businessmen with problems do kill themselves."

I took a deep breath. So what if Jarston considered my help meddling. "Mr. Windemere's personality brought out strong reactions in people." My next words tumbled out. "Several people had the means, the motive, and probably the opportunity, Inspector. When you dig a little deeper, I think you'll agree."

"Dr. Trevor, I'll say murder is my gut sense, if that's any consolation to you. By the way, I must warn you to watch yourself. These notes could portent harm. I assume your local police will be kept informed."

"Of course, I'm well aware of the threat."

I heard Jarston shuffling papers in the

background. "Do call again if you uncover any facts to confirm your assumption of murder." He emphasized the word *facts*. "Now you must excuse me. I'm rather busy." He said good-bye with a barely tolerant air.

I dropped my head into my hands and moaned aloud. "What a painful and useless conversation."

22

The tranquil CD of classical instrumentals I use for counseling sessions played softly in the background, but I felt anything but peaceful.

I sent my children a chatty e-mail before the arrival of my first client Rose Windemere. *Keep them safe, Lord.* I closed my laptop and reviewed my schedule for the day.

Busy but doable. I marveled again at Al's wisdom in setting up this unique counseling requirement prior to distribution of the inheritance monies. Money wields power, even posthumously. Al was accustomed to accomplishing his objective. This strategy might make it happen. I sipped the remains of my tea.

Rose's voice sounded in the outer office through the slightly ajar door. Ellen led her in. A strong floral scent drifted into the office with Rose. Good thing I'm not allergic to perfume.

She selected the straight-back chair a few feet from my own and perched primly on the edge. Her lovely green knit suit probably came from Crystal's clothing shop along with her brown alligator bag and shoes. Total effect elegant. Despite her diminutive height, she wore low heels. Obviously comfort and practicality were most important. I imagined her dwarfed next to Al's tall, debonair handsomeness. I've known many six-foot-plus men with doll-sized wives.

"Welcome, Rose. If at any time you feel you're not up to continuing with today's session, we can stop."

She nodded and picked up the pen I offered. "I almost didn't come, but now that I'm here I glad." She pointed toward the two Norman Rockwell prints on the wall. "I never noticed those before. They make it seem cozy in here."

"I'm glad you think so. When feuding married clients see the picture of a young couple signing their marriage license, I hope to stir memories of a happier time. The Rockwell town meeting picture with the gentleman in the suede jacket speaking his piece, hopefully, reminds clients that courage and truth must prevail."

"I like that."

Possibly athletic in her youth, I observed Rose's arm and leg muscles had atrophied with age and the effects of cancer treatment. Despite her fragile physical appearance, Al said she'd been emotionally strong during it. From counseling cancer survivors, I know those who battle this ugly monster discover strengths they never knew they had. It's a privilege to work with such brave people. Once the threat of death is past, they embrace life with more gusto than ever.

"Now tell me how you're doing."

"I'm coping," she sighed, "at least on the surface. I'm used to being alone a lot, one benefit from our previous lifestyle." Rose's lips formed a sad smile as she crossed her legs. "I always think of myself as a survivor. I couldn't be married to a flamboyant, adventurous man like Al and not worry he'd beat me to the grave. Not that I ever wanted that to happen."

"Of course not."

"Eventually, I learned not to worry every time he went on a business trip. Because of my cancer this past year, our roles switched. He was concerned about my dying and his being left alone. He couldn't have been more attentive. I think before he'd assumed I'd always be there. It pleased me that in some way I was a source of security for him."

"Your cancer treatment made Al more mindful of how much he loved you and how you'd suffered emotionally. He grieved for having hurt you."

"In many ways my cancer became a blessing. We each worked through our own life and death issues. My remission has been an unexpected bonus." Rose paused and took a sip from the water bottle she'd brought.

"I'm glad you're doing well."

"For now at least."

Did she know something she wasn't telling? Or was she simply stating the fear that all cancer patients have regarding the future?

"I hope you never have to go through the emotional loss of a husband. Knowing there will never be another hello, another hug. The circumstances of his death still bother me. I have nightmares of him covered with blood. It's hard to shake the horrid image."

"How awful."

"Crystal complains I talk about him all the time."

"You can discuss your husband as much as you like here."

She gave me a weak smile. "When Paul Jacobsen called to tell me about the trust funds, I wasn't surprised. I know how badly

Al had wanted to make things right with Ken, Crystal and Aaron, too. He never said much about his brother, but I know the emotional distance between them bothered him."

"Any other relational problems you know of?"

Rose pursed her lips.

"Al stored antiques at Rich Nichols' storage warehouse. Al didn't care much for him personally, I'm not sure why. I always found Rich charming. But Al tolerated Rich for Aaron's sake, and had some business deals with him."

Rose pressed her hands together firmly in her lap. "Al had become kind, but you and I both know he wasn't always. The years of his affairs were very difficult for me, but that's all in the past. I resolved my hurt long ago."

"Are you sure you don't need to explore this further?"

"No." Rose's voice turned sharp. "I only need your help sorting out who hated my husband enough to kill him. You went to his office?"

"I did."

"What did you find out?"

"Several people appear to have disliked Al intensely, particularly his business partner."

"I'm aware of that. Dislike is a rather mild word? At times Halston was quite vocal about wanting him dead. Unfortunately, my daughter said the same thing, but I refuse to believe she meant it."

"Based on my first meeting, I'd say she harbors intense anger toward him."

"Crystal and her father were never on good terms, but she wouldn't kill him. She may have fantasized it, but she loves me too much to hurt me like that. She and the grandchildren are all I have now. Our missing son despised his father. That's why Ken left." Rose sighed and swallowed hard before going on. "Something else. I was distressed to learn Crystal and Halston were at the Dells together the weekend of the murder. I believe she dated him just to hurt her father."

"They were seeing each other?" I blurted out, not concealing my surprise.

"She started several months ago. I wasn't in favor — he's much older. Anyway, she told me yesterday she and Halston broke up."

Rose looked so pitiful I patted her hand. "I'm sorry you have this concern over Crystal to deal with, too."

My brain spun. Halston and Crystal both had motive as well as opportunity. Had Halston left town because he thought Crystal killed Al and feared he'd be implicated? Or had Halston killed Al on the golf course, and was he worried that Crystal suspected him?

Rose rested her head against the back of her chair and closed her eyes.

"Who arranged the party at the Dells?"

"Al had invited Crystal for my birthday brunch and to play golf with him beforehand. Crystal declined his golf invitation as usual. I wondered why Al still asked her. She always rejected him, but she agreed to attend my birthday brunch. Aaron and his wife were invited also."

"Do the police know about Crystal and Halston's relationship?"

"I hope not." Rose sat up straighter. "You won't tell them? I certainly didn't." She finished in a tearful voice. "I can't bear to lose her, too."

My blood ran cold. My goodness, she seriously thought Crystal was a possible murderer. How could a father cause such hatred in a child that his wife actually feared their daughter could kill him? Sad! Therapists are trained to hide their feelings and to not make judgments. Still, we can't help having them.

Rose pulled a tissue from a pack in her

purse, patted her eyes, and composed herself. "You're at a disadvantage under-standing Crystal's feelings. You knew Al after he made changes in relating to us. The Al we lived with for over two decades was, well frankly, an extremely difficult person."

"Tell me how that affected you."

"He partied as hard as he worked and ignored us entirely except to pay the house-hold bills. I went through therapy years ago to help me cope. Nothing changed until his Christian conversion. Crystal has every reason to be bitter. Her father was not only a womanizer, but a mean alcoholic." Rose's voice took on a monotone quality, as if she were speaking about a character in a book, not the man she'd lived with.

I pressed Rose for details, although I knew some from my counseling sessions with Al.

"His new obsession became AA meetings four nights a week and events at church. God knows I've had plenty of reasons to be upset with Al throughout our marriage."

"Rose, this next question may be difficult for you. We don't need to go here if you don't want to. In our previous joint sessions we talked about strategies to strengthen your marriage but never discussed details about Al's unfaithfulness. This may be beneficial now if you're up to it. Perhaps we should consider these other women in your husband's life as suspects. One of them could be responsible for his murder, if not by pulling the trigger, then by hiring someone to do it."

Rose took a deep breath and straightened her shoulders. "Nothing is off the table for clues leading to Al's murderer. What would you like to know?" She looked so piteous. I had all I could do to keep my eyes dry and proceed. "Women have told me a husband's death is easier to deal with than his deceit. You've experienced both. Any details about his liaisons could be helpful."

Silence followed. I lowered my face so she wouldn't see my emotion. If only men knew how deeply betrayal hurts their wives. Rose shifted position on her chair. Her eyes darkened. "They were mostly professional contacts at first made through work." She dabbed at a tear with her thumb. "Not with his assistant, Angela, if that's what you're thinking. She adored him, and I'm sure Al played on those emotions, but Angela wasn't his type. He viewed her as a useful tool. I know that sounds terrible. She'd do anything for him, often working nights and weekends to get paperwork ready for deals he'd neglected until the last minute. Impulsive and charming, he attracted women like bees swarming heather." Rose sighed deeply.

"How painful."

"Foolishly, I felt I could keep him content." She looked away. "I suppose in some fashion I did. He stayed with me anyway."

"Did you discuss his behavior?"

"He denied everything. When I became aware how serious his philandering was, I begged Al to go for counseling, but he refused. Eventually, everything had been said, and his ears were deaf to me."

I kept my head bent over my legal pad jotting notes to better maintain a stony expression. I hurt for women like her and often had to suppress anger toward men who didn't keep their commitment to their wives.

Rose stood and wandered to the window. She seemed to be looking out, but I doubt she saw the view. Maybe she'd functioned in her marriage by looking but not seeing.

"Quite honestly, at first I wasn't bothered much. I assumed he was just flirting, an innocent game, and I'm ashamed to say I was willing to tolerate it. Don't all men flirt?"

"Flirting can be dangerous. Few men learn this until it's too late and inappropriate emotional connections have developed."

"My husband could sweet-talk a watermelon." A tiny smile crossed Rose's face as she sat back down. "He'd wink at me when I'd hear him on the phone with a woman, clinching a sale. I hoped naïvely it was only business."

"You weren't initially upset by these manipulations?" I felt as though I were listening to a soap episode about value-free living among the rich and famous.

"No, definitely not at first."

Her response was not healthy. How hurt I'd be if Nick behaved this way.

"Al said a business proposal was a done deal if he could make his presentation to the wife as well as her husband. I knew he manipulated women's emotions unashamedly, but most of the time, I didn't care probably because I was privy to his act and felt secure."

"Then something changed?"

"He didn't sleep with these women, until" — Rose's voice broke — "With Ann Tylore I felt threatened for the first time. I met her at a business dinner function. Seeing the way Al looked at her, I knew she was a danger. Another woman, an investor, Joanna Tuler, seemed to have charmed Al as well. She called the house several times. I'm not sure what their relationship was." Rose gripped the chair arms with white-knuckle force and glared as she spoke. "Ann Tylore came to Al's funeral. The nerve!" Rose clenched her hands and sat back.

"If Ann Tylore still had feelings for Al and thought you didn't know about her, she felt safe to come to the service."

Rose's flare-up at Ann Tylore shocked me. I'd never seen her so distressed. My eyebrows lifted as a horrid thought came to me. Despite my overwhelming sympathy, could I rule out this intelligent, controlled lady as a suspect? Had she been the one who hired someone to kill her husband? Chills ran down my arms.

Rose visibly relaxed. "Shortly after Al got religion, he confessed the affairs to me and promised to change his ways. I believe he was sincere. But seeing her there, well, I wonder, do you think he did end it?"

"Based on his desire to live a Christian lifestyle, yes, I'm sure he ended it."

Rose shook her shoulders as if shaking off bugs. "If Ann Tylore or Joanna Tuler couldn't deal with Al's ending their relationship, they have a motive for having him murdered."

"Highly possible." Could Rose be trying to deflect blame onto these other women to protect herself?

Rose frowned. "Perhaps I should tell the police about these relationships?" She shook her head. "No. I don't want attention given to Al's flamboyant past."

I knew the police would investigate this on their own. "Does anyone else come to mind as a suspect?"

"I noticed Al seemed to be brooding over something the last few weeks. He wasn't as upbeat as usual. I've wondered if what was disturbing him was connected to his murder."

"Did you question him?"

"He said it was nothing we needed to talk about. It wasn't like him to be secretive again, because he'd recently become so open. Then there's the gun."

"What about it?"

"The police informed me the gun found next to his body was his. I explained it had been stolen from our bedroom nightstand after our Fourth of July party last year."

"Which would mean the murderer was in your home. Do you have a list of the guests who attended the party?"

"We had a party after my treatment ended and invited a large group of family and business acquaintances to celebrate."

"Why would guests be in your bedroom during a party?"

"Access to the master bath is through our bedroom. When we entertain a large gathering of guests we allow them to use all our bathrooms."

"I suppose the night table was a logical place to look. Who knew Al owned a gun?"

"He bragged openly about keeping a gun for protection." Rose dabbed at her eyes.

We spent the rest of the appointment focused on healing of memories.

"Maybe when you counsel the others, more clues will turn up," Rose said wistfully before she left.

I drew a deep breath. *Rose*, I wanted to say, *don't put your hopes on me*, but I couldn't. She looked so forlorn. I only nodded.

23

I was running through a carnival chased by a clown wearing a baseball cap. A bell struck by a muscle man gonged. The barker shouted, "Ring it again and win a prize." Incessant clanging jarred my dreams.

I opened my eyes to watch the sledgehammer strike. Instead, I was in bed next to my snoring husband, and the phone was ringing. I clumsily reached toward the persistent noise. My vocal chords moved from reflex.

"Hello," I mumbled into the receiver.

"I'm watching you. When you're alone and least expect it, I'll be there! You can count on it." The connection went dead.

I dropped the receiver onto my nightstand. Revulsion soured my stomach.

Nick awakened, saw my face, and grabbed the phone. "Who is this?" he demanded.

"Don't bother. No one's there." I was shivering and couldn't stop.

Nick tried to trace the call to no avail.

"Was the voice a man or woman's?"

"I can't be sure. It sounded stifled, as though speaking through a scarf or cloth. I could barely hear it." I repeated the words, remembering every syllable.

Nick's expression was grim. "Any distinguishable background noise?"

I pulled the comforter snugly around me. "No."

Nick brushed my arm. "How upsetting. Can you go back to sleep, sweetheart?"

"I doubt it."

"Try." His tone was protective as he laid his hand across my forehead and prayed over me for peace, sleep, and safety.

Amazingly, I did sleep, although at 7:00 AM, I felt as though I'd been up half the night. Nick and I both had early appointments. We made plans to meet back home at noon. Somehow, I got through the morning.

By twelve, my fear was replaced with hard, cold anger.

Nick wasted no time when he walked in the door. "Jennifer, you need to terminate these Windemere clients immediately. I rarely interfere with your work, but this is different. A call on top of the notes is too much." He dropped his suit jacket over the kitchen chair arm. I clamped my lips shut

190

and let him vent.

"Your safety. The threatening call . . ."

"Whoa. It may not have anything to do with the Windemeres. It could have been a prank, one of Collin's teenage friends. Do you want me scared off? I'm doing the right thing. Scripture says we should not fear what man can do." I was already plenty nervous, but I talked steadily to persuade Nick.

"You're missing the point. If you get hurt, I'll be furious with myself for not making you avoid potential contact with a murderer."

"The fact is we have no proof. I simply can't abandon these people." I kissed his forehead, hoping to erase the concern in his eyes.

It didn't help.

"You are so stubborn." Nick gazed at me somberly and then sighed. "I tried." He enfolded me in his arms. "At least you have your revolver and can protect yourself if you need to."

Some time ago, we purchased guns and become proficient in their use. Wisconsin is a concealed carry state, and I keep mine locked in my car's glove compartment and pray I never have to use it.

"Saturday, we'll go to the shooting range

and brush up."

God, help me not hurt any innocent person.

I changed the subject. "When is your next appointment?"

"Two thirty."

"I hate seeing how upset you are." I winked at him and started to unbutton his shirt. "I know how to relax you."

He followed me into our bedroom. I climbed onto our queen-size four-poster bed while Nick turned off his phone. Several deep, tender kisses later, I no longer thought about anything except us. As if making love could dispel fear of death.

24

The next afternoon at 2:00 PM, I was enroute to meet Ann Tylore in her office in downtown Milwaukee. The heavy traffic, despite it being only mid-afternoon, reminded me why I dislike big cities. Our country roads in Walworth County have me spoiled. The last twenty minutes bumper-to-bumper almost did me in.

The mature, dignified receptionist at the Columbia Realty Company treated me with the deference due a new client, which she probably assumed I was. I didn't want to deceive her, but I also didn't bother to correct her since she hadn't asked. My title, Dr. Trevor, may have given a false impression. People sometimes assume doctors have fortunes to invest.

"Please have a seat, Dr. Trevor. Ms. Tylore will be out shortly."

The luxurious reception area was carpeted in a rose floral with a sturdy weave that looked like it would last until the year 3000 and never show wear. An elderly man, with his head buried in Newsweek, occupied one of the other leather side chairs. I used the wait to scan my cell for e-mail.

A male broker strolled past. He wore a traditional navy suit with red tie. His thin hair was slicked down in back and had a front comb-over spreading the few available strands. He whisked his waiting gentleman to the back offices. How nice that brokers personally escorted clients through these hallways to their offices.

I wondered if I'd even get as far Ann's office. I hoped so, for her sake. What I had to say was best spoken in private.

Minutes later, Ann sauntered into the reception area on three-inch beige heels that matched her two-piece suit. A long silk scarf covered her shoulders and draped to her hips. The fabric was an amazing conglomeration of earth tones slashed diagonally in broad streaks. Her straight skirt hung two inches above finely molded knees. Wavy long hair, clipped at the nape of her neck, looked both sleek and professional. Creative office couture. She spoke to the receptionist briefly then announced my name in a rich alto voice.

I knew immediately this was the woman

who eluded me at the funeral. I sucked in my breath and hoped she wouldn't remember I'd tried to chase her down.

Ann introduced herself and led me to her office. If she recognized me, she didn't show it. I exhaled deeply.

On the way down the hall, Ann made small talk about the weather. My chitchat tank runs dry fast. I'm a balanced extrovert/introvert but better at deep, substantive talk, suitable for counseling. Today, my introvert mode was prevailing, and I wasn't expecting to enjoy this conversation.

Inside Ann's walnut paneled office, a large picture window framed several buildings depicting Milwaukee's finest architecture. Huge rubber plants greened two corners. Only partners or near-partners rated a setting like this — elegant and conservative in black and grays. I was duly impressed.

Ann settled herself in a swivel chair behind her desk and invited me to the client's chair. My hands felt sweaty. *Lord, where do I start?*

She looked me over squarely; her gaze traveled up and down my body. I felt like I were being coded and filed. "You look vaguely familiar. Have we met?"

"Not formally, but we both attended Al Windemere's memorial service."

She stiffened and peered at the information sheet in front of her. "Your name rings a bell . . . Al Windemere's therapist, correct?" Her facial muscles tightened before her gaze turned away abruptly. "Then you're not here as an investment client?"

It sounded like an accusation.

"Perhaps in the future." I talked fast, fearing I'd be shown out any minute.

"Al was involved with you, too?"

I swallowed hard, shocked, and felt myself blush. "I'm happily married, Ms. Tylore. My position is assisting the family. I'd like to ask you a few questions."

"Why would I talk to you? You're not the police." Ann Tylore rose and started toward the door.

"Just a minute, please. As Al's therapist I have an interest in seeing truth revealed about his death. Since you had personal history with Al and came to his funeral, I hoped you'd care enough to want the mystery of his death solved as well."

She hesitated. "What do you want?"

"I'll get right to the point. I understand you and he had an affair. The police found a suspicious note in Al's pocket torn from a piece of paper. It simply said in his handwriting 'can't go on like this.' Might he have been referring to ending your relationship?"

"How would I know?"

196

"Did Al write a note to you about ending it? Perhaps someone got hold of it?"

"He never so much as sent me a card. We were very careful to avoid any written record of our relationship."

She turned her face away. To hide what? Sorrow? Guilt? Being rejected by someone you love can hurt for a long time — sometimes forever — and make you do foolish things. Had he told her they were through and then managed to get part of the note back to identify her as his killer before she shot him?

"The murderer was probably someone he knew, like yourself."

"I have nothing to hide. Do I look strong enough to pull a man Al's size into the woods?"

"Al probably walked of his own free will from his golf cart into the woods behind the green. A woman could have fired the gun as easily as a man." I had her attention now. "Where were you the morning he was shot?"

"What a ridiculous question. Home if you must know. I slept in, read the papers, did some laundry."

"Did you see anyone?"

"Not until my dinner engagement at six."

"I'm not accusing you. I want you to help me identify his killer, but I think the police will conclude you had plenty of time to drive up to the Dells and back. With a motive as an unrequited lover, although Al said you agreed to end the relationship without, shall we say," I searched for the right word. "Ugliness. But perhaps you'd made an effort to start it up again, hence the note."

"Isn't what he told you privileged counseling information?"

"Al's will provided a complete release of confidentiality for his past counseling sessions."

She lifted her chin. "What else did he reveal about me?"

I had to select my words carefully with this sharp, sophisticated woman. I didn't want a lawsuit. "Only minimal information, very discreetly shared, I assure you."

"Comforting." Her expression was guarded. "Anyway, I don't care. He was out of my life."

"I saw your reaction at the funeral. I can't believe you don't have lingering feelings."

"Ridiculous." Her tone reeked with sarcasm.

"Ann, I didn't come here to upset you. I apologize. I know I have."

She folded her hands loosely in front of her.

"What more do you want?" Her words

came out in a whisper.

"Help me find the killer."

"How?"

"By telling me anything you know that could be significant."

Ann leaned her head back against her chair. "Al Windemere was the most charming, fascinating man I've ever known. He may have had other lovers I'm not aware of." She spoke his name slowly, savoring it. "When he tried to end our relationship, I wanted him all the more."

I nodded. How many times had I heard that in counseling? Someone unattainable becomes even more desirable.

"For the record, his wife was selfish and demanding." Ann gave a half-hearted laugh. "But then I suppose men always say that about their spouses when out cavorting."

"Did you ever discuss marriage?"

"We talked about it several times. He said the time wasn't right."

Ann looked at the framed pictures on her walls — the Swiss Alps, a beach in St. Thomas, the Seine River in Paris. "We traveled together but were never photographed in the same picture." An involuntary sob came from deep within her startling me. "I shouldn't have gotten involved with him. It was a risk. I sacrificed a lot to get to this stage in my career."

She'd achieved incredible success from the looks of this place. Nevertheless, how sad she sounded. Ann pressed her hands together. "I'll fight anyone who tries to take away what I've built. She pulled a makeup bag from a desk drawer and powdered her face from a tortoise shell compact.

Pain shadowed her eyes. Her features softened as she said, "After two years together, one day out of nowhere, Al announced we were through. Just like that. I tried everything to make him change his mind, but he was adamant. That man made decisions in steel." She brushed away sudden tears and stared at me. "That was the end. He apologized for intruding into my life. Said he was now a Christian, and he'd recommitted totally to the family God had given to him and was working to rebuild these relationships."

"How shocking for you."

"There are no words for it. Yet I still loved him and respected him more than ever."

"I'm truly sorry for your pain. Did you speak with Al again after he ended your relationship?"

She shook her head. "I tried, he wouldn't return my calls.

"Can you recall incidents or any details —

times, places regarding individuals who showed animosity toward him?"

"I seldom saw him in the presence of other people. We preferred to take off to isolated settings. You've heard of being discreet. We often drove an hour and a half to meet for lunch. Neither of us wanted to risk exposing our careers to gossip. In real estate investment, as you may know, reputation is everything. Being in the same industry complicated our relationship enormously."

"You have no idea who might have wanted him killed?" I waited, holding my breath.

Ann stared at the legal pad on her desk. Aimlessly, she pressed the point of her pen on it. Her dots looked like a colony of marching ants.

"His partner was a pain. I'd suggest checking him out. He had an estranged son. Al had been tough on him as a young teen and eventually threw him out. Something tragic happened there, but Al didn't talk about it."

"Anything else about his immediate family?"

"Al had a younger brother, Aaron. Supposedly Aaron resented Al."

Ann became pensive. "Know what?"

I was all ears.

"It's crazy, but Al's breaking up got me thinking about God. When I entered college, I'd put God in the fairytale category. Al said God was his source of strength to live right and be joyful. He didn't seek Him until he'd achieved all his dreams and, to his great surprise, felt depleted Connected to God he felt alive and purposeful."

I smiled. How well I knew.

"Al insisted on giving me advice the last time we were together." Her voice cracked, but she recovered. "He told me to find a good church committed to preaching God's Word and get involved. He said there are some bad churches like bad financial investments. Pay attention."

"He sincerely cared for you, Ann, and wanted to help you spiritually."

"I'm sure he did. From adultery to Christianity — quite a shift in one relationship. Soaps are never this good."

"Have you?"

"What?"

"Taken up his suggestion?"

She lifted the coffee cup on her desk and drank deeply. "Not yet. Dr. Trevor, before I knew you, I disliked you. I hated that Al picked a Christian counselor. You helped destroy my plans for the future. But partly because of your work with him, Al became a man I truly respected, a person of character. At first, he'd been a pleasant diversion."

She thrust up her chin. "I've had numerous men. None with integrity. I didn't consider character a realistic expectation in this age. Honesty seemed to go out with the knights, but I watched it develop in Al. He became" — she paused, looking away as if searching for a word — "authentic. Not just a sweet talker, but truly kind. You did good."

"I can't take the credit. The Holy Spirit was at work."

Ann closed her eyes. "But his new lifestyle made him shrink from me." She opened her eyes and stiffened. "I had to let him go, and I have." She shuddered. "And now people think I could have killed him? Me a suspect?" She shook her head.

Ann's eyes turned dark.

I sensed it was time to leave.

25

Today's progress notes had taken more time than I'd expected, and I still had messages to return. Forty-five minutes past my scheduled quitting hour the phone rang I leaned back and answered, aware of the frown lines tightening my forehead.

"Jennifer Trevor, please."

"This is she."

Where had I heard this voice? I scanned my memory for a matching image.

"Rich Nichols. We met the other day at the floral shop."

"Hello, Rich." I pictured Aaron's shop manager in his preppy, button down collar, khaki pants, exhibiting smooth manners. "What can I do for you?"

Rich laughed, a pleasant full sound. "I'm calling about service to you. My storage building houses the antiques Albert Windemere owned. His lawyer contacted me. You have your choice of any three items from his Eastlake collection. I'm to facilitate your selection and several other bequests before the rest goes to a charity auction."

"Thanks. I have a lot going on right now. Can I get back to you?" I tried to keep impatience out of my voice. At the moment, all I wanted was to get home.

"I'll be brief. Al had a small fortune tied up in these antiques, and they need to be liquidated soon. I'm trying to expedite this process. I'll soon have descriptions and drawings of what's available, so you can make your preliminary selections."

"Until recently I didn't know Al was heavily into antiques."

"On the QT. His partner was a bear. I think Al was looking to scale back from American Realty Investment and expand into other business ventures."

My antenna perked up. I found it strange Rich knew his business particulars. "How did you two connect?"

"Through his brother. I invested with Aaron in a condo development Al had recommended. To be honest, I didn't like the man personally because Aaron told me his brother was a rat during their childhood. However, I recognized that Al was a good businessman."

"How's Aaron coping with his brother's

death? I assume you know since you see Aaron daily."

"I don't bring the subject up because it upsets him. By the way, Aaron told me about the counseling arrangement. How's it going?"

He made the question sound casual. I heard the plink of metal in the background and pictured him scrunching a cell phone against his neck while pushing flowers through wire.

"Fine. We're tying up loose emotional ends and looking for any clue to help identify Al's murderer." I could ethically make this general statement.

"Gutsy dangerous female detective work, huh?"

I cringed. "Maybe a little."

While we talked, I checked the application deadline on an upcoming conference, "Adult Women Dealing with Abusive Fathers." I'd missed the cutoff date, so I tossed the brochure into the garbage.

"Once I've completed inventory, the family will make their choices. Then I'll drop off pictures and wood samples. Next, I'll have your selections touched up or refinished, as they require. When that's done, you need to come to the warehouse showroom for final approval."

"Competent and professional."

"Self-serving. Transporting them multiple times is costly."

"OK. Sounds like a plan." I stood and stretched my legs to rev up my circulation.

"By the way, if I can be of help with your counseling the Windemeres, call me. I know all the family secrets."

Rich rattled off his home phone number, which I had no intention of ever calling. Did he really hope to help or merely want to find out what I knew?

Good grief, Jennifer! He's not a busybody, just a nice person. Time to go home. Your patience quota is exhausted for today.

I wondered what he meant by family secrets.

26

I drove to work the next morning under a weak sky lacking distinct cloud shapes or color. One of those meteorologically blah days, as if the sun couldn't decide to emerge or stay in hiding. Funny how I felt the same way.

Crystal meandered into my office for her session. She wore attire that could brighten any day — a periwinkle shirtwaist with white collar and cuffs and three-inch wide matching belt. She could easily be mistaken for a fashion magazine model. The exquisite tailoring of her little cotton knit guaranteed it didn't come from a department store rack.

If only her eyes held a hint of brightness. A beautiful, yet tortured, woman I noted immediately.

She settled on my sofa. "I'm a mess. It's probably good that I'm here. I have other issues you may as well know. I can't stop myself from shopping. I take far more buying trips than I need. My shop could show a decent profit if it weren't for my exorbitant expenses and my high payroll because I'm seldom at work. I take a lot of time off to do things with my mom and girlfriends."

"Do you enjoy spending time with your mom? Over the years has that compensated for an absentee Dad? I didn't get that impression at the Dells."

"I feel an obligation to care for her. She's been like my fellow prisoner, a wound victim. Does that make sense? Mom doesn't speak about her pain, she doesn't have to. I know."

"You think you have the power to help her?" I laced my question with skepticism.

"I expect you'll say she's an adult yet seems incapable of getting her emotional needs met." Crystal lifted her shoulders, as if being her mother's guardian made her important.

Maybe that was it. "Was this always your role?"

"From the time I was little, Dad was never around. Mom needed me for company. She was never one to do much with girlfriends," Crystal said matter-of-factly. "Either we went out or she stayed home."

I listened hard and prayed for insights to help. Thoughts of solving Al's murder disappeared in this moment. This was a hurting human being. I followed my counseling instincts. "Sounds like you never established reasonable boundaries between your identity and your mom's."

"Maybe not. So what? It's nice to feel important to someone."

"Not healthy, although understandable to enjoy the security of having your mom bound to you in a permanent relationship. Insurance against rejection by one parent, at least." I wanted to convey my understanding and sympathy. "Unfortunately, emotional dependency isn't the basis for mature relationships."

She listened, sad-eyed.

"Usually it's the other way around. You know, moms looking out for daughters." I said this gently, aware how fragile she was.

"I'm not blind. I know what you're saying is true." Crystal shifted uncomfortably in her chair.

In the back of my mind, I was hard pressed to reconcile Crystal's need to care for her mother with Rose's independent, strong-willed personality. Clearly a discordant note.

"Has Rose been the sacrificing type of mom for you?"

"No." Crystal picked at the polish on the

pinky nail of her right hand, already almost bare.

"Did you sometimes deny your own needs or your family's needs to care for your mom?"

"Yes, but that's my job as her daughter."

"Perhaps other people in your mother's circle of family and friends could help her meet needs for companionship and encouragement. Her emotional nurturing doesn't have to fall completely on you."

"We've established a pattern. She'd be lost without my attention," Crystal insisted. "It's been this way."

"Habits aren't etched in marble, Crystal. Sometimes when we peel away a layer of how we think we must act, we find a deeper, better way."

"I'm being unselfish. Isn't that good?"

"Are you? Maybe your mom lets you think she needs your help to make you feel needed and good about yourself."

"That's ridiculous."

"Is it? When we pull back from an inappropriate service to someone, we free others. They can lean too much, maybe without realizing it. Right now, your mom is grieving and needs comfort. That's different. I'm referring to the typical pattern of your lives."

"But Mom depends on me."

It's not healthy to get totally consumed in her. That's harmful to both of you."

"She needs me." Crystal's glare defied me to correct her.

"Sometimes parents hurt children by expecting things kids shouldn't need to give."

She frowned and crossed her arms.

I remembered for a fleeting moment the years of caring for my alcoholic mom. I forced my thoughts back to Crystal. "Might you have also intensified anger toward your dad and harbor resentment by believing you had to assume a huge responsibility for your mom's happiness?"

Crystal cupped her palms against her forehead and massaged it.

I prayed. *Lord, help her to process her behavior honestly.* "Crystal, you could never make up for your dad's emotional treatment of your mom no matter how hard you tried."

"I despised my father seeing Mom under this strain. Plus driving my only brother from our lives added to my hatred."

"Was it all your dad's fault? I understand your brother made some poor choices."

Crystal shifted in her chair. "Ken wouldn't have run off, done drugs, and joined a cult if he'd had more love and attention. I can never forgive my father. We didn't always

212

get along, but I loved my brother."

"I'm sure you did." I reached over and patted her shoulder.

Crystal relaxed a bit, probably pleased I understood. "Now, Mom's obsessed wanting Father's death to be murder instead of suicide, because that would be her ultimate rejection. I get that. You talk as if our past can be resolved. I think you're wrong." Her slouch reminded me of a puppy neglected too often. No mistaking the pain in her voice.

"I truly do understand. My childhood was anything but fun, with a mom who didn't drive — just as well, since alcohol was her constant companion — and an alcoholic dad who avoided being home. Crystal, you can go on to have a happy, fulfilling life. I did."

She started to cry. "It's true. I gave Mom energy that John and the children deserved. My mother lived in visible anguish. She was alone so much."

I looked down at the pre-visit notes I'd made and plunged into my next topic. "Your mom wants to protect you now. This is a rather delicate topic, but I want to be completely open with you. She's concerned about your presence at the Dells with Halston."

"She n-needn't . . . worry," Crystal stammered.

I bit my lip. She does need to be concerned if you're an accomplice to murder. "What about Harold Halston?"

"It was nothing. A way to frost Father by chumming with his enemy. I don't even like the man much. I broke our relationship off after the Dells."

"Your mom's concerned Halston may have been your father's killer."

"I wouldn't put it past him to commit murder, but I wouldn't have helped — I couldn't for Mom's sake." She sat up straighter. "You won't tell the police about our relationship? This is confidential, right?"

"I expect the police already know. They'd check the guest register."

Crystal groaned. "Do you think mom will ever get over this?"

"Overall, she appears to be doing well."

Crystal sniffed in disdain. "I know her. She pretends to be strong, but she's not."

"It takes toughness to fight cancer assertively."

Crystal slumped down in her chair. "Even in death my father destroyed her peace! He's hurt us both enough."

"She says she's over past hurts. In time, perhaps with counseling, you'll be free of anger as well." I let my voice trail off.

Silence momentarily filled the air. I glanced down at my notes. "Crystal, are you familiar with false memory syndrome?"

"Not really, although I've heard the term." She tossed her head.

"It would be irresponsible of me not to inform you. This refers to a situation where adult women rework their memories and create either false or exaggerated memories of their victimization. They make their past seem worse with each rethinking and retelling. Now, certainly, you have reason to feel hurt and angry, but statistics show intelligent females like you are more inclined to exaggerate perceptions about emotional abuse."

Crystal's intense green eyes planted themselves on mine and her back visibly stiffened. "You think I've imagined my father's horrible treatment?"

I leaned forward to project sincerity. Counseling an adult who was abused as a child is difficult. "You haven't experienced physical violence or sexual abuse, Crystal, but you were emotionally neglected. No abuse of any kind is acceptable, but be sure your mind doesn't play tricks of exaggeration. That's all I'm saying."

"I can assure you I'm not conjuring up

the image of my father as an absentee parent." Crystal's tone grew haughty. "I would have preferred harshness or abuse to total indifference!" She spoke with barely controlled fury. "Can't you understand that?"

"Absolutely."

"All I had from him was rejection. He never came to school events. He'd say, 'I have to work. Ask your mother to take you. Here's money for shopping. Don't bother me. Can't you see I'm busy?' " She threw her head back. "When I was a kid every one of his hours was programmed. And not one line of his calendar had my name on it. He came one time during four years of high school, the day I graduated. I remember reading about how devastated Winston Churchill felt when his mother would never visit him at boarding school, and I cried for him. I lived in the same house with my dad and never saw him."

"How difficult, especially during adolescence when a young girl most needs to experience a father's love."

Crystal pressed her hands together as though squeezing water from a sponge. "He'd say, 'Let the teachers do their job educating you. Keep me out of it. I don't need them to visit my business. That's why I pay private school tuition.' "

Crystal's mascara dissolved into thick brown streaks beneath her lower lids. She hunted in her purse. "I have a handkerchief somewhere."

I handed her the box of tissue from my desk. My heart ached for her, for myself, and for every child who never had responsible parents. Some things simply should never be.

"So you felt worthless? The exquisite clothes and perfect makeup became a symbol of validating your worth?"

Crystal nodded. "I mastered the art of staying busy non-stop, leaving no time to think. I never talked about Dad's neglect. It still hurts."

"I know."

She broke out in fresh sobs. I waited until her tears subsided.

"Mom sensed how angry I was, but I never talked about it. He wasn't there for her, or me. He was so . . . so . . . *cold.*" She bent her head, still crying.

"I'm sorry." I gave her time to collect her emotions. "Parents don't realize how much they can hurt their children. It's good you're sharing now. How I wish emotional abuse didn't happen. But when you acknowledge the hurt, it can become easier to move on. Let it all out."

217

Her words tumbled forth: hatred, pity, fury at Al's alternating verbal putdowns and complete indifference. "A few months ago, he said he changed and wanted to make things right with me," Crystal admitted, "but I wouldn't let him. I liked knowing I could hurt him back finally by rejecting him."

"Unfortunately, you hurt yourself, too, by keeping these wounds open."

"I was evening up the score!" she answered emphatically, rubbing a mole on her right forearm.

I glanced at the sign on the side wall of my office and read, "There's no such thing as a perfect childhood or a perfect person; each of us lives our best imperfect life in an imperfect world."

"That's for sure," Crystal agreed. "Rob and I had issues, too."

"Our session is nearly over. We'll start by discussing those next time."

"One last thing. I'm not sleeping well. I fret over stuff."

"About what?"

"The kids, my marriage." She forced a little laugh. "Last night I fell asleep at two, woke at 4:00 AM, and I've been up ever since. Can I get some sleeping pills?"

I swiveled my chair to my desk and examined her intake form to review the medication section: Current meds: none. No reported drug use or abuse.

I walked over to my file cabinet, shuffled through folders, and pulled out several papers. "Here are some relaxation exercises to try that will be helpful. I can't prescribe medication, but your internist can. Perhaps short term sleeping meds would be helpful."

"I get tense even thinking about relaxing."

"Focus on rhythmic breathing, not relaxing. Next time we'll discuss the specific issues disturbing your sleep. Bitterness can be a factor."

She stood, straightened her skirt, and actually smiled. "How you do listen to people's problems every day? I feel like the survivor of a six-car collision."

"As long as you're the survivor," I bantered before she left.

I sat immobile for several minutes reviewing our session. I sensed a measure of progress creating trust with Crystal. Hopefully, I was no longer perceived as the enemy, but a caring professional.

A client with Crystal's apparent exterior of steel, is, in reality, often fragile as eggshells. The ones who seem soft on the outside and pour themselves out quickly can fool you. They have spiels down pat, and their heavily armored interiors are nearly impenetrable. Crystal Vandley, thank God, opened up to me. We'd established a working relationship. If her previous hatred hadn't motivated Crystal to kill her father, I would be able to help.

If only I could be sure.

27

Heavy rain slapped steadily against my office window. I didn't mind the puddles everywhere, but grayness depleted my energy level. Better rain than snow. I dreaded the thought of winter.

Ellen knocked and entered my office in one motion. Her black gabardine pants and black blouse, simple, professional attire, were a contrast to the bright colors she usually wore. "I dressed to match the weather. Can you tell?" she joked.

I smiled. Faithful assistant and friend, never emotionally up, or down, she often makes me laugh and helps me stay anchored.

"Actually, I'm in mourning. A pro bono client, Ms. Convers, who's usually quite sweet, just read me the riot act because I couldn't fit her in until next week."

"Sorry. Some clients aren't nice, I'm glad I can always count on your gracious manner and treating our pro bono clients with the same respect as those with megabucks."

Ellen pretended to bow. "Keep the praise coming."

"That's enough. Any more, and you'll be wanting a raise, and I couldn't afford you."

"Your next to last client of the day, a new one, just cancelled."

"No problem. I'll use the time from the no-show to go through Al Windemere's file again. Please get it." I stared at my calendar. First time cancellations never surprise me. Their no-show rate is high because new clients are jumpy. Some view counseling as their last hope, and fear finding out it might not help would be more than they could handle. I thought of one client who scheduled an appointment for four weeks in a row and didn't show. After every missed session, she'd call with a plausible excuse and reschedule. When she finally came, we resolved her issues rapidly.

I looked up as Ellen quietly returned with the file.

I determined to check the file more thoroughly this time. First, I noted the appointments Al made for Crystal and Aaron were both no-shows, not once but several times.

Some individuals like Crystal are so accustomed to dysfunction they really aren't aware they're unhealthy. To keep family members off their back, they may schedule and break numerous appointments — or worse, show up unmotivated to work on getting better.

I reviewed the assignments I'd given Al on communication, conflict resolution, and restitution. Like many men, he simply hadn't known how to be a loving husband and father, but he was willing to learn. I used the psychodrama technique among others. Some clients, like Al — perhaps because he was in sales — learn best by role-playing new communication skills, the auditory approach. Al practiced until he could express his feelings naturally and sincerely.

I hunted through my progress notes, session by session, for any detail I might have missed during my cursory glance at Al's file when I returned from vacation.

In the second session, we'd agreed on a treatment plan, which Al signed. I could see him sitting there, eyes filled with hope.

My notes showed I started the third session with an explanation of the levels of communication. I remember Al had laughed at the lowest level, cliché conversation. "How are you?" He'd winked and wisecracked, "Whadda mean? That's how the

223

world talks."

"You mean discussing sports scores isn't emotionally bonding?" Al had been great fun to work with due to his natural sense of humor.

I glanced out my office window at the small parking lot, almost empty. The rain had finally spent its strength. As I stared, a car pulled into the lot and circled the perimeter, creeping around like a turtle, not once, but three times, as though the driver couldn't decide to park. It struck me as odd, but I dismissed it and returned to my notes.

Explained Communication Level 3, expressing ideas or opinions. At Level 2 Al W. stalled — no notion of the kind of relationship that occurs at the top two levels: Level 2 — openly revealing feelings or emotions and Level 1 — complete personal transparency — the ultimate goal in a relationship like marriage." He's open to experimenting with these levels.

I fiddled with my pen, remembering Al's words. "Of course, I want emotional closeness with my wife. In school, I never had one course that taught me how to relate intimately. I've never been totally open with anyone."

"You're not alone, Al," I'd said. "At least you're learning now."

I resumed reading until I came to the

reference about Aaron. Al had said, "Our talk is always surface stuff. We've never revealed our real feelings to one another. Sometimes Aaron refuses to talk at all." My note read, 'Al said Aaron's living dangerously. I need to get through to him before it's too late.' "

I wished I'd explored that in depth. Now I wondered too late for what?

Looking out the window again, I saw the car that had circled the lot still there, a black Honda, a fairly new model, I guessed. The driver would have a clear view of me, and I didn't like being in a fishbowl. I walked over to the window, pulled the vertical blinds down, and twisted them shut.

I returned to Al's file. What did it mean? "Too late." I searched my notes to see if Aaron came up again. I found a reference on Al's five-page social history. Under Comments Re: Family of Origin, Al described his background. *Family ties not fostered with sibling, feelings seldom discussed at home.*

I dug into Al's files further. Nothing else of value as far as I could tell. In the last sessions, we'd explored techniques for resolving conflicts with Al's wife and daughter, despite Crystal's constant blaming and withdrawal.

My stomach growled. Nick was cooking

his specialty for us tonight — chicken stir-fry with fresh broccoli, cauliflower, mushrooms and brown rice. Yum!

I stood and stretched and then walked over to the window and peeked through the blinds. The car was still parked outside, headlights off. Smoke from the exhaust indicated the engine was running. I shivered involuntarily. I was strangely uneasy. This car had parked two spaces from mine? Why so close? The rest of the lot was empty. Who was this person waiting for? The two previous notes and ominous phone call produced a rush of fear.

I checked my watch. *Jennifer, you're exhausted. Go home.* I closed the folder and placed it in the filing basket for Ellen. Before leaving, I looked out my window a last time. The car was still there.

I locked the door behind me and hurried to my car wishing I hadn't worn two-inch heels, even if they did match my gray suit. When I drew within a few yards of my car, the other car pulled away. Thank goodness. I breathed a little easier.

My curiosity was piqued. Who had been in the car? No other office appeared open.

"Stop it, Jennifer," I coached myself aloud. "Shake these heebie-jeebies."

28

Disappointment set in the second I got home. Where was my welcoming fragrance of food wafting from the kitchen? No sign of my husband, either.

I checked my cell phone, which I'd turned off during counseling and had forgotten to turn back on. Nick's apologetic voice came through voice mail. "Sorry, sweetheart. I've been detained. Dinner will be late. Feel free to start cooking. See you around eight-thirty."

Feel free. What a joke. I was exhausted but dutifully changed into a T-shirt and jeans and dragged myself into the kitchen. From the pot drawer, I pulled out a ten-inch non-stick frying pan and gave it a few squirts of olive oil spray.

I'm a decent cook when the mood strikes, and I have time, but I eagerly surrender the task any chance I get. Nick took a cooking class this past year, and became a master chef, in my opinion at least. Planning our menus is still my forte. I keep a supply of ingredients for our favorite healthy meals.

I pulled frozen whole-wheat rolls from the freezer and set them in the microwave to thaw. I was sorry I'd planned stir-fry tonight with fresh veggies that needed chopping. I have devices intended to simplify the chore, but usually revert to my big knife. I'm not as adept as Nick with it. If he ever chose not to practice law, he could get a job at a Japanese steak house.

I opened the fridge and tossed the lettuce resembling wet tobacco leaves and a tomato with enough fuzz to be shaved. The cauliflower, red cabbage, broccoli, mushrooms, carrots and onions I plopped on the cutting board and chopped away marveling at the veggie colors and shapes. This routine household chore revived my droopy spirit like therapy. I should be Suzie Chef more often.

Nick arrived at eight forty-five all smiles when he saw the table set with china and the crystal candleholder in the center. Two glasses of Moscato crowned our plates. Maybe the flickering flame would hide my tired eyes.

"How was your day, Love?" Nick asked before serving himself a heaping helping of stir fry over rice.

I resisted the urge to say difficult. I didn't want Nick to hear me admit again that I'd overextended myself. I dislike his told-you-sos. Finally, I opted for honesty. How can I teach people to engage in intimate, honest communication without practicing it?

"Trouble's brewing. Not only did I bite off more than I can chew, Nick, I stuck the whole rope in my mouth."

He laughed.

"It's not funny." I heard petulance in my voice.

"Your choice of words gives me a great visual."

I punched him lightly in the arm.

He chuckled again.

"Hey, a little support is what I need." I recounted the details of the day, which seemed even worse in the retelling.

"You'll be done soon."

"I hope."

Nick pushed back from the table and opened the newspaper, apparently without a care. I envied his ability to turn off his work brain when he walked in our door.

I carried the dishes to the sink. He was right; this extra counseling wouldn't go on much longer. I'd make it through. Tomorrow, I might even be excited about my work again — I hoped.

I went to the study and grabbed the folder with the notes I'd made on Al Windemere's file. I set it by Nick on the kitchen table. "This is no longer confidential. Can you take a quick look and see if I missed anything?"

"I suppose. I'm not sure you can afford me though."

While he read, I busied myself cleaning the kitchen.

"What do you think Al meant about Aaron?" Nick called out.

I returned and sat down across from him. "Wish I knew. Maybe Aaron's a chain smoker, and Al wanted him to stop. Al made it sound like something serious."

"Smoking is a life and death matter."

"True, but you know what I mean."

"You said you think the murderer has to be a close associate or family member. Why?"

"I'm guessing."

"Based on . . . ?" Nick's legal brain wanted evidence.

"Only someone in his intimate circle would get a handwritten personal note from him. The police verified Al's signature. Also the murderer knew Al was golfing, only the family knew that."

"They all knew? You're sure?"

"I think so. Rose said Al had asked his brother to go to the Dells to play golf with him. Aaron refused but agreed to come for brunch later with his wife, Lorraine, and his partner, Rich, and Rich's mom. They were having Rose's birthday brunch in the clubhouse after golf. The entire family knew Al would be on the course that morning."

"Yet someone may not have physically killed him but could have hired a killer.

"Al's business partner, Halston, knew of Al's golf?"

"I bet Crystal mentioned it. Al had invited her, but she also declined. Halston was with her at the resort."

"How about his secretary, Angela Thursted? She probably knew where to reach Al practically every waking minute."

"True."

"Is that everybody in the inner circle?" Nick stacked the pages together.

"Except for his former son-in-law, John Vandley, who was bringing the children to the Dells for the party with their grandparents. John resented Al because of the pain his workaholism brought Crystal, his former wife."

"I still don't get why rule out some outsider who might have been following Al and knew his routine, an enemy he didn't know he had? Somebody on the fringe of his life."

"I couldn't come up with anybody else. Plus, Al was sharp. I think he'd have picked up on being followed on the course, and there would have been signs of a struggle."

"I suppose all the family has an alibi?"

I shrugged. "Yes and no. It's tough when a murder occurs during an hour when most people are in bed asleep. Corroboration's fairly impossible. The person who sent me those notes may think I uncovered some evidence."

"And wants to keep you from investigating further."

"Yes." I tapped my fingers on the table. "Maybe if the killer thinks I know, he or she will come out in the open. I could spread the rumor."

Nick's eyes widened. "Absolutely not. You're not to put yourself in more danger."

My bold idea lasted approximately three seconds. "Right. Skip that."

"When you get impatient, sometimes your stupid cells overrule your smart ones." Nick handed the file back. "Enough. I'm going to bed. You can knock yourself out over this, but I'm tired. Good night, wife."

He was right. I had to avoid obsessing over this killer and focus on completing the counseling process.

I might not ever discover who killed Al Windemere, but I wouldn't quit trying.

233

29

The next day started horribly.

I breathed the prayer *Lord, help me not grumble* after a client mistook the time of her appointment, arrived an hour late, and then was angry with me because I couldn't fit her in. I simply didn't have another fifty minutes.

My colleague, Lenora, called and cancelled our lunch ten minutes after I'd turned down another date with an old friend. When I tried to reach her, she'd already left.

I finished with my four o'clock client at five, and Ellen poked her nose in. "See you tomorrow." She tapped her finger on her watch. "Shouldn't you be leaving as well?"

"Heading home as soon as I complete my notes. Ten more minutes. I feel like I've been whirled in a blender all day."

Ellen harrumphed. "Probably because you have."

Ten turned into twenty minutes when I heard a noise in the outer office. Ellen must have forgotten something.

I sauntered out to her office to check on a client's file. Ellen wasn't there. Her desktop was clear except for TO DO and PEND-ING manila folders in her stand-up file. The empty reception area emitted only quiet-ness. Strange, I thought sure I'd heard her return. Her swivel chair faced her computer station instead of her desk. I didn't register this as out of the ordinary until later. Obses-sively orderly, Ellen would never leave her chair out of place.

The noise I heard must have come from the office next door.

Squelching my notoriously creative imagi-nation, I stepped back into my office to fin-ish paperwork and closed the door from habit. I'm good at ignoring my prickly sen-sations.

I smelled a faint scent of smoke about ten minutes later. Someone burning leaves? I kept writing and then stopped abruptly mid-sentence. How could I smell leaves outside with the sealed windows in here? I have a climate-controlled heating and cool-ing system with overhead fans in each office to keep the temperature comfortable.

A mix of scorched wood and the putrid

odor of melting plastic filled my nostrils within seconds. I whipped open the door to my outer office. Flames shot from the center of Ellen's desk and licked across the room in both directions. The fire seemed to come from the floor.

A fire extinguisher against the far wall next to the supply cabinet mocked me. To get to it, I'd have to pass through the blaze around Ellen's desk. Way too dangerous if my clothing caught.

Magazines and pamphlets in the reception area shriveled into ashes as the fire intensified. The exterior door was on the other side of the flaming desk. No way could I make it through.

I was trapped.

Sweat ran down my face and under my arms.

I turned back into my office and slammed the door. I ran to my desk and banged out 9-1-1 on the phone. I shouted out the building address as I grabbed towels from my bath to seal the space under the doorway.

Panic surged through me. I didn't want to die and certainly not like this. *When you pass through the fire you will not be harmed for I am with you.* Everything stilled as the Psalm came to mind. A tiny, then deeper, layer of calm slid over my fear.

I eyed the double-hung windows, rushed over to the one on the left, and pulled with all the full force of my body to raise the heavy, old sash.

It wouldn't budge. I searched for something heavy to break the glass — my wide-armed antique desk chair. I tried to lift it but could only raise it only a few inches. The metal swivel apparatus at the bottom added too much weight. Oh for sleek, light stainless steel.

Where were the firemen? Smoke billowed into my office.

I dashed to my bookcase, grabbed a fist-sized paperweight, and threw it at the window.

A pane of glass shattered. The burst of air gave me momentary relief. No way could I wedge myself through the tiny twelve-inch rectangle. I threw another book and missed. Next throw, I heard another cracking sound.

Even if I shattered all the glass panes, how could I fit through the wooden frame? Why try? Flames lapped around the edges of the office door. Panic gripped me.

I gasped and dropped to the floor, choking for air vaguely aware of my brain deadening. I couldn't seem to signal my lungs to draw another breath.

A loud clamor caused me to look up. A

shadowy figure stood above me.

Seconds later, big, bulky arms dragged me across the window ledge and down the ladder.

Someone asked with utmost concern if I was all right while an EMT checked my vitals. I was in an ambulance.

Nick met me in the emergency room. The horror on his face frightened me afresh.

"You're going to be OK," he said and repeated the words as he leaned closer perhaps to make himself believe them. He kissed my forehead over and over.

"Thank God the children can't see me now. I must be a fright."

Nick stroked my cheek. "You're beautiful as ever."

I strained to sit up and coughed out the question searing my brain. "How did the fire start?"

"Don't know. There'll be an investigation."

I groaned and fell back on the pillow. "I want to go home."

The doctor insisted I stay twenty-four hours for observation. I talked him into letting me go home under Nick's supervision.

I have no recollection of riding in our car, but I awoke as Nick carried me into our bedroom. I slept until almost ten, which is rare for me.

But then, almost being killed doesn't happen to me every day.

30

The next morning, I felt a hundred percent better and refused Nick's offer of breakfast in bed. I ate oatmeal in the kitchen while he read me the online news story of the fire.

"Firemen contained the fire to the back half of the building. The blaze destroyed the rear of the first and second floors. Estimate of total damage is yet to be determined. The fire apparently started in a waste can under the secretary's desk in the reception area, which must have been full of paper. It ignited when a lit cigarette butt was dropped in."

"Ridiculous," I interrupted. "I have a no-smoking policy in my offices. Ellen doesn't smoke, and we shred our papers. This was a personal attack. I didn't take those threats seriously. A huge mistake."

Nick glared. "I'll say."

I called Jacobsen to tell him what happened. Next, I contacted the fire chief and got a callback minutes later.

"Arson is suspected. We surmise the lock had been picked and then relocked by the arsonist when he left. The whole lock mechanism has been removed and sent to forensics for examination. Depending on how busy the lab is, we'll know in one to two weeks."

"The noise I heard in my outer office must have been the arsonist entering."

"Very likely. A person in overalls, wearing a baseball cap, and carrying a trashcan was seen entering your building shortly before five. A secretary on her way out noticed him but assumed he was maintenance until hearing about the fire. No workers were scheduled last evening."

"Can she identify him?" I asked.

"Unfortunately, the secretary didn't get a good look at his face. One other thing . . ."

I scooted to the edge of my chair. "What?"

"Whoever started the blaze was familiar with the building layout."

"And knew where my office was?" I said. "You suspect a personal attack?"

"Very possible. The investigation will take time, but initial sight work and photos are completed. The documents within the steel file cabinets should be retrievable. You can go over and pick up any papers inside them."

"Good. We'll go right over. I need to protect my clients' confidentiality. This whole incident seems surreal."

"I'm sorry you've had to go through this. We'll keep you posted regarding our investigation."

"Thanks."

"This could have been one of your clients?" Anger laced Nick's voice. "You're trying to help them, and in return, one of them is trying to burn you alive."

"Or thinks something in my files is incriminating. The intent may have been to destroy my records, and I just happened to be there working late." I shook my head. "I can't imagine what someone could think I know. I've checked over and over."

I remembered the car in the parking lot the night before, and my legs turned to liquid. The certainty of foul play overwhelmed me. How could I be so naïve? I started to shake.

Nick pulled me toward his chest and gave me a strong hug. "I don't want to lose you," he whispered in my ear. "It's scary. When they finish the arson investigation, we'll know more."

"In the meantime, let's go see what we

can retrieve."

Part of me never wanted to go near my office again. Nobody knows better than a psychotherapist the ravage of fear. I wasn't going to succumb. Restorative, brave, positive thoughts take effort, so I began. "Soon I'll be feeling strong again." I spoke aloud to pump myself up.

I stood weakly, gripping the back of the sofa for support.

Nick took my arm. "Are you sure you're up to this? I can get everything while you stay here and rest."

I shook my head. "You won't know what to take. Besides I need to get this behind me. There's nothing physically wrong with me. I'm just tired from the ordeal."

Nick continued to try to talk me out of going, but I was adamant. I hate fear, especially when it tightens around my chest like now.

I changed from my nightgown and robe into a sweat suit. We were out the door within half an hour.

"First stop is Sentry Foods to pick up a few cardboard boxes."

Nick loaded several into the back of the van.

We'd driven less than a mile when I became nauseated. "Please run in a gas station and get me a coke."

"I knew this was too soon." Nick clucked.

I pressed my arms against my belly. "My stomach is still queasy from the smoke. I'll be fine."

Nick pulled into McDonald's drive thru.

I sipped the drink slowly, lowering my head between swallows. "Thanks, hon," I said weakly. "I feel a little better. Now, let's get this done."

The front exterior of my building appeared untouched. We pulled around the back and saw a bizarre contrast of blackened mess. An acrid odor of smoke and wet debris penetrated the air. Only the iron stairs on the right rear remained intact.

Nick helped me gingerly make my way upstairs. At the second-floor landing, I shuddered. "It's like seeing a skeleton."

We strode through what once had been the door. My orderly office, which had brought me such pleasure in the past, was a trauma site. Sooty file cabinets stood like weary sentinels along two sidewalls.

"Lord, how quickly things are destroyed, but creating takes so long!" I wanted to sink into a corner and cry. Instead I started to hum the tune to "Tomorrow" to block sad thoughts.

Nick found a blackened chair and threw

his jacket over it. "Sit here and direct me."

"The only retrievable items in the suite are in the fireproof locked files. I'll arrange for a mover to take these to my new location if they can be cleaned. In the meantime, we'll take the files I'll need immediately."

Nick worked his way through the debris to the cabinets and began pulling and sorting. I scribbled labels with a black marker on the boxes he filled: insurance papers, professional license, and current client files.

After he filled the second box, Nick came to stand over me. "After this disaster, I want you to consider closing your practice temporarily for a long rest. I wish I could seal you up in a plastic bubble and keep you safe forever."

I looked up, startled. "You don't really mean that, Nick? Continuity in counseling is important. I'm not going to do anything foolhardy, but God's got an appointed time for me to die. Fear isn't from God. That's not how we've lived. I won't start now."

Nick knelt and took my hands in his. "You're right, but I don't like it. My job is to protect you from danger, and I can't."

"Let's trust God. Help me find another office. We aren't quitters." I opened my arms, drew him closer and hugged him.

"I still don't like it." Nick set his mouth in

a grim line and went to take the boxes to the car.

"Remember Psalm ninety-one," I said quietly when he returned. "God will protect me from the fowler's snare and the deadly pestilence." I smiled.

"Nothing like pulling my favorite Scripture on me."

Nick helped me into the car before getting behind the wheel. I fell asleep before we pulled off Main Street. My nap was wild and non-restorative. In my dream, I slept in my house as it burned down around me.

31

Morning arrived, and with it an intense determination and fresh energy kicked me into high gear.

I considered several possible office suites Ellen had located. Two were prime prospects. One, a first-floor vacant storefront would need painting. The other consisted of three rooms on the first floor of a pristine Lake Geneva Victorian mansion converted for businesses. Small and pricey, but very attractive in pictures online. Best of all, I could move in immediately with a one-year sub lease. The lawyer, who occupied the suite, was on an around-the-world trip with his new bride. By day's end, I'd negotiated the price down to a manageable amount — a lesson from my papa: always ask.

The furnished Victorian suite was near Nick's building. I like to think of myself as a strong woman, and I am. However, at the moment, I liked the idea of having Nick nearby. My sense of personal security could use a boost.

The lawyer's business items had been packed in several boxes in the storage closet, and his confidential file cabinets locked. My new file cabinets fit in next to his.

By the time he returned from his extended honeymoon, my original office building would be rebuilt — hopefully.

The phone system was switched to my number while the lawyer's number was rerouted to a service. The local printer did a rush job putting my new address on the basic forms I use for intake, progress notes, and treatment plans and guaranteed business cards in twenty-four hours — the marvel of speed printing.

I placed a framed picture of my children, taken from my dresser at home, on the oak desktop. Now it felt right. I looked around. *Thank You, Lord.*

The wall hangings from my former office were ruined, but I'd replace them later when I had more time to shop. Ellen ordered new file cabinets from a local office store, which delivered them three hours later. They would hold my most critical papers for now.

"Remind me to give you a raise," I teased Ellen again.

"Sure. I've heard that often enough." She laughed. We both knew I already paid her handsomely. I sent her out for a few more office supplies.

I'd forgotten about lunch, but food could wait. I organized my DSM, Diagnostic Statistical Manual, and a few salvaged books on the oak bookshelf.

An hour later Ellen bustled in along with whiffs of mustard and oregano on sub sandwiches.

Soon, I was operational again, thanks to Ellen's efficiency. We toasted to my being back in practice with lemon LA Croix.

The desk phone rang. Ellen reached over to answer. Her hand shook as she put the caller on hold. "How eerie. It's him, Aaron. I wish you wouldn't see him. Call it my intuition."

"Relax. I'll finish my counseling commitment. This will be our second session."

I grabbed the phone. "Hello."

"Dr. Trevor, I need to see you immediately." Aaron's voice had lost its composure. "What time can I come today?"

Today? I opened my appointment book. *Why not?* "Actually, I could be free at four thirty." I gave him the address of my new office.

"I'll be there." He hung up.

Aaron didn't seem to find my move or my immediate availability unusual. Strange. I walked over to where Ellen stood organizing my file cabinet, undoubtedly straining to overhear my conversation.

"Aaron didn't mention the fire. He must not listen to the local news," I said.

"Because he's the arsonist and knows what happened." Ellen sucked in her breath. "He's called to see if you survived."

"You're jumping to conclusions."

"He's a dangerous man to be alone with. I feel it in my bones."

"I'll be careful."

"You know I'm a sleuth. I'm sure he's the one who killed Mr. Windemere then went after you with the fire."

I smiled. "Ellen, you have no evidence to make him into a murderer or arsonist."

Nevertheless, her words made my skin prickle. I pondered Al's comment about Aaron being involved in something he shouldn't be. Whatever had Al meant? I forced myself to reject the image of Aaron as the fire perpetrator and ignore my amateur detective assistant.

"Aaron's coming at four thirty. Put his appointment on my calendar."

Her eyes bulged. "To check out your new location and finish the job."

"Stop!" My hands trembled, and I frowned, annoyed with myself more than Ellen. Should I be afraid of Aaron?

Aaron charged in a few minutes early. I welcomed him despite chills creeping up my arms. He sat on the edge of my office chair and never asked about my new setting Maybe he read about the arson in the paper. Red-faced and apparently distressed, he gripped his crossed arms tightly which only added to my tension. *Lord protect me and guide me.*

He'd hardly settled in when he bounced up. "It's preposterous!" he shouted. "The police are trying to turn conflict with my brother into a motive for murder." He paced back and forth across the room twice then paused in front of me. "They grilled me for an hour, insinuating I'd killed Al."

"They're only doing their job."

Aaron pointed his index finger at me. "I want you to tell them to stop harassing me. The police wouldn't know about the arguments between my brother and me unless you told them. I never should have signed a release of confidentiality."

"Calm down, Aaron. You're making erroneous assumptions. I never discussed your strained relationship with the police." I managed to keep my voice controlled. His behavior made me apprehensive. Harboring such pent-up fury, this man could be the killer. I reached for the sweater across the back of my chair.

"You didn't tell them?" Aaron eyed me with disbelief.

"Certainly not. Aren't you forgetting friends and family knew about your anger toward Al? It's not like you kept your feelings secret. I'm a counselor. My job is to help alleviate anger, not create it." I spoke as gently as I could.

The tightness in his features lessened, and he seemed to relax a little.

"For the record, didn't you hate your brother?"

Aaron lowered his head. "Yes, I mean no, not like I used to. We'd started getting along for the first time ever, like I told you."

"Although I haven't observed an expression of grief over the death of your brother."

"How do you know what I'm feeling?"

"Body language and tone as well as words. You speak objectively about Al's death."

Aaron squeezed the arms of his chair. "You're missing something. Al told me he believed in an afterlife. If he's in heaven, why shouldn't I be happy for him?" He dropped his head into his hands and rubbed his temples. "I saw the impact Al's faith had on him." Aaron stared me in the eye. "He actually became a nice guy. I didn't dislike being around him as much as before. I could hardly believe it. Rich and I even started meeting him for lunch every few weeks."

"Rich Nichols, your manager?"

Aaron nodded. "When Al had a great real estate deal, he'd pull me and Rich in if he needed a few more investors. Eventually he and Al had some antique furniture storage business dealings." Aaron brushed back his blond hair with his palm.

"Did they get along well?"

"Always fishing, aren't you?" Aaron's words sparked with scorn.

"I want to help you." My displeasure must have shown on my face because Aaron answered in a kinder voice. "Rich had respect for Al's business skills. He appreciated tips Al gave us."

I noted this association on my clipboard pad. "About your relationship with Al, how did your wife react to his change?"

"She wanted me to have nothing to do with him. Lorraine remained bitter over our past." Aaron stiffened. "Why are you asking about her?"

"To get the whole picture of the family

dynamic."

"Leave my wife out of this. I don't want the police bothering her." Aaron pounded his fist into his palm. "Even in death, Al's the center of attention and messing up my life. Now he's got the law hounding me."

"Sounds like you still harbor resentment toward your brother?"

"I'm supposed to turn it off like a faucet? Let's just get this counseling done."

"Help me discover the real killer. You must have some ideas."

Aaron leaned forward. "You bet I do. Al's investors were all types. My guess is he was involved with the mob."

Before I could respond, he barged out of my office as quickly as he'd come.

I hadn't seen this nasty side. "Healthy anger under the circumstances." I noted in his file after he left. Was it a killing anger?

Rain pattered my windshield non-stop. I gripped the steering wheel, wanting the downpour to end quickly. I needed a run. I had one goal in mind once I reached home and threw on my sweats and tennis shoes: to hit my treadmill.

Nick met me at the door. "Glad you caught me, hon. I'm heading to a board meeting." He recited a litany of instructions for me as if I were a child. "Don't open the door for anyone. Let the answering machine take all calls." I gritted my teeth to keep from answering.

"Stop it. You're making me nervous."

"You should be!"

On the treadmill I pounded off my frustration with Al's murderer and life in general.

I needed to be mentally refreshed and at my full strength for tomorrow's meeting with Al's former client, the mysterious Joanna Tuler.

32

Between sips of apple cinnamon tea at my desk, I read again the list of ten clients Paul Jacobsen had e-mailed me. Each had been defrauded by Al's deceitful financial advice and had lost half a million dollars buying into a property with zoning problems. Al had been aware of this, although his duplicity couldn't be proved, or there'd have been lawsuits.

Debold's reimbursement check was in process. I crossed his name out. Joanna Tuler was another story. Every other client had been compensated except her.

I empathize with people who are swindled. My first IRA investments went into bonds with two companies our broker assured us were as safe as Grandma's apron pocket. Both declared bankruptcy, I learned later they were actually high risk. The financial advisor wasn't the least conscience-stricken, although he went out of business shortly afterward.

God keeps me neither rich nor poor, a good place. I need to trust in His provision at all times. I stopped musing and focused on Joanna. She'd returned to town two days ago. Ellen had pinned down an appointment this afternoon.

"Bad news." Ellen walked into my office frowning. "Joanna Tuler called. She can't get away after all, but she'll see you if you can stop by her business at 4:00 PM. I checked your schedule. She's your last appointment of the day. You could manage, barring construction or heavy traffic."

"Stop by" wasn't the way I'd describe a two-hour jaunt to and from Milwaukee. I hated driving home during rush hour, but I needed to see her, and Al Windemere's estate was paying me generously to be accommodating. "Tell her OK."

I drove to Highway 43, checking my rearview mirror occasionally while reassuring myself no one would mess with me on a busy road or at a prestigious place of business.

I focused on the road, keeping my speed at a steady sixty-five to seventy miles per hour. At the turnoff to downtown Milwaukee, I reviewed what I knew about Joanna Tuler: trendy, well-respected designer for upper-class clientele. Milwaukee had welcomed her with wild enthusiasm three years ago. No fashion business the caliber of hers had ever graced the boundaries of a city historically famous for breweries and the Brewers baseball team. Joanna had invested and lost heavily with Al Windemere's company.

I left my car in a parking garage across from her building. A uniformed window washer diligently squeegeed the sparkling expanse of glass on the storefront. Either the window scarcely required his attention, or I needed to have my eyes checked.

A doorman popped out before I could push on the elegant door emblazoned with the discreet Tuler brass nameplate. I stumbled on the threshold, queen of grace that I am.

My shoes sank into a plush mauve carpet inside the living-room-style showroom. Dresses hung in arched white display alcoves arranged between sitting areas.

I paused to study the setting, enthralled. I love fabrics. The use of vivid colors and designs was Joanna's trademark, according to her website. Gorgeous silks and lush brocades surrounded me. I wasn't even tempted to shop. Loving a bargain as I do, I didn't expect to find one at Creative Clothing by Joanna Tuler.

Fashionably dressed women sat on loveseats in pods separated by tapestry-covered drapes, occasionally sipping from a wine or water goblet. Equally well-dressed saleswomen carried samples of clothing on hangers draped over their arms.

A cadence of friendly chatter filled the air.

I overheard a matronly customer describe her style preferences while being escorted to a large walk-in dressing room. Velvety, draped curtains blocked the private rooms from other clientele in the showroom.

A saleswoman smiled as she approached me. "Welcome to Joanna Tuler's. I'm Coletta. May I help you?" The fiftyish brunette had one of the friendliest voices I'd ever heard.

"Thank you. What a fun place. However, I'm not here to shop today." Best to inform her before she got her sale's style in gear so as not to disappoint her later. "I have an appointment with Ms. Tuler."

Her eyes dulled and her smile faded but didn't vanish. "This way please."

We walked through an expansive soundproof room, twenty by thirty feet, where live models intermingled with mannequins in various degrees of dress. Several seamstresses surrounded a few of the gals, pin-ning, tucking, draping fabric, and occasionally consulting a pattern on the worktable next to them. I passed a maze of men and women hunched over worktables with assorted fabrics and sewing machines humming in disparate rhythm.

Coletta pointed me toward Joanna's office in the corner, a glassed-in extension of this workroom.

"C'mon in. Door's open." A brusque, female voice responded to my crisp knock.

Joanna lifted her eyes from the fabric swatches she was intently comparing and stared blankly. For a moment, I feared she'd forgotten I was coming. A light spread over her face as she emerged from her work trance.

"You must be Dr. Trevor. Your assistant didn't give me details but intrigued me enough to see you. Glad you could manage the appointment switch and run over."

"Me, too," I said, holding out my hand to shake hers. *Quite a run.* I put the dreaded trip back out of my mind — I've never been fond of hour-long car rides. Too much carsickness as a child.

A glint of hardness showed in the tense lines engraved around her serious brown eyes. Above her lips, a row of fine lines formed a parade beneath her nose.

She wore a white cable knit sweater over designer jeans and gold flats. An engraved locket watch hung from a thick gold serpentine chain around her neck. The ring finger of her left hand was covered to the knuckle with an emerald the size of a large marble.

"We ran into a couple of glitches with a fabric order today for my new collection," Joanna explained in an apologetic tone. "I can't leave my desk." She reached down and patted her cell phone and intercom. "This is my lifeline to meeting deadlines and getting key staff in the loop on follow-through. I absolutely must be here."

"I understand."

She didn't invite me to sit. The only chair not covered with fabric books and swatches was against a sidewall. Her message was implied: Don't take too much time. Not to worry, Joanna.

I shot her my politest smile, pulled the lone empty chair closer to her desk, and sat.

She followed my gaze to the jammed award wall behind her and laughed — a deep, raspy, not unpleasant, sound. "OK, I admit to being vain. I like symbols of my success around me for inspiration. When I want an even bigger high, I look at my investment portfolio. Or at least I used to before investing in an American Realty REIT."

"Exactly what I've come to discuss . . ."

"I must say Al Windemere's death was a shock. Frankly, I dislike having reminders of the shortness of human existence penetrate my world of beauty. I like to focus on the fullness and abundance of life." She waved her hand at a bolt of fabric cascading over a chair. "These fun prints of riotous flowers and vivid birds made me famous. They are as much for my delight as my customers."

"They're beautiful, but I'm sure you're wondering . . ."

"Yes, get to the point," she interrupted. "Exactly what is this about?"

I gave Joanna the general reimbursement information between numerous interruptions from staff barging in.

"What kind of game is Al playing and from the grave yet?" She eyed my turquoise rayon paisley dress and brown pumps with apparent approval. "He certainly knows how to pick pretty women, I'll give him that. You sure he didn't just string you along with a sweet story like the rest of us?"

Blood rushed to my face. I worked back my annoyance. I'd driven a long way and hoped for a more professional response. "I assure you this settlement is on the level."

"There's gotta be a gimmick. American Realty wants me to invest more money to average out my losses, right? I won't put in another cent. Do you understand? Don't pressure me."

"Of course I won't. And I'll be out of your way in a few more minutes. I'm not in the habit of wasting clients' time or mine. You had an unprofitable business deal with Al Windemere." Digging into my briefcase, I pulled out a paper titled, Joanna Tuler Creative Clothing. "Here's your Investment Summary Sheet. Correct?"

Joanna leaned her elbows on her desk, propped her chin in the palms of her hands and watched me through half-lowered lids.

"Looks right. So?"

"Mr. Windemere has arranged for his estate to cover the losses you experienced because he unethically withheld important information on certain properties. He regrets his behavior and wishes to make amends. When you agree to accept this settlement, you'll get back your original payment back in full, plus interest. If you still have bitter feelings toward Mr. Windemere afterward, my services are available for free counseling to help you work through your anger."

Joanna leaned back in her chair. After a few seconds of silence, she spread her hands on her knees and laughed raucously, as if I'd told a clever joke. "Al is dead, but he wants me to like him again. Well, now, ain't this a piece of —" Abruptly she stopped, pondered, and looked me straight in the eye. "Hey, you're serious about this, aren't you?"

"Absolutely."

"Jennifer, that's what your first name is, right? I have only one real enemy. Aging. How do I destroy this competitor? Every time I look at the advancing creases marching from my neck to my forehead, I'm reminded of death. If I weren't afraid of dying under a plastic surgeon's scalpel, I'd at least reduce the speed of my enemy."

"I'm not sure what this has to do with . . ."

"You want me to get excited about finances? I have oodles of cash, more than I can spend. Money matters most when you have youth and beauty to enjoy it. Still I'm a businesswoman and a substantial loss is nothing to ignore. If he wanted to be stupid . . ."

I inhaled deeply. Patience is essential in counseling and not my strong suit. "Whatever your personal opinion of Mr. Windemere or his behavior, this restitution is a stipulation of his will." I braced myself for more sarcasm and spoke fast. "Mr. Windemere was determined to make amends to all those he wronged."

"I don't get it. Why?" The question, only one word, suspended itself in the air between us. She looked bewildered and fragile, like a feather.

"After becoming a Christian, Al desired to act like Christ with integrity in all his business dealings," I explained.

She pressed a palm against her forehead, as if pushing away a headache. "Spare me the religious talk, honey."

"Mr. Windemere had already reimbursed other clients before his premature death. He'd hoped to be giving you these funds personally and to ask your forgiveness in person. Unfortunately, you were out of the country when he began and now he's" — I gulped — "been murdered."

"Must I do the counseling?"

"Your receipt of these funds is not contingent upon receiving counseling or extending forgiveness. You'll get the money regardless."

"Well I'll be a . . ." Joanna's eyes darkened. Then she whistled. "Did you know Al well?"

"Yes, but only during the last months of his life."

She stared out the window. "When he was with you, his eye contact never wavered. You were the most important human being in his life at that moment. He made everyone more alive in his presence. Those kinds of business friendships, let alone personal, are rare. I truly enjoyed our relationship. Still business is what it is. I invested, lost, and never expected to see my loss made good. If every broker covered sour deals, who'd survive?"

"This was beyond normal risk. Mr. Windemere advised you and several others to invest in a project he knew had zoning problems, which was unethical."

I checked my watch. "Do you want this reimbursement executed?" My tone implied why wouldn't you?

"You bet I do. I've got nothing personal against you, honey. This is just hard to figure, and as I said, I don't like to think, let alone talk, about death. A man who sat in this room with me is now worm food in the ground." She shuddered.

"I understand." I'd counseled many older adults facing the pain of aging and loss of vibrancy. "You might be comforted to know that Albert Windemere didn't fear death because he knew what was coming next — eternity with Jesus." I smiled broadly. "Now if you'll sign this release, I'll let you get back to your work."

"I've got nothing against Windemere. This just seems too bizarre to be real." She shook her head. "But people do screwy things all the time." She shrugged. "I'll believe it when I cash the check."

Joanna wordlessly picked up a pen and scratched her signature. I wished she'd have counseling with me so I'd have an opportunity to help her work through her fears and introduce her to Jesus. If people knew the life to come was more splendid than anything they'd ever enjoyed on earth, they wouldn't be afraid to die.

"Thanks for your time. I can find my way out." Joanna reached for her cellphone. Before I closed the door, I heard her demanding the latest details on delivery of her order.

In my car, I made a mental note to send Joanna a Bible and a copy of a book my friend had written called *Love Always, Mom* about her son's brush with death and the reality of God.

Joanna seemed to speak fondly of Al. Was it a ruse? Might she be another angry jilted lover as Rose implied? I wanted to dispel the thought but couldn't.

Had Joanna hired Al's killer?

33

Funny how priorities change when thinking about life and death. Usually, I feel good at day's end when I've accomplished objectives I set for the day. Tonight, just being alive made me grateful.

I slowed my car by the park at the corner. Our family often walked here after dinner for an impromptu baseball or soccer game. How I missed my kiddies and wanted them home. I entered our wooded subdivision and pressed down the car window to inhale the fragrant evening smells of the woods.

Nature's ebbing melody bringing closure to the day soothed my spirit. I visualized squirrels and raccoons, flowers and trees settling into sleep. Corny? Blame my love of God and His creation, plus a poetry course in high school.

Ascending the drive to our home, typically peace enfolds me. Not tonight. Without the children, a sense of sadness drifted over me. Someday, these little ones I'd birthed would be on their own. I prayed Nick and I were preparing each of them well for their life's adventure. Their temporary absence made my schedule easier but didn't make up for the huge hole without their presence.

On our closet wall, I had taped a note that listed the months we had left with each child until they turned eighteen. Nick and I vowed to make each one count. He feels the same as me about treasuring our time. I couldn't ask for a more caring Dad! *Thank You for him, God.* I breathed out. If only my husband were more understanding sometimes about the demands of my work.

I found Nick in the kitchen busy at the stove.

"Smells good. I'm starving."

He spun around. "A kiss will buy you a feast." He ticked off his fingers. "Baked sweet potato, fresh broccoli spears, multigrain rolls, and green peppers stuffed with rice I've labored over for hours."

"You sold me. I'm having dinner here." I dropped my briefcase on the kitchen desk and headed to the sink to wash up.

Nick slipped up behind me and enfolded me in his arms, avoiding touching me with his oven mitts. "I must confess. The deli had a special on stuffed peppers."

I laughed. "Great! I love their entrées."

After dinner we lingered at the table for small talk, read the newspaper, and sipped hot drinks — tea for me and coffee for Nick. "That food was wonderful."

"Excuse me. I need to call our little darlings. Want to talk to the kids with me on speaker?"

"You go ahead and tell me what they say."

I carried the cell phone into our bedroom, changed into my nightgown and robe, and put the call through.

I value physical connection even if it's only by voice. I tensed when the phone rang four times before Nick's mother answered.

"Hi, Mom. How are you, Dad, and the munchkins?"

"Super. Can they stay another week. We're having so much fun!"

"Never!" We both laughed. "Mom, I couldn't handle it, but I'm delighted your time is going well." We briefly exchanged news before she assembled the kids. I spoke with Jenny first, youngest to oldest. "Hi, I miss you precious."

"Me too, Mommy! We played miniature golf today." I listened to a litany of each child's activities for long enough to fill my hollow mama's heart with their personalities.

I padded in my fluffy fur slippers down the hall to the living room where Nick was reading, his face illuminated by a warm glow from the brass floor lamps at either end of the sofa.

"The advantage of this vacation is I'll appreciate my urchins even more when they return if that's possible. Best of all, Grandma and Grandpa are being blessed. I need to remember how much I missed Tara the next time she gets in one of her teenage girl moods."

Snuggling up next to him, I pulled a cotton throw over my legs. He drew me close. "How are they?"

I recounted my conversations. "They're so unique and fascinating?"

"You're biased, so am I. I'd like to keep them young and carefree forever, but that's not realistic. Life is hard at times. I'm glad they weren't around the night of the fire. Any news about the perpetrator?"

"No." My eyes clouded. "Hopefully not busy planning a new surprise for me." I tasted fear as I said the words. *Lord, give me courage and peace.*

"Better not." Nick's tone was harsh. "The quicker life returns to normal the better. The police will catch the arsonist and the killer, and this drama will be over.

"I might even settle for a little boredom."

"You? Not a chance." Nick chuckled.

"I'm making progress. I met Joanna Tuler and got her signature on the restitution affidavit." I described Joanna's attitude. "I don't think I can rule her out as a suspect. Even though she was out of the country, she could have arranged for a killer." The words gave me a chill. I nestled closer to Nick.

"Why do you suspect her? Does she seem devious?"

"Hard to say."

From what you've said about her assertiveness, if she wanted to kill someone, I'd picture her holding a noon shootout at the OK Corral with an audience."

A smile tugged on my lips.

"What about motive? You said she'd already reconciled herself to the financial loss."

"She could have been jilted after a clandestine affair with Al. Although she gave no indication."

"Of course she wouldn't. That would make her a suspect."

"A professor during my psych studies taught us when assessing clients to trust your gut. Joanna's overall reaction to the restitution makes me think she'd already put bitterness behind her. She's a tough woman who's used to taking life's knocks."

Nick pulled me closer. "Maybe that's why Al's reimbursement seems incomprehensible to her. With some people, being the receiver of a kind deed shocks them."

"Just to be safe, I'll try to confirm her alibi for the morning Al Windemere was killed. She was supposed to be out of the country, but I have only her word."

Nick kissed me. "At the moment we have something more important to think about."

"That doesn't feel like a good-night kiss."

"It isn't. The honeymoon continues. Tomorrow's a long way off; tonight is ours."

34

The voice sounded nervous, fragile. "I'd like to make an appointment. How soon can you see me?"

While making my client prep notes for the day's appointments, Lorraine Windemere's surprise call came in.

"Your attending counseling isn't required to fulfill the requirements of Albert Windemere's will. I already offered your husband the option of couple's counseling, but he declined."

Lorraine's voice quivered. "Whether he wants it or not, I need counseling as soon as possible."

"Of course you can come if you wish." I opened my appointment book and stifled a sigh. Clients usually want to see me ASAP. Sometimes it truly is an emergency, but often, they simply want to get in quick before they change their mind. Accommodating these demands zaps my energy.

Ellen's worth her salary for handling my schedule because she refuses to overload me. It's easier for her to say no to a hurting client than for me to do so. Next Friday is the first available date."

"Oh dear. I was hoping you'd have something this afternoon."

"I'm completely booked. Sorry."

"Could you put me on a waiting list? Maybe you'll have a cancellation." I heard sniffling. "It's very important."

Goodness, she's frantic. My compassion kicked in at her tears. Plus, Lorraine might have some information relevant to her brother-in-law's murder.

"Let me think a minute." I rationalized I'd sacrificed my lunch break the other day to see Angela. The kids were still away. Nick wouldn't mind a late dinner. "I could stay an hour later this evening if it's an emergency. Can you come at five o'clock?"

"Oh yes. Thank you so much. I'll see you then."

"Be here fifteen minutes early for paperwork." If I could help this distressed woman, it was worth stretching myself. A murder in the family can unsettle everyone. I put Lorraine out of mind and focused on my morning clients.

Crystal Vandley arrived on time for her

10:00 AM appointment. I considered her promptness a good sign.

I started with high anticipation and fervent silent prayer. *Lord, I so want to help this wounded woman. Guide me.*

She squirmed getting comfortable in her chair. Immediately she brought up her dad's infidelity, her posture taut, as if on a juror panel, judging him. "I can't figure why my friend thought she was doing me a favor telling me about seeing my father with another woman, and why did it freak me so much? You know who I'm talking about?"

"No. I'm not sure who you mean?"

"Ann Tylore. Their affair went on at least a year, maybe longer. The friend who saw them together wanted me 'informed for my benefit.'" Crystal shook her head. "Like I didn't already know my dad often was unfaithful to my mother."

"Maybe she'd hoped you could talk sense to him."

"Fat chance. It's not like I had any power to change his behavior." Crystal's face reddened. "A lot of men and women my age fool around. When I was still married, I had a few extramarital flings. Weird how it became a big deal to me when my dad cheated on Mom."

"We have different expectations for our

parents. In my counseling, I've been amazed to see the depth of pain an adult child experiences when a parent breaks their marriage vow. The infidelity feels like personal betrayal."

"What made it so terribly hurtful was he never had time for us but managed to fit in dating other women. You want to help me get rid of my bitterness toward my father. Start with that!"

"I'm so sorry. Truly that was a terrible violation to you, your brother, and your mom." *Lord, I hurt for her, but I can't heal her. Only You can.*

"Several months ago, my father actually confessed his affairs to me in a moment of rare honesty. Guess he thought I didn't know. How arrogant and blind of him. If it was his intention to hurt me more than he already had, by talking about it openly, he did."

"Not to cause you more pain, maybe I can explain. After he'd repented and broken the relationship off with Anne Tylore, he wanted to ask your forgiveness."

"Like I'd ever believe him!" She stiffened. "Mom lived with the agony of truth. She was rejected for a high-priced slut." Crystal's eyes turned hard and cold.

"Thank God he ended his adulterous

behavior. Your dad's being honest with you and your mom and expressing sincere sorrow was intended to open the way to a honest relationship. Deceit — trying to keep this hidden — would always have been a block."

"Poor Mother. Sometimes she cried non-stop for weeks, couldn't eat, and rarely slept. I feared she'd have a nervous breakdown." Crystal set her mouth in a line. "It was so unfair. But then nothing in this family has ever been fair."

"I agree. Life is often unfair. If your dad were here right now, what would you like to say to him? Pretend he's sitting in this chair." I pulled up a side chair in front of her.

"Don't be silly. I can't."

"Just try."

She looked from me to the chair and back again.

A minute, maybe two, passed before she stammered, "Nice going, Dad. You messed up my life. You weren't a good father or husband. You never knew how. And now your death left us with a big mess."

She darted a glance at me.

"Go on," I encouraged.

"The woman you had an affair with may well be the person who murdered you for

278

all I know." She stopped. Had she said aloud something she hadn't voiced before?

"And?" I coached.

"I don't blame that Tylore woman for killing you if she did. Serves you right for deserting her like you did us. Mom didn't deserve what you did to her."

Immersed in the drama, Crystal started to shout. "You ruined all our lives! Now you're dead and left these stupid conditions in your will. I feel nothing for you except hate." She paused, dropped her head into her hands and sobbed.

I touched her shoulder. "Crystal, hate is dangerous. It eats away at the person who holds it. Your tears tell me you hold sorrow in your heart as well as hate. If you didn't still love your dad, you wouldn't have these strong emotions."

She lifted her head and sniffled through her tears. "Hate keeps me going."

I shook my head. "I'd never try to minimize the huge violations against you. Your dad was a human being, responsible for very grievous wrongs. None of us are perfect. Unfortunately, our transgressions hurt the people we love."

"Alive or dead I can never forgive him." Crystal compressed her lips. "All I wanted was a real father. Several months ago, he came to me and said he found a relationship with God the Father, Son and Holy Spirit and knew Jesus as his Savior. Where was my father? Where's my savior?"

"Your father wronged you. It pained him deeply, and he hoped to make it up to you. He wanted you to know his love for you was real and prayed you'd come to trust him in time. Now his death has robbed you both of this chance."

"He told you all that?" Her eyebrows lifted.

"Yes, he was very sad over your rejection, but he understood. Mourn your lost childhood with an involved dad, but for your own good, try to see the new dad God created for you, maybe in response to your anguished, if unspoken, prayers. Your Father in heaven loves you unconditionally and always has."

She sighed. "All those years without a normal family life."

A Scripture verse came to mind. I spoke it into the almost palpable tension in the air. "The Lord will restore the years the locust has eaten."

"Whatever does that mean?"

I put down my pen before answering. "It's a Scripture verse that means God can make good come from all things. Pain is horrible but it can make you stronger and more caring." I paused and prayed briefly about whether to disclose some of my own past. *Lord, only if it will help.* I sensed the Lord say go ahead. "Crystal, I also had a painful childhood with narcissistic, alcoholic parents. It gave me great compassion for others who are hurting. My difficult past is part of why I went into counseling."

Crystal pulled back in her chair. "You really believe my dad changed, don't you?"

"Without a doubt. If Al Windemere were my father, I'd want to know more about the God who changed him from a dishonest playboy into a faithful man, filled with parental love, and gave him sound business ethics. You can't deny something extraordinary happened to him, can you?"

She sat wide-eyed as I told her about my faith. "I know God is real. You can experience Him for yourself. The choice is yours."

Crystal sat very still, gazing past me, her demeanor subdued.

I prayed again. *Lord, help Crystal release her bitterness toward her father and realize You love her.*

She seemed totally spent. I ended the session. "We'll continue from here next time."

Crystal reached for her bag. "One thing I'll say about counseling is you have a calming effect."

"Good." I hoped what I'd shared about her dad's transformation would get through to her.

I pondered how to sum up our session in my notes. Did she know who murdered her father? Had she in fact set it up? Was she avoiding guilt now by angrily rationalizing that her father's death was justified?

35

Inspector Jarston's call came in as soon as I returned from lunch. "Did you come up with any new information?"

I hated the timidity in my voice. "No." I gulped. "Have you?"

"We're viewing Al Windemere's death as murder. We haven't come up with a strong motive for suicide. His business is solvent, his marriage restored, no obvious health problems. However, he had quite a few enemies. I imagine this pleases you, Dr. Trevor."

"Yes, and the note? You're willing to ignore '. . . can't go on like this. No more!' "

"We find it questionable. The words could have come from a letter written to, for example, a former girlfriend, about breaking up. He seemed to have a problem in that area."

At last, you're seeing this my way. "Have you zeroed in on a suspect?"

"No. The whole family — daughter, brother, in-laws, even his wife — and business associates are being checked. Anyone who would benefit from his death. You're still seeing the family for counseling?"

"How did you know?"

"Rose Windemere told me. What have you found out?"

"Nothing specific. I do agree there's plenty of motive for Al Windemere's being murdered."

Inspector Jarston harrumphed. "I'm going to make a suggestion since you're already involved with this family. If you tell anyone I said this, I'll deny it. Off the record, watch yourself around Aaron Windemere. You've been a victim of arson. I wouldn't want anything else to happen. In fact, I suggest you stop probing altogether for your own good."

"Thanks for the warning."

"Something will break sooner or later. It always does. Until then," Inspector Jarston added in a stern voice, "leave the detective work to professionals."

I hung up and stared at my notepad. His concern surprised me. Maybe he wasn't such a cold herring after all. Nevertheless, I refused to abandon my investigation.

Inspector Jarston was the second person

getting bad vibes about Aaron. What was it about that man?

I finished counseling my regular scheduled clients and assembled intake papers for Aaron's wife's session. My gaze drifted to the sofa where she would sit. *Holy Spirit, show me how to help this woman. I need your wisdom.*

Ellen showed Lorraine in before she left for the day.

"Dr. Trevor, thanks for fitting me in. We didn't speak at Al's funeral, but my sister-in-law, Rose, pointed you out. May I call you Jennifer?"

"Of course." Lorraine's blue and gold warm-up suit blended with my sofa fabric. She adjusted a throw pillow at her side using quick darting movements. I placed my clipboard on my lap and noted observations. Full oval face, eyes hollowed with dark circles, nose rather wide. She would not be considered pretty but had a gentle demeanor. When she smiled her bottom teeth looked like seedlings planted too close; in contrast, her top teeth formed an even row. Definitely nervous gestures, although her voice sounded more composed, as if she'd come for afternoon coffee.

I remembered Al's words that something

285

about Aaron disturbed him. Maybe Lorraine would reveal it.

I computed Lorraine's age at forty-two using the DOB on her intake form. Her toned body signaled regular workouts. She was what you'd call unremarkable, a woman who would fade into the background in a crowd.

"You needed to see me today on an urgent matter?"

"Yes." She cleared her throat. "I've come to discuss Aaron's . . . problem."

I bit my lip. It's frustrating when clients want to talk about somebody else's problem, not their own. "Lorraine, I need to clarify. Emphasis on others' problems, even your husband's, prevents working on your own issues. You can never change someone else, only be supportive and encouraging. If they're not motivated" — I shrugged — "sadly, nothing you do will help."

"Well, I'm concerned." Lorraine reached for words. I got the impression she was trying to recall her memorized script.

"Please explain why." I gazed into her eyes.

"I'm not sure what's going on, but I believe we need to work on our marriage although he's not interested in coming for counseling, says he hates discussing personal matters."

I felt my eyebrows lift. Aaron had co-operated in our session.

She seemed to read my mind. "He's coming for the inheritance, but that's all. How much is he revealing?"

True. I hadn't gotten close to touching Aaron's feelings. Except for his anger with the police incident, and his brother's earlier treatment, he'd put on an "everything's OK" demeanor about himself.

"Lorraine, please be more specific about your marital problems?"

"We've been married seventeen years. He always seemed happy and content until a year or so back when he became distant. Now he stays up until 1:00 AM, far later than ever. I often hear him up during the night. He's not sleeping well. And . . ." She paused.

"Yes?"

A red flush spread across her face. "Our sexual relationship has been non-existent this past year. He doesn't even sleep in our bed."

"Have you asked him about this?"

"When I bring it up, he claims nothing's wrong, says he's just getting older."

"Despite all the TV commercials about erectile dysfunction, in real life people are still reticent to face such ailments and

287

discuss them with their spouse or doctor. You both need to know even people in their eighties can have satisfying sex lives."

"I'm aware some men have problems as they age, but I don't think that's true of Aaron."

"Does he take medication for other health issues? That may be a factor."

"No. Something else is bothering me. What we discuss here is confidential, right?"

"Absolutely. Unless your sharing has bearing on Al Windemere's murder."

Lorraine nodded. "Now that the police have been investigating his brother's death as a murder I'm worried they'll think Aaron could have hurt Al. Aaron loved his brother."

The euphemism "hurt" for the act of murder? I let that pass.

"Aaron's a good person." She dug her thumbnail further into her cuticle.

"My lady doth protest too much" came to my mind. Was guilt the issue keeping Aaron up at night and avoiding intimacy with his wife?

Lorraine's strong emphasis on his innocence made me wonder if she were trying to protect him or convince herself. Various options paraded through my mind. Was Lorraine a nag who had blocked her husband's affections? Had Aaron become depressed, even homicidal? Evaluating a husband's behavior from his wife's assessment wasn't easy.

"What else can you tell me about Aaron's relationship with Al?"

"From the time I met Aaron when we were both in high school, he hated his brother. Aaron called Al nasty names behind his back. From childhood they fought for their dad's attention. Aaron always wanted to prove himself as good as Al."

I rubbed my arms feeling a sudden chill. Jealousy is never healthy between brothers. It could become a motive for murder.

"So Aaron had a competitive childhood relationship with Al?"

"Yes. I don't know details, but they had constant squabbles. Their dad was gruff and undemonstrative." Lorraine chose her words. "Al was favored because of his athleticism and good looks. His Dad frowned on Aaron's artistic interests."

"Did the brothers have anything in common?"

"Not really. Recently the relationship was better. Al shared his investment expertise. Aaron disliked asking but did because Al was the best financial advisor he knew."

"Both men apparently wanted to make a

success of their lives. Correct?"

"To a degree. Aaron resented that Al became more successful than him — I did, too." Her face reddened. "It seemed as if Al hardly worked and Aaron labored so hard at the shop, putting in long hours. In recent months the animosity seemed to lessen."

"Aaron's negative feelings from childhood changed?"

"Yes and Al began to treat him better."

I smiled inwardly. I knew what was responsible for Al's changed behavior. "Go on."

"In the past six months, Al went out of his way to visit Aaron's shop and show interest in his activities." Lorraine looked down and smoothed her blouse. "It seemed as if they were beginning to actually like each other." She looked up. "Write that down."

My eyes widened. I wasn't accustomed to a client ordering my note taking. Was she trying to build a case for Aaron's innocence?

"How did you feel about the change?"

She lowered her lids. "Sadly, I resented it getting better while my marriage was going aground."

"Did you get along with Al's wife?"

"I always felt sorry for her. She seemed the last to know about his philandering."

"What about you and your brother-in-law? How did you get along?"

"We didn't. He was self-seeking and arrogant. I disliked him for the way he treated my husband." Lorraine started to fidget.

Exactly how deep was her resentment of Al? I wondered if it could have incited Lorraine to arrange for Albert to be killed.

"I hope what I'm telling you isn't giving you reason to believe Aaron could have killed his brother. He'd never resort to violence. The police questioned Aaron. He was furious."

I remembered Aaron's explosion during his recent visit. I understood why Lorraine had come — worried, no doubt and wanting to protect her husband. "Where was Aaron the morning of Al's death?"

"Home with me asleep."

"I thought you said you no longer slept together?"

Lorraine turned red. "That night we did."

"I see." I'm supposed to believe that?

Lorraine crossed her arms across her chest. "I refuse to think Aaron is capable of murder! Aaron's killing Al would only be hurting himself. Al's financial advice increased our portfolio hugely. It was to our advantage to keep him in charge. The police will find his murderer, and Aaron's innocence will be obvious." She clenched her fists. "Jennifer, in the meantime I've got to know what's gone wrong with us. Goodness knows, I've tried to be a good wife."

"Are there any other factors in Aaron's life which would explain the change in your relationship this past year, new staff at work, etc.?" I wanted to broach with tact the subject of a possible affair.

"Not that I can think of. His business is doing well. It's improved more this year since Rich became assistant manager. As I said, Rich and Aaron also have joint condominium investments. Money is not a problem."

"Lorraine, this may not be about you at all."

"What do you mean?"

"It's possible Aaron has been experiencing a male, mid-life crisis. The symptoms you've described, becoming withdrawn, cynical, sometimes impotent are common to this syndrome. What about Aaron's work habits?"

"No change there. He loves his work, always has."

"With an acute mid-life crisis, his enthusiasm for work wouldn't typically remain the same. It's more common to have a general apathy." I hated to ask the next question but had to. "Sometimes men indulge in an affair in an attempt to re-experience their youth. Have you seen any signs that would indicate this possibility?"

"He doesn't flirt. He never even looks at other women."

"But then he's gone so much and doesn't sleep with you. Might you be in denial?"

"No."

"Has he ever used physical violence?"

She shook her head. "Never."

"Good. When he's upset, has he threatened divorce?"

"No." She sat straighter and tried to stifle a sob that eked out. "But I sense he may be close. Lately, he rarely even comes home for dinner." I heard sorrow and shame in her words. Marriage counseling — better communication — is what we need. He disagrees. I don't dare bring it up again. He gets very angry. But if you recommended couples counseling, wouldn't he have to go? Could you make him?"

"No. I can't force him into marriage counseling. However, I'd be happy to bring up the possibility during our next appointment."

"Thank you so much! Should I let him know I've seen you?"

"You don't need to go out of your way to

tell him, but if he inquires, don't lie. Honesty is vital in relationships."

Lorraine tugged on the sleeves of her jacket. "Aaron's my first and only . . ." Her eyes clouded as her voice faltered.

I patted her hand. "You obviously love him very much."

"Yes."

I'd put her feelings into the simple, ancient words.

She smiled for the first time.

"Jennifer, I feel lighter just having told you all this. I hope you can help. Thank you."

"I'll do what I can."

I walked her to the door.

After she left, I took a deep breath and wished for the thousandth time I were a miracle maker. Only God could recreate love that had been extinguished, but if there was still a spark, I might be able to stir the ashes and get a blaze going. For Lorraine's sake and Aaron's, I'd try.

A more pressing thought gripped me. Did Aaron's unusual behavior signify guilt? Had he been responsible for arranging his brother's murder?

Hadn't Inspector Jarston implied that very thing?

36

A young mom in a gray sweat suit herded two pre-school age girls out the YMCA locker room door as I entered. I dropped my duffel bag on a bench and changed into navy nylon shorts and a white T-shirt.

The weight area reeked of rubber mats mingled with sweat and antiseptic spray. Several men lifted free weights. All but two elliptical machines were available.

Nick waved at me from the rowing machine. "Hi, sweetheart. how was your morning?"

"Don't ask."

"That bad?"

"I'm just tired." Oops. That left me open for a "you're overdoing" lecture, the last thing I needed today. I put a finger to Nick's lips, pecked his cheek, and headed to the bicycles.

I met Nick at the health club over lunch hour at least once a week when our schedules permitted. Our family membership, one of Nick's company benefits, keeps their key men health insurance rates low and contributes to the community YMCA, a bonus all around.

I pulled my iPhone from the zippered pack at my waist and positioned my ear buds.

The room had one mirrored wall and another of clear glass facing the pool area. I quickly assessed myself for motivation: legs not bad, but after two C-sections, my waist had acquired a couple of extra inches. The abdomen is a hard spot to streamline if you hate crunches and leg raises, as I do.

Nick mounted the bike next to me. "Race you."

"You're on."

I pumped furiously trying to out pedal him and didn't notice John Vandley, until he mounted a bike the other side of mine.

He looked lean and muscular in black gym shorts and white T-shirt advertising Pepsi in bold blue letters.

I waved as I set the uphill grade on the bike's electronics.

"Dr. Trevor, nice to see you again. We met at Al Windemere's memorial service if you recall."

"Of course." I held up my hand in a

"hold-it" gesture while I turned down my music. I introduced Nick.

"Nice to meet you. I've never seen you here before. Are you a new member?" Nick asked.

"I come occasionally and pay the daily fee."

"Great." Nick continued pedaling.

John hopped off the stationary bike to adjust the seat and then turned toward me. "I know this is rather irregular," he said lowering his voice, "but I'd appreciate the chance to talk with you privately a few moments, Dr. Trevor."

I didn't conceal my surprise. "About?"

"Your involvement with the Windemere family. I'd like to run some things by you."

I groaned inwardly. It's not uncommon for people to want to give me their perspective when they know I'm counseling a family member. A red flag goes up. "John, I welcome family counseling in the professional setting because it's an efficient way of working and often speeds up the process but . . ."

"Sure, individually you may get lies."

I winced at his sharp statement. "But," I continued, "ethically you need to ask Crystal if you could join her for a joint session." I stated this as kindly as I could.

"I wouldn't dare suggest it. I know how it would be received. I'm willing to pay for an hour of your time, if you'll just listen to me for ten minutes." His piercing green eyes beseeched me. "I think the information I give you may help solve the mystery of Al Windemere's murder."

Now he'd pushed my hot button.

"Before you answer, I want to be totally upfront with you." John wrung his hands. "I didn't plan meeting you today. I saw you walk in here a few minutes ago as I finished a sales call across the street, and . . ." He shrugged. "I always keep exercise clothes in the car. He bent closer. "I'd been hoping to connect with you, just a few minutes, please."

His honesty prompted my cautious agreement. In this Windemere murder case and bizarre counseling situation, I needed to follow my instinct, as long as I stayed within legal parameters. I welcomed any information that might lead to the discovery of Al's murderer. Did John have evidence pointing to Crystal? Or might this son-in-law be Al's murderer trying to divert suspicion?

"OK, John, I'll hear you out as long as you understand I'm not at liberty to discuss anything Crystal said during her sessions. If you're planning to pump me, forget it."

"Fine."

"Fifteen minutes is all I have. Let's go to the juice bar."

As I dismounted, Nick gave me a look I read as *what are you up to now?* I shot him a smile and led the way to the reception area.

The health food bar on the ground floor faces the indoor tennis courts and was deserted. I perched on one of six lime green bar stools with comfortably worn vinyl seats and rested my arms on the smooth bar coated in polyurethane as thick as my little finger. My history as a child of an alcoholic makes me uncomfortable at bars, but here the smell of pineapple juice replaced the typical alcohol odor. Several small bowls of popcorn were welcoming, too.

John slid onto the stool next to me.

A front desk employee wandered over to assist us. We both ordered wild berry smoothies with glasses of ice water. The young man blended our drinks and returned to the check-in desk.

"Now what's this about, John?"

He swallowed and cleared his throat. "I'm not good at talking about myself, but I want to get some things off my chest that might help you."

"I'm listening."

"I'm worried that Crystal's going to give you the idea that I was the big, bad wolf in her life just like her dad was."

I imagined Crystal for a brief moment in a little red cape and bonnet. I loved fairy tales. "You weren't?"

John waved his arm in protest. "Absolutely not! I'm not perfect, but our marriage ended because of her, not me. Crystal believed everybody else's life was perfect; only hers was flawed. True, her dad wasn't a family man. She always said she wanted a simple, loving family life — her exact words — but did nothing to make ours that way." His tone turned sarcastic. "You don't find this at the party scene, the only place she looked. Has she told you about her wild past?"

"I can't comment. Don't ask me details again, or I'm out of here." I spoke as kindly as I could.

"OK! See this?" John held up his empty glass. "Crystal had an insatiable thirst for attention and affection that I couldn't fill. I cared about her like nobody ever did, but she barely noticed me. She was always looking for the thrill of new guys."

"Why did you marry?"

"I loved her and thought I could settle her down."

300

My throat constricted with sadness. Nobody can change another person. Why don't high schools teach students about relationships?

"I learned the hard way." John glanced down at his glass. "Crystal started drinking heavily and reusing pot after our first child was born. Having a family didn't bring her the satisfaction she expected. She moved on to other drugs, mostly uppers as far as I know until she got clean." John pulled out a handkerchief to wipe tiny beads of perspiration that had formed on his forehead, despite the air conditioning.

"When did Crystal shake drugs?"

"About a year and a half ago. She'd been in treatment several times before. "She's off everything now, I think. She used the AA route after inpatient. By the way, I warn you she hates counseling. She never felt like it helped her."

I recalled our first visit and her intake form. She'd checked no previous counseling experience. No history of drug use. I tried not to let surprise show in my eyes. *Huge lies, Crystal?* The hair on my neck bristled. I dislike dealing with clients who distort facts.

Then, again, maybe John wasn't telling the truth. I'd find out. "You've gone out of your way to talk to me. Why? What are your feelings toward Crystal now?"

"She's the mother of my kids and still hasn't got her life together. From what I piece together from them, she's on a roller coaster from one affair to another. When loneliness threatens her fairyland, she makes the ride go faster. She's good at it. I can't begin to tell you how sad and angry she makes me."

His pain was palpable. "I'm sorry," I said with deep sympathy. "You share custody of your two children?"

John tossed his head back. "Yes and I'm a good dad. I could have won full custody when she was using if I'd wanted, but I gave in provided she hired a nanny to watch the kids. I hated to take them from her. Although, sometimes, I swear she doesn't even care about our children. She's totally self-absorbed."

"If you haven't been loved, it's hard to parent well."

John sighed. "Crystal claimed she wanted to be a mother but never considered the commitment required. She likes the kids around when she wants to play. I swear it's as if she were a child with them. She never learned how to be an adult."

He gulped his drink. "The kids spend

more time at my house than with her, even when it's her turn to have them. The only person Crystal seems to care about is her mom. She spends a lot of time with her. Crystal has help at her store so it runs itself. She does a decent job selecting merchandise on buying trips and her sales are OK, probably makes more than me. She always had good taste in clothes, I'll give her that. I keep up with my custody payments, even though things have been tight lately."

"You're sure she's not using again?"

He shook his head. "Don't think so. Crystal quit, but for all the wrong reasons."

"What do you mean?"

"She fueled her recovery with bitterness and channeled all her energy into hating her dad even more." John fiddled with a napkin, rolling it.

I shook my head. "Not healthy."

"Don't I know. I wish she'd be a better mother. The house is usually a wreck except days the cleaning lady comes. The kids end up taking care of Crystal half the time."

"A terrible role to stick on children." I know. I lived it, but I wouldn't let myself think about that now.

"Does her mom help with the children?" I'd seldom heard Rose mention them other than showing me their pictures.

"Very little. By the way, I doubt our relationship could ever be called love. I thrilled her for a time but couldn't give her the constant excitement she needed. I hated watching her destroy herself and the life we could have had."

"What was your relationship with her father like?"

John took a deep breath and lowered his voice. "That's what I wanted to talk to you about. Al Windemere had the nerve to blame me for Crystal's addictions, the jerk." Veins popped from his neck. He reached for another paper napkin and began to shred it.

His response scared me. Had John shown his love for Crystal by removing her father, the greatest source of her pain?

"A few months ago, her dad called. We met for lunch, and he actually listened to my side, which he'd never done before. I think for the first time he understood what went on in our marriage. He said he hoped Crystal and I could get back together."

I wasn't surprised. This would be the Al I knew.

"Crystal's getting older, and soon her life-style will affect her appearance. I don't think she'll be able to handle aging well. She's has guys at her beck and call now, gets frantic about being alone. Someday, they'll quit coming around, and she'll have no one."

"Except Rose?"

He shrugged his shoulders. "Her mom's a taker who demands Crystal's time and attention. Crystal feels guilty if she backs off. Rose seems sweet and rather passive, but she gets Crystal to jump hoops for her."

I couldn't picture Rose manipulating Crystal but said nothing.

"Crystal won't admit it, but because Crystal's never had a relationship with her dad, she's petrified to lose connection with her mom."

"Off the record, do you think Crystal would be capable of arranging to have her dad killed?"

"She couldn't, as much as she hated him. That's another thing I want you to know. She's not emotionally strong enough."

"In your opinion."

"It's true. Crystal's self-esteem is almost gone, not on the outside; she's all bravado there. Crystal's mother could help her more emotionally. Talk about self-focus. Guess that's where Crystal got it from."

"Maybe Rose was too busy dealing with her own battles and losses," I spoke on her behalf grabbing a handful of popcorn from the bowl on the bar. My stomach churned.

This distraught man had stirred my sympathy. "How are you doing personally?"

"I've had some financial problems lately . . . and no this has nothing to do with my feelings for Crystal. I'm working them out on my own. I'll admit Al Windemere's death shook me up emotionally."

I checked my watch. Five more minutes, and I had to leave. I couldn't be late for my next client.

John dug into the other popcorn bowl. "Crystal's broken, and I'm not Humpty Dumpty who can put her back together again. I don't even know if I'd want to try. Maybe I do, or else why would I be talking to you? Crystal said I was a freeloader when she'd withhold sex, which she did all the time. I've always paid my own way. I could support her, if she'd live by a realistic standard."

"John, I get the gist. I have only a few more minutes. Anything else?"

"Yes." He lowered his voice. "Al had talked to me about his Jesus. He said Jesus removes sin and guilt and His Holy Spirit has power to restore people and relationships, even remake memories. He said Jesus could still make something good out of my relationship with Crystal if I'd ask Him. Do you think that's true? I mean if Jesus is real and powerful, could He change things between us?"

"Is that what you want?"

"Truth is: maybe I still love Crystal. It's been so long I'm not sure. Now there's nothing but the shell of a connection left, but I'd like to find out. I see a glimmer of hope for us." John looked into my eyes. I sensed how important my answer was.

"When you understand the love Jesus has for you, your desires change, and you receive an amazing power called grace to live in a way that honors God."

"I'd like to know Him better. What do I do next about Crystal? Maybe pray?"

"That's a good start."

I pulled out a business card and scratched down the name and number of our church on the back. "My pastor can help you. Thanks for trusting me with this information."

He nodded. "I appreciate your listening to me. I hope what I've said assists you in counseling Crystal. I'll be out of town a few days. When I return, let me know if there's any way I can help."

I shook John's hand. "You appear to be a sensitive husband and father. I wish you all the best."

I hurried out.
Lord, I need discernment.

37

In the midst of attacking the persistent pile of paperwork on my desk before heading home, Ellen came into my office and announced, "Joanna Tuler on line two."

"Jennifer, my check arrived. So this was on the level!"

"Absolutely."

"Want my opinion on this?"

I smiled.

She assumed I did, because she kept talking.

"At first, I considered Windemere's behavior nutso. Now I'm intrigued."

"I can understand your reaction." I spoke warmly, choosing to ignore her initial rudeness when we first met. I watched tree shadows play on my office walls. Through my open windows the fragrance of pine-laden air was heavenly.

"You talked about forgiveness. I've been thinking about how good Al must have felt making things right before he died. I've got a couple of accounts I should straighten out, too. I don't want to come in for an appointment or anything, but tell me how you do this stuff."

"Forgiving wrongs encourages humility, which forces out pride. Unforgiveness is like sipping on poison — dangerous to physical as well as emotional health."

"And what about this restitution stuff?"

"It's sometimes hard, but it's always possible with the grace of God who wants everyone to live in honesty and harmony. The restitution aspect requires going out of your way to do good to those you have harmed. It's amazing for creating peace of mind."

"Honey, I never knew diddly-squat about this! I was raised to kick back at anybody who wronged me."

"If you read the Bible and go to a Christ-centered church, you'll learn more, Joanna. Or I'd be happy to meet you for coffee to discuss this further if you don't want to come in for formal counseling, that is."

She laughed. "I'll think about it. This is intriguing."

Click.

Lord, please help connect her with You.

■ ■ ■ ■

By nine, a hot shower played a sweet, rejuvenating tune on my skin.

Nick returned from his men's group meeting and found me. "How'd your day go?"

I wrapped myself in a towel and stepped out. "Great. Two encounters with people bowled over at God's principles for living a great life."

"Was one your talk with John at the Y?"

I gave Nick the details. "He'd been trying to get up the nerve to call me for some time. What a bolt out of nowhere that conversation was."

"You lead such a fascinating life. Take off that towel, and I'll make it even more interesting."

I chuckled and complied.

Loving beats talking about murder any day.

38

The next morning, I took the back roads to work through brilliant pink and orange sunlight. Perky pansies, petunias, and hearty marigolds graced the walkway leading to my temporary office. How I wished summer could go on forever. Anything below seventy degrees is too cold for me.

My first counseling session of the day was a follow-up with a thirty-eight-year-old single mom who'd abused her kids several months back. They were put into temporary foster care. Individual counseling and an on-going parent support group helped her. I discharged her today with no anticipation of a recurrence. I treasure success stories. Unfortunately, I know the pain of failure often, too. People don't always live the life I want for them. I know how God must feel.

I finished returning a phone call as Rose Windemere drifted in wearing a gold madras dress with dark green metallic threads woven throughout the fabric. From the way she moved, I knew her energy level had waned since our last visit.

She slouched into my client's chair. "I went to my oncologist for a checkup and got my report yesterday. Seven months of being cancer free; now it's back." Rose dropped her head into her hands and sobbed.

"Oh, Rose, I'm so sorry."

She lifted her head and pulled several tissues from the box on the coffee table.

"My primary doctor is hopeful, but this oncologist all but guarantees my doom."

"Do you have any experimental treatment options?"

"I wish. Jennifer, you've been a good friend to me in the short time I've known you."

"How are you emotionally?"

"Horribly at first. I was furious with the young doctor who gave me the news casually like he was giving a weather report. I wanted it to be him with the relapse to know how devastating it feels. Why can't modern medicine come up with an end to this scourge with all our marvelous technology and millions of dollars spent on research, some of which, by the way, came from my husband's and my gifts."

The surge of anger electrified Rose briefly, and then her energy was gone.

"Rose, I'm so sorry."

She attempted a smile. "Such a waste. I endured the horrid, long treatment protocol for nothing." Her voice became subdued now. "I've got to be realistic. There's seldom a cure for breast cancer after recurrence and metastasis."

"But some women survive." I tried to give Rose encouragement even if it was just a shred. No one can live without hope.

"Death is a matter of time." Rose swiped at the tears brimming over her eyelids. "I won't have Al to help me through."

"Have the doctors said how long?" I always speak openly with individuals battling terminal illness. Beating around the bush doesn't help.

"They can't say for sure, but my oncologist guesses less than three months."

I reached over and squeezed her hand.

"Thank you. It helps to tell someone. I don't want Crystal to know yet. You'll be careful not to let it slip out in your counseling? I need to work this through for myself first."

"Of course."

"I'm trying to be especially sensitive to Crystal. Our life has always revolved around pain. With Al so emotionally cold toward us, she was terribly hurt. I'd like to wait until she finishes counseling to tell her. At that point, I'm hoping her bitterness toward him will be diminished if not eliminated."

"Whenever you choose to tell her is your decision. Just so you know — I believe Crystal can handle it whenever you feel the time is right for you. If you tell her while she's in counseling we can work through her feelings together."

My head was spinning. Rose's concern for Crystal didn't add up with what John Vandley had said about her demanding attitude toward her daughter. This wasn't the time to explore the mother-daughter relationship. Rose had enough to process.

"I'll continue our counseling. You're a great support to me. I need all the emotional encouragement I can get. And I want to stay on top of your investigation into his murder. Any news?" Rose managed a feeble smile.

"Nothing to report, sorry. You're being very brave."

She waved away my words. "Jennifer, whatever happens is OK, because I'll be with Al again. What we shared these last few months has been precious. Al said we'd never be separated. He believed in a literal heaven that lasts for eternity."

My eyes misted.

After she left, I wondered how, for even a moment, I could ever think this woman could have arranged her husband's murder.

Minutes later my phone rang. "Jen, don't be alarmed." Nick's voice chilled me. "Think carefully before you answer."

I stiffened.

"Mom and Dad called. Tara had a phone call that spooked Mom. The person had a high-pitched voice, but Mom thought it was a man. She said 'Tara's not available' and asked who was calling. He wouldn't leave a name. Is there any reason why an adult man would be calling Tara at my folks — music lesson, sports coach, that sort of stuff?"

"Nothing I can think of. If so, they wouldn't be reluctant to leave a name."

"OK, hon. Mom wanted to check with us. I'll call her back and tell her to screen and record all future calls on her answering machine."

"Nick, this frightens me."

"Don't worry. Dad's not going to let anyone near the kids. Gotta go. Love you."

I turned off my phone with trembling fingers.

39

Midway through the next afternoon a floral truck delivered a gorgeous garden bouquet in a foot-high milk glass vase to my office. Tiny yellow mums, velvety snapdragons, and zinnias stood against a backdrop of stately gladiola spikes. Magnificent fragrance filled the air.

Ellen crooned as she arranged them. "What a man you married! He's so romantic."

I laughed. "True, but these can't be from Nick. He knows I prefer a single yellow or peach rose to a huge bouquet."

Ellen hovered as I ripped open the envelope after noting the logo — a flying heart. The sender had used a florist other than Aaron's.

For her benefit, I read aloud. "Received my check. How can I ever thank you? How about dinner this Friday? Fondly, Robert Debold."

"What's with 'fondly'?" I flicked the card into the garbage. "Send a formal thank you, Ellen, and put the flowers in the reception area."

Half an hour later, he called.

"Jennifer, Bob Debold here."

Now it was Bob? No way was I getting on a first name basis. "Mr. Debold, I received your bouquet. That wasn't necessary, but I appreciate your kindness."

"You like the arrangement? I insisted they make it extra special."

"It's lovely, Mr. Debold." As if anybody wouldn't appreciate it.

"Call me Bob. The flowers and dinner are the least I can do to make up for being rude at our first meeting." He sounded like the script of a soap opera.

"I didn't take it personal. Only doing my job. Are you calling because you want anger management counseling?"

"Don't need that. But I'd like to take you to dinner so I can show I have no hard feelings about Windemere and properly express my gratitude. I've a great restaurant in mind. I'll keep it a surprise. How about I pick you up at your office around six tomorrow night." Debold sounded as though he were gifting me with a corner of the world.

"Were you planning to invite my husband

and your wife to join us for dinner?"

"Not exactly. I had something more intimate in mind."

"I'm sorry. My schedule's jammed, and my next client's here. Need to go."

"Wait, don't hang up. I want to get to know you better to —" I held the phone away from me like it was a piranha.

"That's what I thought. Good-bye."

"Ellen, if Debold calls back, I'm unavailable permanently."

I sensed frown lines tighten on my forehead. Perhaps Debold should stay at the stove in his kitchen and out of trouble. I hoped this huge cash settlement didn't do more harm than good in his life. Suspicious gremlins began dancing in my brain. Had he invited me to dinner to find out what I knew about Al's murder? Or to arrange a convenient accident for me somewhere? My logical self kicked in. *Don't overreact, Jennifer. Debold made a plain and simple pass.*

I glanced at my reflection in my picture window and combed my fingers quickly through my blunt cut, blonde-brown hair, in need of a trim.

I sighed. His invitation to dinner made me feel queasy. I suppose he expects me to be flattered if that's all it was. Had I given any hint that I was a woman with loose values? I hoped not.

Nick called at three to discuss our dinner plans. I told him about the flowers.

"Rather brazen. What's with this guy?" he demanded.

"Don't worry. He got the message that I don't do extracurricular."

"I don't like anyone assuming you're the type of woman who fools around. It's demeaning."

"We both know some people think nothing of a 'business' dinner alone with the opposite sex. Sadly, I often see them later in marriage counseling."

"And I get them a year later in divorce court. I wish more people practiced what you teach clients about the danger of spending time alone with the opposite sex. Obviously, this Debold guy doesn't have a clue."

Nick was in rant and rave mode, so I let him go on a few minutes before I said, "Nick, enough."

The door opened, and for the next four hours, I submerged myself in the emotions of hurting clients.

Five thirty in the afternoon. Time to turn the key on another day. First, I needed to check phone messages and make calls, which could take fifteen minutes to half an hour.

Subconsciously my brain burst with thoughts about the Windemere situation. His murder lingered beneath the surface of my thoughts all day. I called Angela at American Realty Investment. I had no doubt she'd still be there. I hadn't heard from her since our lunch.

"Angela, Jennifer Trevor. Got a minute?"

"Just," Angela said reservedly. "I'm busy preparing a contract, but I've been meaning to contact you to let you know I changed my mind."

"About what?"

"Mr. Halston being a suspect."

"Really?" Surprise. I gripped my phone tighter.

"I did some more research. As you said, the buyout agreement is standard with a partnership like theirs."

I blinked rapidly. "Yes." Quite a turnabout!

"Also Mr. Halston couldn't have done it. He told me what happened between Mr. Windemere and John Vandley, Crystal's ex-husband. Mr. Halston heard Vandley threaten his partner. He told Inspector Jarston about it."

My face flushed.

"Put Mr. Halston on, please."

"He's in a meeting. We're both working late." Angela was in a chatty mood. "We've re-organized office procedures."

"I see."

"Mr. Halston's very generous and grateful for my help during the transition. I got a big raise." The words Mr. Halston rolled out as sweetly as she'd mouthed Al Windemere's name when I first visited her. "Mr. Halston and I are having dinner later, so I need to finish."

I blinked rapidly. Her words floored me.

"How interesting." I stretched out the syllables.

"It's not romantic or anything like that." Angela's words may have been more to remind herself than me.

"Don't bother telling Mr. Halston I called. I'll try to reach him another time." I smothered my motherly advice, although my instinct screamed for her to be careful. "I'm glad you're doing well. I sincerely wish you the best, Angela."

"Bye."

Since Angela had stopped fighting Windemere's war against Halston, she'd be a valuable ally. Was he being kind to stop her accusations?

While not exactly a lady-killer, Halston was attractive, well groomed, and articulate. Women would find him appealing. Competent and caring? Maybe. Angela had another boss now to nurture and protect. Some women are content to give of themselves without expectation. Mr. Halston probably enjoyed being adored in exchange for Angela's loyalty and competent managerial skills.

My mind wandered to what might have motivated John Vandley to threaten to murder Windemere. Or had Halston made this up to throw suspicion off himself?

I had to find out what really happened between John and Al.

40

During dinner on our deck, I reveled in the hum of motors powering crafts along Lake Geneva, the myriad sounds of people having fun, which I love.

Nick set his fork down and stared at me. "Jennifer it's only eight, and you look done in."

I turned my head from studying a persistent squirrel attacking our bird feeder.

"Guess I am. It's been a busy week."

"Every minute you're either working or thinking about the Windemere situation." Nick's words took on a slight edge.

"You're exaggerating. Aren't we out here now enjoying this gorgeous evening?"

"Your mind is elsewhere."

"I can't deny it. The Windemeres may cure me forever of over-extending myself." I laughed to break the tension.

Nick reached over and pressed his finger lightly to my lips. "Don't even say the name.

How about some tennis? This is our time, remember?"

"Great idea." Guiltily I knew I'd prefer to stay home. I had a strange foreboding that something bad was about to happen.

We drove to the park's lighted courts. I focused as best I could and played a decent game, but Nick beat me 4-6 and 6-7.

When we returned home, Nick went to shower. Out of habit, I checked the answering machine on my desk and found it blinking red. Why couldn't its light be a soothing green or peach? I punched PLAY. My father-in-law's voice came on, not steady as usual, but shaky. Instantly, my heartbeat quickened. Usually it's Mom Trevor who reports on the children.

"We're OK. Don't worry," he said, "but we had a problem today. Call us as soon as you can. We weren't able to reach you on your cell phones. We'll wait up."

I ran into the kitchen to grab my cell where I'd left it recharging on the counter, yelling on the way. "Nick, it's Dad. He wants us to call immediately."

Nick came in, a towel hooked around his waist.

"He doesn't sound like himself. Something's wrong."

"Don't jump to conclusions."

325

I punched my in-law's number in all the while pacing back and forth.

"Stand still," Nick insisted.

The line was busy. How maddening!

Gripping the phone, I opened a cabinet, snatched a glass, filled it with water, and downed gulps. I continued to press redial every few seconds until I heard the ringing sound.

"Nick, it's going through." He leaned close to hear the speaker.

Dad answered in a weary voice. "Hello."

"We called as soon as we got your message. What's up?" I nearly shouted into the receiver.

"Sorry if you've been trying to get through. I was on the phone with the police."

"The police?" My heart jackhammered.

"There's been a car accident . . ."

My feet froze to the floor "The children?"

"They're fine. But they had a close call."

"You and Mom? How are you?" Nick's voice rose.

"Just a few cuts on my forehead. Mom's pretty shaken up, but she'll be fine."

"How did it happen?" Nick demanded.

"We took them to the lake to swim after lunch. Stayed until five o'clock. On the way home, a car drew up behind us, suddenly sped up, and pulled alongside as if to pass. That section of road is usually pretty deserted. The driver drew even with our vehicle and veered his car into us and bounced into the side of our car several times, forcing me off the road." Nick's dad stopped and drew a breath. "Scared me to death. Mom says she almost had a heart attack."

I felt like I'd been punched in the stomach, and I collapsed onto a kitchen chair.

"It was all I could do to keep control. Next thing I knew we were in the ditch." His voice trembled.

"How terrible," I said.

"The girls were screaming. Poor kids were pretty frightened."

Nick jotted down details. "Dad, I'll take over following up with the police report and insurance. I want you to call our family doctor to get medication to help you relax.

"Dad, can you please put the children on for a minute." I needed to hear Collin, Tara, and Jenny say they were OK.

"Can't. We just got them calmed down. Mom read the girls to sleep and then dozed off herself. Collin went to bed twenty minutes ago. It's probably best to wait until morning."

"OK," I said, not bothering to hide the

disappointment in my voice.

"How did you get out of the ditch?" Nick asked.

"The car was at a precarious angle; we crawled out the high side. Fortunately another car came by because" — Dad's voice broke — "the driver who side-swiped had started to turn around to come back. Another driver, a woman, came up behind and stopped to help. When he saw we were getting help, he took off."

I clutched my chest and inhaled deeply. "Thank goodness."

"I called the police and a tow truck. We all got into the woman's car to wait."

"Dad, how did you know it would be safe to get into her car?" Nick asked. "What if the second car had been part of a plan?" We were on the same wavelength with visions of a setup.

"I recognized the lady as the waitress at a restaurant in town." His tone took on an air of defensiveness. "The children and I couldn't sit out there with that other car coming back."

"Right. Then what?" I asked impatiently.

"The police made out a report but told us not to expect to track the guy down; road rage happens a lot. They said maybe I was going too slowly. We all know that's not true. I drive the speed limit," he said. "I can't figure it out. I guess some people are just looking for a way to release their anger. But we had kids in our car."

"Dad, you said he. You're sure it was a man?" I asked.

"Can't always tell nowadays with those short haircuts, but I thought so."

Nick took hold of the phone. "Did you see the car well enough to identify it?"

"Came right by me, but I was too busy trying to control my car to get the license number. I know it was a gray sedan of some kind. My car's in bad shape. I'll drive Mother's until it's repaired. The children are worried you're going to make them come home early. Please let them stay. Jenny's having a grand time playing with the two girls next door. And I'd planned to take Collin and Tara golfing day after tomorrow at Timber Ridges."

"Are you sure you and Mom feel up to having them stay?" I asked, trying to keep my voice calm.

"Of course we want them to finish their vacation. Let's not let this crazy driver ruin our time together."

"OK, but stick close to home if you don't mind," Nick said. "Please lock the doors and keep a constant eye on the kids."

"We will. Now I'm going to take two aspirin and go to bed. I feel better since we've talked."

"Dad," I said, "We love you."

"We sure do," Nick added. "Now get some rest. We'll check back with you tomorrow."

After we hung up, Nick glared at me through blazing eyes. My body turned ice cold all over.

"I know what you're thinking. I'm wondering the same thing. Man in a baseball cap. This could be connected. We need to find him." I headed to our bedroom.

Behind me, I heard Nick calling the police station for further information and to arrange for the accident report to be faxed to his office.

I was too exhausted to talk to Nick, but my body was wired against sleep. I kept berating myself for making our children vulnerable. Had I put them in danger so their mother could be a savior to others?

More than anything, I wanted them sheltered from harm. It appeared too late for that. Hadn't John Vandley said he was going out of town? Was he a violent man hiding under the pose of a rejected husband?

Or was Halston capable of arranging something like this?

Lord, reveal the identity of Al Windemere's

330

murderer quickly and in the meantime, keep my family safe.

41

Off and on throughout the night, I awakened with cold sweats dreaming of the frightening accident involving our children.

My distrust of Halston intensified by the hour. When I first met him, he'd tried to put blame for Al Windemere's death on Aaron. Yesterday Angela said Halston implicated John Vandley. Multiple ploys to throw suspicion off himself?

At 9:00 AM, I called American Realty Investment.

"Angela, I need to talk with Mr. Halston immediately."

"He's in a conference. I'll have him return your call."

"Get him on the phone. It's important, a matter of life or death."

A slight exaggeration? No. My kids had been endangered, and I was furious after a night of being nearly sleepless. I pictured cool, professional Angela squirming as she tried to decide what to do.

"Hold on." Seconds later, her voice came back on. "I'm sorry. Mr. Halston really can't be disturbed. He's in the middle of —"

"Never mind." I slammed down the receiver and grabbed my purse.

Twenty minutes later, I strode into the American Realty building. I knew the location of Halston's office from my earlier visit and headed straight past the receptionist who was busy on a call. She didn't look up.

Angela's office door was open. She jumped up and blocked my access. "You can't go in there. He's in a meeting," she insisted.

"Get Halston out here, Angela, or I will." I was being rude; my "mama bear" came out with the threat to my kids. I was acting totally out of character but didn't care. I had to talk to him.

She pursed her lips, knocked on his door, and disappeared into the office.

Less than a minute later, Halston stalked out with Angela trailing behind. He swore like a sailor, his face the color of violet as he gestured me into an open office across the hall.

"Excuse me," I raised my voice over his. "My children's lives were endangered yesterday. Did you hire the car that side swiped them?" Tears stung at my eyes.

"Dr. Trevor, I know nothing about your children. This is a place of business! I insist you leave immediately."

"Not until you answer my questions. He turned to go back to his office. Worried he was ducking out, I put a restraining hand on his arm. Was I losing it, or what?

Halston tossed off my hand with a look of disgust. "I'll be right back. If you must interrupt my meeting, have the courtesy to give me a few minutes."

I heard him in his office excusing himself briefly to his clients and saying Angela would bring coffee.

He stepped back into the room where I stood. "Now what's the problem, Dr. Trevor?"

I told him everything I knew about what had happened.

"I had no knowledge you even had children. If I were a murderer who wanted to stop you, wouldn't it be more logical to eliminate you? Now what do you want to know?"

"Why you held back the information about John Vandley's assault on Al and then conveniently disclosed it to the police?"

"I originally believed Al's death was a suicide. I didn't want to bring personal gossip into this." Halston's tone held controlled fury. "When the police called with questions about Al's murder, I felt an obligation to tell what I knew."

"To throw suspicion off yourself!" I edged my words with sarcasm. "Exactly what did you tell Inspector Jarston?"

"Find out from him. I've no time for this."

"If John Vandley is dangerous, I need to know now!"

"You're obviously distraught. If you must know . . ." Halston dragged out his words and shook his head, "Al and I were having lunch downtown at the Cactus Club in one of the alcove rooms —"

"When?"

"Two weeks or so before Al was shot. Around 3:00 PM, we'd finished going over our business and were about to leave. The place was almost deserted. Suddenly, Vandley showed up at our table." Halston stopped as if choosing his words with care.

"And?"

"He'd been drinking, I smelled whiskey on him. He slurred his words. I don't recall exactly what he said — something like, 'If you hadn't been such a lousy dad, my marriage might have had a chance." Then Vandley grabbed Al by the throat, and the next thing I knew, Al was gasping for breath."

"You didn't stop him?"

"I tried, of course, but couldn't pull him off. John's one strong guy. A guy from another table in the restaurant came over to help. I told John to get himself together, or I'd call the police. That quieted him down."

"And Al? What was his reaction?"

"He stayed amazingly calm. After John stormed out, I wanted to report the incident, but he refused. Said he planned to talk to his former son-in-law when he cooled off to get some issues straightened out between them."

"I told Al he better have an armed guard with him when he did."

"Do you know if he ever met with John?"

"No idea."

"Were there other witnesses?"

"Not that I'm aware of, other than the patron who helped out. He left immediately, and I never got his name. As I said, the place was almost empty."

I studied Halston's eyes. "How convenient."

"What's that supposed to mean?"

"You better not be lying. If you recall, I left my card with you and specifically asked you to contact me if you thought of anything significant regarding Al's death. Obviously, you ignored that request."

"What good would it have done to tell you? I'm not sure there was any benefit to informing the police either. Vandley will only deny it. Now if you'll excuse me, I need to get back to my clients." His sarcasm was thick as sludge. Halston tossed his head back. "I don't appreciate your self-appointed investigator status. You're a psychotherapist. Stick to your profession."

For a split second, I saw red, but I walked out without another word. I didn't know who to believe. Halston had to know I'd try to confirm his story.

I returned to my office and waited for the clock to move toward my session with Crystal. I wanted a better understanding of her former husband's personality.

Four fifteen came and went. No Crystal. Where was she? *Don't get frazzled, Jennifer.*

If she arrived late and I tried to fit in a full session, I'd be behind the rest of the evening and be angry with myself for modifying my schedule for Crystal's tardiness. It's hard to be of service in less than fifty minutes.

Praise God in all things, even delays, I reminded myself as I enjoyed a late afternoon banana-nut muffin and herbal tea. Afternoon teatime is a personal custom I began after a visit to England — nothing like the calming, tonic qualities of steaming tea — must be the English blood in me. I surely needed it today.

At four thirty Ellen buzzed me. "Inspector Jarston's on line one."

"Any word from Crystal?" I asked Ellen before I took the call.

"No."

I returned the inspector's curt hello.

"Managing to avoid crises, Dr. Trevor?" From his bland tone, I couldn't tell if he was teasing.

"Barely." To my surprise, this man was growing on me. I liked him in spite of his formality and eccentricity.

I told the inspector about the danger my family had experienced last night and my suspicion. "Even though our family is in Arizona, I believe the incident is linked to my Windemere work."

"Road rage is common. Is your father-in-law an extremely slow driver? It may be coincidental," he said, brushing off my concern.

I ignored his comment. "What can I do for you?"

"Mrs. Windemere is a feisty lady. She badgers us daily to find her husband's murderer."

"Of course. She's worried she could be next."

"If you discovered anything significant in the course of your counseling, despite the confidentiality issue, you'd tell me, correct?"

"If someone's life were in danger, certainly."

"I understand John Vandley spoke with you?"

"How do you know?"

"I'm in the process of checking out Al's former son-in-law's alibi." Jarston's voice grew cold. "You didn't think it necessary to bring his anger to my attention?"

So that's why Jarston had called.

"I just heard. It didn't occur to me. Sorry."

Jarston changed the subject. "Within the realm of my police career, I've learned to study people's body language carefully. During our last conversation, Rose Windemere didn't seem very concerned about your being the victim of arson. In fact, I wondered if she even cared."

Was he baiting me? I tried to sound unconcerned. "I don't expect sympathy from my clients."

"I should think compassion would be nice, especially since you helped her husband so much. How can you remain positive about those individuals you try to help, when they're detached and self-focused?"

"Because I truly care, Inspector. Some people don't show personal feelings well." *Like you.* A smile warmed my face. Jarston was revealing concern for me. Did he have a beating heart after all?

"You'd think with all the problems you hear," he continued, "you'd become numb like the surgeon for whom patients become simply another body."

"Quite a comparison. I operate on people's emotions, which are delicate."

"I wouldn't know, being purely cognitive and factual myself," he countered.

"And I dwell in the realm of feeling. I often enter a client's life through their intense moments of pain."

"Some people tolerate emotional distress better than others."

"How true. I only wish I hadn't put my family and myself in jeopardy."

"That's what I mean. Stop hunting for this murderer," Jarston barked without a second's pause.

"I'm determined to help my former client's family. That's my main goal, but perhaps I can also help discover who killed him."

"I could arrest you for intrusion and obstruction."

"But you won't, will you, inspector?"

He sighed heavily. "You really believe you changed Al Windemere?" The inspector's words reeked with cynicism, no mistaking the put-down in his tone, but at least he'd dropped the obstruction of justice threat.

"God changed Mr. Windemere, not me. I was privileged to be an instrument through our counseling."

"Perhaps what you're defending is only a matter of professional pride?"

I winced. That hurt. Pride can tempt me — I regularly take stock and try to quench it. Of course, I didn't want my reputation smeared because I'd failed with Al Windemere and he'd ended his own life. That was natural. I fiddled with the phone before answering.

"Still there, Dr. Trevor?"

"Inspector, I work hard and I pray hard. I'm grateful when God uses my counseling along with my clients' efforts to create emotional healing. I'm especially thrilled when He saves marriages."

"I doubt God has anything to do with it."

"We differ on that point."

"I see a great deal of violence stemming from marital problems. The sooner spouses in conflict are separated or divorced the better."

"We have different perspectives, Inspector."

"What about when you fail to facilitate change?"

"I can only do my best. Some people refuse to take suggestions and modify their behaviors. But, Inspector, you didn't contact me to discuss my counseling philosophy."

"No, I called because I also get upset with people who won't take my advice. I urged you to watch yourself. That fire was no accident, and it's possible neither was your family's accident."

My shoulders shivered beneath my suit jacket.

"An acquaintance of Crystal Vandley's informed us that Crystal was at a gun range ten days before Al's death."

I gripped the edge of my chair. "So?"

"She was practicing shooting with a hand gun. Highly suspicious, don't you think?"

I gasped but quickly recovered.

"I understand Crystal had an appointment with you today. She won't be coming. We brought her in for routine questioning."

Jarston certainly had taken a long enough time getting around to telling me. The information, while not totally unexpected, pierced me like a steel rod.

Jarston had another call and clicked off.

Crystal's failure to appear made sense now. This complicated woman had many defense mechanisms including using a handgun. Was murder in her repertoire or was she practicing at the shooting range for self-protection?

42

Sunday, we went to Al's church to hear his pastor. The sermon title listed online in advance, "Freedom of Forgiveness", intrigued me. How would he handle the subject?

The service started at ten thirty in the main sanctuary. We arrived ten minutes early. Nick and I waded through a stream of welcoming handshakes from greeters in the entrance area.

The sun poured in through huge windows forming shadows on chrome chair backs in the sanctuary. I debated where to sit as I eyed the few still-vacant gray chairs. We ended up halfway down the center aisle.

People around us of every age, gender, and skin color seemed to know one another based on the waves of chatty talk and occasional springs of laughter.

A young black man, early twenties, sat on stage in front of an electric organ. Next to him, a sixtyish white man with full gray beard and burly arms cradled a guitar against his black shirt and jeans, stereotypical biker looks, probably a living saint. The few strands of hair on his head had been pulled into a long ponytail rubberbanded at the nape of his neck.

Around us, guys in jeans and slacks sat next to men in pinstripes with ties. Kids with well-worn gym shoes mingled with children wearing patent leathers. Families of different social classes had come to worship together. I loved the eclecticism and warmth.

A heavy woman drew next to us in the aisle. Her herringbone blazer clashed with a black and green plaid blouse. She graciously introduced herself as "Nancy." When she smiled, her ordinary-looking face warmed with sheen like a well-polished antique. "Welcome." Her sincere tone left no doubt she meant it.

Despite her chunkiness, Nancy moved with the rhythm of a figure skater as she threaded her way to a seat beside a black-haired, distinguished gentleman in a gray sport coat and peach knit shirt. He put his arm around her as we all sang the introductory song.

The churchgoers alternated between

standing and sitting for almost fifteen minutes of clapping and repetitious song words. Some people closed their eyes and lifted their hands.

The pastor stepped to the podium. His deep, resonant voice made me want to close my eyes to enjoy the full effect.

After the singing, adults flipped open their Bibles and notebooks, and young children were dismissed to Sunday school classrooms. I whipped out my pocketsize pad and my pen to take notes.

"Our stiffest enemy isn't always Satan," the pastor began. "Our enemy is often the self-centered schedules that stress us and fill our lives, leaving no time for reflection and connection to God. Then when disaster strikes we have no foundation for dealing with it.

"We want ease and success," the pastor continued, "but suffering can be God's gift to us and makes us grow spiritually in ways we never could have imagined. Suffering strengthens our inner self like ease never can. However, if we don't respond well to inevitable times of suffering or lack, bitterness can develop, poisoning body and soul."

I mulled over his words thoughtfully and remembered watching a bitter client's arm stiffen with arthritis when she dealt with a tough circumstance in her life. I learned then the power of bitterness was real.

The pastor went deeper. "If somebody steals all your money and your home, and you don't get it back, can you forgive that person? Even do good to him?"

Scattered amens followed.

"Why endure such a violation from another person?" He paused, looking around the assembled group and then answered his own question. "Because when you forgive the unforgivable and love the unlovable you grow closer to the character of God and you give your offender a chance to experience the love of Christ on the human level."

Nick poked me. "He's right on. Shades of Albert Windemere."

"It's foolish to think because you're serving God, your life will be problem-free. God allows hurts. It's OK to get mad when you're hurt, but don't dwell there. Remember God's not obligated to provide a perfect life for you now. He's far more interested in perfecting you for eternity."

The pastor used as text for his teaching the story of Joseph and his envious brothers who tossed him into a pit to die. Eventually, Joseph became an Egyptian ruler with the power to save his brothers, father, and the entire Israelite people, and he did.

When the service ended, Nick and I followed the crowd down the aisle. People drifted out slowly, stopping in knobs of conversation here and there.

I turned to Nick. "Some would say Al carried forgiveness to the extreme, but he was only following our Lord's example. I bet he'd even forgive his murderer if he'd had a chance!"

"Let's say hello to the pastor," Nick urged.

"Sure." I hadn't met him at the funeral.

When he finished chatting with the pod of people surrounding him, we approached and explained our connection to Al Windemere.

Pastor Forester shook my hand warmly. "Al spoke highly of you. You helped him greatly. What a tragic death."

"You're very kind, Pastor. I totally agree with the ideas you presented in your message today and use the same principles with my clients, although not everyone is open to the spiritual basis underlying them."

The pastor smiled. "When you encourage people to eliminate bitterness and initiate forgiveness in their lives, they may become intellectually convinced of their value, but can still be unwilling to do it. As Al discovered, there's no easy way to turn bitterness

348

into love. It requires the grace given through Christ."

I nodded.

"Pastor," Nick added, "you've given your congregation quite a challenge."

"I hope so. Jesus challenges us to love well, and His reward is always worth the price."

That evening, Nick and I rented a video described as a drama. It turned out to be a mistake. The subplot focused on a female killer and smacked too closely of the Windemere saga.

43

Monday, an eighteen-year-old female drug addict in recovery came for her first appointment. Her mouth and nose were pincushions hosting multiple rings. The momma in me wanted to say, "Precious, don't hurt your delicate body." Such a discussion might come at a later visit. Definitely not yet. Instead, I concentrated on taking her history and forming our relationship.

"My AA friend said you're a Christian counselor who can help me with my addiction."

"I certainly am. Thank you for being honest with me. That gives us a great foundation to work from."

Midpoint through reciting her family background, she blurted out, "I miss my dad so much. I haven't seen him for ten years. I'm afraid he's dead, gone forever." She fell silent.

"What makes you think so?"

"Mom said she didn't love him anymore and asked him to leave when I was eight and my brother was fourteen. She wanted her freedom. She kept us with her. Dad was crushed and wouldn't fight. He said he must have been a terrible husband and father and he accepted her rejection. But he wasn't. He was always good to us, and to her, too. He was devastated. I hate her for destroying our family."

"I'm sorry this happened, hon, but you know what? Destroying your life won't bring him back."

"I know. I learned that in rehab. But I don't know how to make good decisions. I've been told I put my mom in my control booth and do exactly the opposite of what I think she'd want."

"It's better to figure out God's plan for your life. He's your Papa who never will leave you, loves you forever, and has created you for a beautiful purpose in this world," I said. "We can search that out together."

My heart leapt inside me. *Lord, help me guide this girl.* The phone chimed. I ignored it. Ellen had left at five thirty, and I never take calls during client sessions. The recorder clicked on with the voice level inaudible.

After the sweet young woman left, I played the phone message, my pen poised to write the number for callback before heading home.

Crystal's agitated voice startled me. "Dr. Trevor, call me as soon as possible please. It's an emergency." She rattled off a number in a shaky voice.

I punched her digits. Crystal answered on the second ring. "Hello."

"This is Dr. Trevor. How may I help?"

Crystal took a deep breath. "An intruder armed with a gun broke into Lorraine's home where Mom was staying. Mom's OK but Lorraine's German shepherd was shot."

"How terrible."

"My poor mom. Yesterday I was taken in for questioning; I'm a suspect. Can you believe it, in my dad's murder?"

Sadly yes, I could believe it.

"Although they released me on bond," she rattled on. "Mom was already upset about that, then this. Aunt Lorraine invited her to dinner and a play to take her mind off me. Mom stayed overnight since it'd be late when they got back."

I'd never heard Crystal talk so fast. "Slow down," I said. "How is she now?"

"The doctor prescribed a sedative for her, and she slept most of the day after the

352

police left. She's up now and asking for you. Can you come to Aunt Lorraine's?"

I reached for a pen to write down directions. "I'll stop on my way home."

Crystal met me at the door and led me directly to the oak-paneled den.

Her mom was stretched out on a recliner with only her neck and head visible above a thick white comforter.

My heart did a flip-flop. "I came as soon as I could. Are you OK, Rose?" I drew close and hugged her.

Rose pulled herself to an upright position. "I think so."

"What happened?"

Crystal began to answer.

Rose held up a hand and stopped her. "Crystal, darling, I can tell Jennifer myself. Please leave us alone for a few minutes."

Before she exited Crystal threw me one of her spectacular glares that could have frozen water.

"I was in the guest room" — Rose pointed a tiny hand — "next to this den and couldn't sleep. About 1:00 AM, I came in here to read. Lorraine's dog followed me and snuggled at my feet. Suddenly, the shepherd growled and started to pace. I heard a noise in the hall. Then the doorknob to the room turned. I froze. Instantly, I feared it was Al's murderer coming for me. I couldn't even scream."

"How frightening."

"The door opened slowly. I ducked down to the floor, a shot was fired, and the dog dropped as the door was closing. The poor animal never had time to bark even."

"Who would know you were here?"

"Just family and a few friends I told at lunch after golf yesterday, unless someone tapped into my phone or e-mail."

"You're more accessible here than in your huge home. It makes sense. Where was Lorraine?"

"Upstairs in her bedroom. She never heard a sound."

I shivered although the room was warm.

I couldn't help picturing my own office. How easy it would be to gain entrance, stand at the door, and shoot. The threatening notes I'd received flashed before me. Invisible coils of fear ringed around my heart. I made myself refocus on Rose. "Did you see the intruder?"

"Only a blur of black and a ski mask."

"Was anything stolen?"

"Not that we know of." Rose began to tremble. "After firing the shot, he or she must have run out. Maybe instead of Albert's killer coming for me, it was a robbery. My presence startled the thief and he or she fired randomly then raced off. I'm so distressed I don't know what to think."

"What happened next?"

"I was in shock for a few seconds, maybe minutes; I don't know. I couldn't move. When I collected my wits, I awakened Lorraine, and she called the police. They found the back door ajar but no sign of anyone or footprints. The walkway and drive are gravel. The police were wonderful by the way — so kind."

"I'm glad. It's unfortunate Lorraine didn't see or hear anything. Where is she now?"

"She's driving to the deli to pick up carryout for dinner."

Inspector Jarston's warning rang in my ears. "Where was Aaron during all this?"

"At a florist's convention in Milwaukee with Rich."

"Could he have left there and driven back and forth?"

"I suppose he could. But why? It's about an hour away." She bolted upright. "What you're implying is ridiculous. Why would Aaron want to hurt me? All I know is someone had the perfect opportunity to kill me — but missed." Rose rubbed her hands together nervously. "It was so frightening."

"Thank God you're OK." Something bothered me, but I couldn't wrap my head around it. Maybe Aaron meant to kill his wife, and Rose's presence took him by surprise. Could he harbor that much anger toward Lorraine? My jaw clenched. Nothing this family did would surprise me.

We chatted for another fifteen minutes until Rose appeared sufficiently calm. Crystal poked her head in. "Would either of you like a cup of coffee?"

"Thanks, but I'm about to leave." I said my goodbyes. "Call me tomorrow at the office if you need to talk further, Rose."

"I feel better after seeing you. You're always a peaceful influence in my life."

Crystal escorted me out to the deck where we were alone.

"When did your Uncle Aaron return?" I asked.

"Around noon today." Crystal didn't flinch. "I will say Uncle Aaron sure is an emotionally cold duck."

"What do you mean?"

"This crisis with Mom didn't seem to faze him."

"How do you know?"

"When he came in, he made lunch and acted casual like usual. Far more upset about his dog than his sister-in-law, I'd say.

But then he's my father's brother. What can I expect?"

Was Crystal trying to subtly deflect attention to Aaron as a possible murderer? I considered asking where she was last night, but I expected she'd have an alibi. "Is your mom staying over at Lorraine's again?"

"No. We're leaving after dinner. The doctor said when she woke up she could go home. I'll stay with her until I'm sure she's OK. She refuses to let me hire someone to guard her. This has been a rough two days. She's still upset over Inspector Jarston's questioning me yesterday about my handgun practice at the shooting range a couple weeks back."

"I imagine she would be."

"I had to do a lot of talking to convince him that I was simply learning self-defense. Inspector Jarston talked to the manager of the range and found out, among other things, I'm a lousy shot. Can you believe Mom worries that I shot Dad? Not that he didn't deserve it." Crystal snickered.

"Jarston would have completed a ballistics check."

She shook her head. "I didn't even buy the gun I tested because I couldn't handle the recoil."

I knew Al's own gun had been used to kill

him but said nothing further. Crystal mentioned the incident in such an offhand manner I found myself inclined to believe her. I turned to go.

"One more thing. I called my ex-husband after I heard about Mom." Crystal coughed and then paused.

"And?"

"He was upset about what happened. Mom and John had been sorta close. He came right over. We did some talking . . ." Her words trailed off.

"Yes . . . ?"

"I shared some of the things you and I have been discussing."

She sounded fluttery.

"How did he react?"

"Very sympathetic, more than I can ever remember. I know this sounds weird, but he seems genuinely concerned. He wants to come with me for my next counseling appointment. Is that all right?"

I stared at her for a moment. "Sure, if it's OK with you." She'd spoken to me like a friend. Had I finally broken through her callous armor. Was she opening the door to her ex-husband and me, too?

God, You never fail to amaze me.

Tinkling bells of reconciliation. That would be a miracle. I cautioned myself not to anticipate.

My favorite Scripture came to mind. "All things work together for good for those who love the Lord and are called according to His purpose." Maybe a forced entry and a dead dog could serve a good purpose.

44

I slithered home through the tail end of extreme rush-hour traffic made worse by construction delays. Finally pulling into our drive, I plunked my automatic garage door open. My heartbeat quickened at the sight of Nick's car. It always does. I located him in the kitchen, his head in the fridge.

"Hey you look like you're hunting for hidden gold. It's not in there."

Nick pulled out a coke, turned, and gave me a hug. "What's for dinner?"

"A surprise I ordered on my way. I'm amazed you got home before me. You're not a mirage?"

"I keep telling you the age of miracles is not past." Nick grinned mischievously, his boyish look, which I still find irresistible.

I laughed. "What a lovable guy."

"Correction, your guy."

Fifteen minutes later Pino's Pizza delivery truck pulled up. I answered the doorbell and returned with a large flat box emitting pungent smells of oregano and basil blended with savory tomatoes.

"Let's eat, I'm starving."

"As usual." I poked his stomach teasingly. "How can sitting most of the day create such appetite in you?"

"I've no idea. What kind did you get?"

"Loaded veggie and a side tray of relishes."

"Great. I'll wash up."

I set blue place mats on the dining room table and pulled two china dinner plates and crystal water goblets from the breakfront. Dinner might arrive in a box, but I could still serve it elegantly. I grabbed forks, knives, and cloth napkins.

Nick returned and took a seat. "How was your day?"

"Fine, now." He looked into my eyes, and I felt the upheaval of the day slip away.

Nick blessed the food and prayed for us, the children, and our family and friends. Since becoming the "real thing" Christians, we eat only holy, prayed-over food. I can't say the taste has changed, but the atmosphere is definitely better.

I battled a gooey strip of mozzarella stubbornly resisting capture and thought about, but didn't mention, Rose's incident. Too much stress there for my digestion.

After we ate, I suggested a walk. We hurried into jackets to catch the last trickles of light before darkness enveloped the woods.

In our subdivision, hike is a more accurate word than walk. The hilly, narrow roads provide great exercise. I moved, race-style, with Nick slightly ahead. After we made the turn to come back, I shared the latest Windemere news about Rose's near shooting.

Nick sucked in his breath, clearly shocked. "One of Windemere's unhappy business cronies?"

I shrugged. "Using my wildest imagination, I'd guess Crystal may have pulled this as a clever diversion. I can't figure her out. She'd have to be a good actress."

"You said Rose was once. Maybe it runs in the genes. You can't discount her as a murder suspect, sad as the thought is."

"The possibility seems less likely since Crystal answered Inspector Jarston's questions satisfactorily when he brought her in." I waved at a neighbor passing by in his car.

"Crystal told you that, correct? Jarston didn't."

"True, but he let her go. It's confusing. Her concern for her mom seems definitely real." I quickened my pace, which had slowed as I talked.

"Possibly she's merely playing dutiful

daughter. If Crystal killed her dad, maybe she intended to kill Rose last night too, but got cold feet when she saw the dog." Nick took my elbow guiding me around a large stone on the road. "This could be simply about greed, a very dangerous emotion."

"Their relationship is strange and so was this incident. In a ski mask and loose black clothing, Rose couldn't be certain the intruder was male or female."

"The flip side of love is hate. Maybe that's what Crystal really feels for her mother."

I shrugged beneath my light jacket. "Her ex-husband John's coming with Crystal to her appointment tomorrow, to work on their relationship."

"John needs to learn a woman who pushes him away may really want him closer." Nick ran in place and pumped his arms vigorously.

"One psychotherapist per family!" I shot him a fake indignant look.

"Then again maybe her ex is coming with her to shake off suspicion he's Al's killer."

"I hope not, I'd like to try to help them rebuild their relationship."

"What's your take about the attack on Rose and Lorraine's shepherd?"

"The poor family's been through so much. Why would anyone want to kill Lorraine or

Rose or the dog? And why in Lorraine and Aaron's house?"

"Rose may know something that has the killer scared."

Nick slowed. "Might Rose have staged this to throw suspicion off her if she arranged for her husband's murder?"

"Highly improbable." I matched his speed. "Why?"

"I can't believe Rose had anything to do with Al's death."

"Then who's your prime suspect?"

I whacked a mosquito on my arm. "I still don't trust Halston, and I'm not sure about John Vandley. He admitted to having financial problems this past year."

"Then John had a motive for murder and for getting back with Crystal if she's coming in to a lot of money." Nick started to pick up his pace again.

"He seems to genuinely care for her but I can't discount John's desire for revenge over the lousy way his wife was treated by her father. Still hardly the time to kill when Al had begun to treat Crystal decently."

"Logical though," Nick said, slightly breathless, "if you hate this family and want to destroy it."

"I'll race you to the row of mailboxes."

"You're on."

Nick won as usual. I only compete because it makes me run faster. Back at the house, we collapsed on deck chairs. The whishing sounds of nightfall entering the forest soothed me, as always. In the far distance, a pencil-thin line of cobalt blue revealed Lake Geneva.

I sighed. "Nick, counseling is great, but as I help others, I'm in the crucible with them. Seeing their ragged edges makes me see a few of my own."

"Like?"

"Crystal reminds of my own difficult childhood."

"Your parents were alcoholics, not workaholics."

"Same consequences, a child knows it isn't valued. A client like Crystal forces me to ponder painful issues within myself. And Rose and Crystal remind me of Tara and me. Our relationship has been strained lately. When she returns I want to affirm her more. I love her so much. I hope I tell her enough."

"She's growing up fast. Soon, they'll all be married and have children of their own. The years to teach our values are running out." Nick switched on the outside light then sat back down. "It's lovely being here with you at this time of year. I wish I didn't have to go out of town for a deposition."

After several minutes, his head bobbed. I admire how quickly Nick can fall asleep. I called his name softly. He awoke with a start. "I'm going inside to shower, Hon."

I hoped Al's murderer was experiencing remorse that interfered with sound sleep.

45

The steady spray of warm water refreshed my body. I lingered in the shower as my brain went to autopilot thinking about Al Windemere. I reviewed again what I knew about his death. No evidence he'd been dragged into the woods. The murderer had gotten Al there of his own accord. He had to have known him. Or her?

At a counseling convention two years ago, I heard a lecture on the psychological research used by the behavioral science unit at the FBI Academy to catch criminals. I'd listened intently because the subject was a novelty, not because I expected to use the info. Now I wish I'd taken better notes.

I lathered shampoo into my hair, barely aware of what my hands were doing.

Analyzing the crime bit by bit, could I piece together a personality? The key was getting into the head of the killer. If only a person with the capability to kill would look like a killer. I thought of Wayne Williams, the serial killer of over twenty children, including two young men who were larger than he was. Williams was reportedly short and had soft hands. Investigators said victims were put off by his friendly, mild-mannered personality.

I conditioned and rinsed my hair still deep in thought. Al's murderer had to be arrogant and organized, obviously with a careful plan. Someone meticulous about details? This could be Halston. But was he brazen?

Actually, Halston seemed a bit of a coward. Otherwise, he would have struck out on his own long ago and not put up with Al Windemere's business shenanigans for years. And I doubt he'd have interrupted his appointment to speak with me when I barged into his place of business.

Bold? Al Windemere was shot straight on, no chance of missing. I wrapped myself in a large terry towel and put a smaller one around my hair.

What kind of person could arrange a carefully crafted early morning murder? Crystal had said during our counseling session that she never rose until eight and needed three cups of coffee to get moving. Most killers come from a dysfunctional family. She qualified there. Crime stats are higher for those who went through a family breakup. But could Crystal face her father and pull a trigger? I wasn't sure. I hoped not. I dusted my body with talc and slipped into floral pajamas.

Was Aaron capable of killing? He had a damaged ego, but could I picture him hating Al that much?

What about Rich, Aaron's business partner? Practically family, his allegiance to his employer could have made him resent Al's behavior toward Aaron. Was that a strong enough motive to kill? If so how would he benefit? I needed to check that aspect.

What of Ken, Al and Rose's son. I had to assume he was dead, or he'd have come forward for his share of the inheritance when he read about his dad's death online or saw the news in the paper.

Rose had opportunities daily to shoot Al in their home without resorting to an out-of-the-way setting. Her past hurts diminished with every passing month since Al had committed his life to Christ and started to treat her well. I had to rule her out.

Any sense of relaxation from my walk and shower was long gone.

I heard Nick in the living room. Apparently, he'd gotten a second wind and was watching the late show. I shut our bedroom door and pictured myself shoving the Windemere entourage into a mental closet. I wouldn't think about this anymore — tonight.

I dropped to the floor, did a dozen push-ups and tummy crunches, then got into bed to read, my mind still wired like blinking party lights. I picked up a copy of an investment magazine, usually a sure-fire sleep inducer. Not tonight.

Nick came in. I lay motionless, face down on the peach floral sheets. He kissed my neck and then rubbed my shoulder with tender pressure. I lost awareness of everything.

Tomorrow, I'd find the killer. Tonight I'd simply be a woman.

46

The details of life couldn't be put on hold simply because my job was in crazy busy mode. I left the house at 8:00 AM to drop off my van for an overdue tune-up, driving beneath gray spongy masses — gunmetal clouds. They formed horizontal streaks that seemed to meet the earth. On most days looking heavenward, even for a few moments, enchanted me; today, the sky had the sensory appeal of cement.

It didn't help that I'd had to shorten my morning devotions to ten minutes instead of my usual thirty and had no time to read Scripture.

En route, I prayed for Nick and the children and asked God to guide my day. Without my quiet time, I can get frazzled dealing with clients and their issues. *Outreach after enrichment,* I remind myself often.

On the walk from the parking lot to my

office, a black cat pounced from behind a shrub and shot across my path.

To say I wasn't looking forward to John and Crystal's joint session would be a gross understatement. Some sessions, even a counselor dreads. My pet peeve is clients who want a mental health practitioner to gift them with the golden key to problem-free living without any work on their part. I like diligent clients with problems I can help them tuck into place. If Crystal and John had learned communication skills earlier, their divorce might have been avoidable. Could I teach them now? For the sake of their kids, I hoped they were truly willing to try, provided one of them wasn't Al's murderer. At the moment, that was a big "if."

I was sipping cinnamon herbal tea at my desk and finishing client prep as Crystal and John walked in together around nine.

John moved gingerly into my office.

"Hello, Dr. Trevor." Crystal strode in like a queen. She tossed her sweater and purse on a side chair and made a snide comment about John's being late to pick her up. They'd arrived in the same car, which I considered positive along with the fact that he ignored her dig.

Crystal settled into a soft, upholstered chair while John bent his tall frame into a stiffer-backed one, perhaps suited to his comfort level — *discomfort,* a better descriptor. Typically, my role with couples like the Vandleys is helping them learn new strategies for relating after divorce. Child custody arrangements often present the first conflict issue a couple absolutely must resolve to mutual agreement.

I smiled a welcome, silently praying, *Holy Spirit, You're on. Help.* "I'm glad you both were willing to come."

"Her invitation sure surprised me," John spoke first. "Most of the time she acts like she hates me, and I've no idea why."

"We never emotionally connected," Crystal explained.

A pang of sorrow shot through me. How sad a man and woman, who love each other enough to want to join their lives together, and whose combined genes produce delightful children, can come to intently dislike each other.

"Emotional intimacy is important as sexual intimacy in marriage. Both alleviate the strains of everyday life."

"We had neither," she retorted. "But we're here today for our children."

"Good. Let's discuss what you'd both like to accomplish during our session."

"I suppose it seems strange, we never had

marriage counseling," John added. "Now we're here for divorce counseling to see if we can get along better for our kids."

Crystal nodded. "We have unresolved issues. Things would be better if John would stop blaming me for everything that went wrong between us. He doesn't hide his feelings from the kids, which upsets them. Besides our divorce was primarily his fault . . ."

"That's the past," I interrupted. "Let's focus on today and the future. It's absurd to think once two people hold divorce papers in their hands, conflict and tension ends forever. Nevertheless, you can form a working relationship where the children are concerned, and I can help you."

"Actually, Crystal needs to quit backbiting about me. It bothers the children."

"The children mustn't become pawns for your anger or sources of disagreement. Let's address the issues blocking communication between you."

They each rattled off a list. Good so far.

"We'll return to this. Now think back to when you first met. John, please look directly at Crystal and tell her what attracted you back then."

John reflected a moment, shifted in his chair, then turned to face his ex-wife. "You were, still are, gorgeous. You seemed to appreciate me — my presence, my attention. When we were together, I felt good. I thought you did, too."

"Crystal?" I raised my eyebrows at her. "Same question."

She didn't look at John but complied. "He was charming, good-looking."

The expression of shock on his face made me think compliments had been rare. John sneaked a covert look at Crystal.

"Was?" I questioned.

A faint blush washed over her. "Is. I like his gentleness along with his toughness." She pulled the words out begrudgingly but seemed to warm a bit in the telling. "John had qualities my father didn't have. Maybe it wasn't right to compare him to my father, but I did," she added, looking confused. "Then, again, maybe I was wrong to think John ever could be the husband I needed."

"Or was he sensitive, and did you destroy your relationship by expecting too much, or perhaps simply too quickly?" I asked the question in a matter-of-fact tone. "And John did you give up on your marriage too easily because of your pride? I'm not judging, just something to think about. I'm on both your sides and on the side of marriage. Tell me what topics created tension?"

"From the beginning," John jumped in, "we argued constantly. She always has to be right. I've seen the damage quarrelsome parents can do to their own children. I wanted none of that tension for my kids."

"Argued about what specifically?" I asked.

"Everything!" John's voice seethed with built up layers like lava. "You complained about my work being menial. You didn't want to go where I did. You name it; any subject became a battle."

I braced myself. "As you discuss the problems between you, please direct your words to one another using 'I messages.' Tell how you felt about what the other person said or did."

John looked at me puzzled. "I thought I just did."

"No. When you use a 'you', it's like pointing a finger in someone's face and saying what *you* did wrong. In an 'I' message, you express your feelings about a situation. For example: 'I felt devalued because I didn't have a fancy job.' "

John turned to Crystal. "I know I yelled too much. I got fed up with your criticism. I felt like I could never do anything well enough." John's words held longing and pain. He averted his gaze from Crystal. "Whatever your dad did to you, I paid the price over and over again. He was far from perfect, but I felt you expected me to be."

"Ridiculous," Crystal snapped. "You . . ."

"Thank you, John," I intervened. "Good job. The way we speak, the tone, is as important as the words we use. You expressed your hurts healthily."

Crystal unclenched her teeth. "My turn?"

"I'm not done." John swerved toward me. "Mostly I felt ignored. She'd go from one extreme to the other. I couldn't get her to stay home. Running here and there, that's all she wanted. Then after she started drinking heavily, I couldn't get her out of bed to go anywhere."

Crystal shot John a disdainful look. "I refuse to listen to his harangue!"

"It's true! You didn't even want to see our old friends." John reminded me of the "Little Engine Who Could" all warmed up. He'd probably never had a chance to say this much before without being verbally shredded.

Crystal crossed her arms and scrunched down in her chair, as if staying and retreating simultaneously.

"Now the kids tell me she's having a ball, out every night with guys again! What a switch!"

"Crystal, perhaps you were also dealing

with depression. Did you get help?"

John answered, "No, not then anyway."

"Please don't talk for Crystal." I pulled my chair closer to her, an intuitive move to strengthen our relationship and disarm her resistance. "John got his issues out. I'd like you to tell me yours."

"It's true I used to self-medicate with alcohol and uppers." She sent a pathetic look at John. "A long time ago. That's why I behaved like I did." Her shadowed lashes blinked rapidly.

"Thanks for being honest. I doubt the two of you ever actually heard each other's feelings before." I paused and waited. The silence in the room was thick.

Crystal bit her lip. Finally, she agreed. "John was right, there would always be another man, another search to fill the hole in my heart."

"I'm so sorry. It's not uncommon for women who didn't experience a father's love to behave like you have."

"I knew you weren't happy with your life, Crystal." John lowered his voice, and he gazed at her with undisguised tenderness. "I know you better than you think."

"Crystal, what did you hear John saying here?"

She pursed her lips and John took a deep breath.

I waited. Clients often struggle with emotion, but it can be powerful. The more self-centered the person, the more difficult it is to get into their spouse's feelings.

"John said he felt he couldn't measure up to my expectations."

"Was he right?"

Crystal stared past me at the opposite wall and twisted a strand of hair around her finger before answering. "I suppose so."

John sat quietly in his chair. His eyes looked like they might spill over any second.

"Crystal, you must have been experiencing a lot of emotional pain to divorce John. You say you expressed your needs to John. He says he tried to meet them, but you were never satisfied. You needed his comfort and support. John may have failed in your eyes, but he did try. Is that right?"

She concurred.

"Crystal, might you have dumped some of the anger you felt toward your dad onto John? Perhaps any small inadequacy on John's part seemed even larger in your eyes? Will you admit that's a possibility?"

"I suppose so," she said quietly.

"It sounds like you had three people in your marriage."

I turned toward John. "For your part, you resented Crystal's father. You recently threatened your former father-in-law in a restaurant. Did Crystal's unfair comparison of you with her dad create extreme anger, maybe even violent feelings toward him?"

John visibly stiffened. "I've already admitted that I resented Al, but an incident in the restaurant was the only time I confronted him. I swear."

"Have you ever been violent with Crystal or the children?"

John's face reddened. "What kind of jerk do you take me for? I didn't hurt her dad either. I may have said some things I shouldn't have, but I never laid a hand on him."

"I understand Harold Halston witnessed the incident of aggression," I said calmly.

John's neck turned red. His denial of intense anger seemed sincere. He had me wondering if Halston had exaggerated the scene. "Back to the two of you. We can agree each of you experienced pain in your relationship?"

John nodded first and then Crystal.

I took them through conflict resolution skills for the remaining time. They both seemed to become more co-operative by the end of the session.

Once they left, I wrote up my notes immediately while my perceptions were fresh.

John and Crystal are balanced in temperament and lifestyle but too blinded by the wounds they've experienced to see this.

Productive interaction, good expression of emotions, progress tentative. Memories of Crystal and John's once loving relationship were revived today. Perhaps a window to a better future.

I said a prayer for them and shut their file. I've helped clients on the brink of divorce and ones already divorced go on to have a great marriage, which is my greatest joy in counseling. In Crystal's case, a restoration would be a miracle, but I'm not God. I spoke aloud in my office, "I did my best, Lord. My job for Al's estate was to help Crystal get rid of her bitterness toward her dad, but maybe I can help dissolve her anger toward her husband, as well.

Then again might John be her dad's killer?

47

Rose Windemere called my office at 9:00 AM. Because of the intruder incident, she needed a sympathetic ear to help her work through her continuing fears. I fit her in at noon.

She arrived in yellow golf shorts and a matching polo shirt. I listened patiently to Rose verbally relive the incident in detail. "I want to convince myself the event was a foiled break-in, not connected to Al's murder. Otherwise, it's far too frightening. I don't want to live in a state of constant panic."

"I understand. Of course not." I wasn't about to brew distress with my opinion. I discussed the importance of caution and perhaps hiring security for a time. I reassured her that every effort was being made to identify Al's killer as quickly as possible.

Rose brought up the relationship with Crystal. "She's still very angry at her dad, at John, and at life in general. There's nothing I can do but love her."

We explored ways to help her heal, and after our session, I escorted Rose to the door as Ann Tylore barged unexpectedly into my outer office.

The long ends of her black tunic flapped behind her, giving the effect of a vulture in flight. Mistress meets grieving wife — disastrous, soap opera material.

Rose's small eyes opened wide as eggs. The two women stood face-to-face barely three feet apart. Ellen, standing behind, shrugged helplessly.

Rose buried visual swords into Ann then directed her anger at me. "Ann Tylore! What is this woman doing here? Jennifer, how can you be working with her and me? I thought I could trust your loyalty."

I grabbed the corner of Ellen's desk to steady myself. The idea of retreating to my office was tempting but out of the question. I longed to explain, but what could I say? I didn't have an appointment with Ann Tylore, but I'd gone to see her to investigate Al's death.

Rose didn't give me a chance to speak. She stalked hotly past both of us and stomped out the door.

Ann seemed taken aback momentarily. As

soon as Rose left, she regained her composure. "Obviously I wasn't expecting to see
Rose Windemere today. I imagine you're
surprised I've come, but then I didn't
anticipate your personal visit the day you
showed up at my office either. I need ten
minutes of your time, and it appears you're
free."

Ann strode past me into my inner office. I
followed wordlessly with a backward glance
at Ellen, who watched the entire exchange
with her mouth hanging open.

"I have time," I tried to sound gracious,
though I felt anything but. "Please sit."

"No thanks." It took Ann less than two
seconds to launch her verbal tirade. "I heard
about what you're doing! It's disgraceful,
shameful."

My brain reeled. "What do you mean?"

"Debold has been broadcasting his unexpected windfall to every investment group
in this community. Al Windemere and
American Realty are up for sainthood to
hear him tell it. He's as vocal as when he
spread sour grapes about Al months back."

"I don't get it. Why are you upset about
Al's restitution process?"

"You should have made Debold swear to
keep his mouth shut!" Her natural beauty
was masked under an expression that could

only be labeled as vicious.

"Secrecy," I said simply, "would have been contrary to Al's purpose."

"His purpose? What about me?"

Wrong comment.

"Well, this action is not acceptable." Her mouth exploded again like a firebox. She gasped to get breath. "These huge payouts are hurting me and every other broker in our profession. Clients will expect to have all investment capital protected against losses. The rest of us can't make guarantees like this. We'll go broke!" She spit out her words with scathing condescension.

"Wait a minute here. This wasn't an ordinary investment. Al acted unethically and knew he should have stopped the deal. He intentionally passed his losses to other major investors. That's plain wrong. He felt a responsibility to reimburse these clients. Certainly, your customers can understand."

"The only thing that matters to them is how their financials read in the end."

"The motive is also important."

Ann took a deep breath and slid onto a chair. "I've told Halston exactly how I feel. I just came from his office."

"And?"

"He can't keep up with the new clients flocking to invest with American because they're so impressed with the integrity of his company. Wait 'til these clients start wanting their losses covered," she added.

"It's clear you see this as simply a competition issue."

"You bet! I wonder if Halston killed Albert Windemere because he anticipated this could happen."

"I'm sincerely sorry this has caused you so much distress." I attempted to soothe her. Evidently her fondness for Al ended when her pocketbook got hit.

She slammed her fist on my desk. "I need to know. Are you finished with these reimbursements now? Or can I expect more jolts to my business courtesy of Albert Windemere's final wishes?"

She stood and thrust her shoulders back. "I'm having my lawyer investigate this as well as your authority to be involved in our profession."

My face flushed with anger. Before I could respond, Ann made a flourishing exit, slamming the door behind her.

She hadn't bothered to ask about my progress in the investigation into Al's murder. Was anything uglier than rejected love, except maybe greed? Or revenge, the kind that could lead to murder.

48

At 7:00 PM, I let myself into an empty house. Nick was at his two-day deposition in Atlanta.

Kicking off my shoes at the front door, I padded to our bedroom and tugged on fuzzy white socks. I changed into a still-new, large yellow sweatshirt I'd purchased at the Dells. I ripped off the price tag still dangling from the sleeve, pulled on jeans, and dragged myself into the brightest room in the house — the kitchen. I needed all the light I could scrounge up.

A day of my life had passed never to be again. Had I accomplished anything? I'd listened to hours of anger and hurts and, hopefully, planted a few seeds of healing, which might or might not produce healthy emotional growth in a few lives.

All the time, a part of my mind dwelt on a dead client who had become my friend. Helping his family was emotionally hard when distress over his death still plagued me.

The silence around me seemed weird. I'm rarely home alone in the evening. Usually when Nick was out of town, the kids were around. Our house is too quiet without them. How many times had I told my darlings, "Walk, don't run in the house." Now I longed for their noisy scurrying through the rooms.

I plunked down on a kitchen chair, opened my briefcase, and spread my Windemere notes over the polished wood table.

A subtle, but pervasive uneasiness hung over me. I'd been doing too much, too fast. without enough extended times for prayer and reflection. Had I exposed my family to potential harm trying to be a light and help to others?

I knew what Nick would say. Lighten up, slow down, and take it easy. I'd become too intense about my work. Determination helps me succeed, along with my faith, which keeps my priorities in perspective usually. Tonight, I felt only out of kilter and exhausted.

Half past seven, I wanted to crawl between the sheets at a toddler's bedtime. If I went to bed now, I'd be up at 3:00 AM. I had to last until ten.

Actually, an entire day in bed sounded blissful. I never do that unless I'm physically ill. God forbid. The green and white striped wallpaper with its clumps of pears, grapes, and cherries strung out every few inches reminded me I hadn't eaten. No wonder my blood sugar level was hitting the basement.

I dragged myself to the fridge and pulled a bag of popcorn kernels from the freezer where I store them to keep eenie-meenie critters out. At the rate my family eats popcorn, nothing nests long.

I poured oil into the popper, heated it, added corn, and listened to the familiar crackle and hiss of the pot. My mouth watered as the *clomp, clump* of the kernels hit the lid. While it popped, I washed off an apple and sliced half a banana.

I salted the popcorn and munched as I carried the bowl to the table. I'd never get this dinner past Nick, but it worked for me.

I flipped through the notes I'd spread on the table. Was what I needed to know about Al's murder right under my eyes? Don't look at things of "B" level importance — not wise for a woman who taught priority management.

Frustration charged through me. I had to admit Al probably deserved his enemies;

he'd cultivated them well. But who was capable of murder?

I grabbed my legal pad and started writing unrequited love, a brother's hate, a close friend's protective anger, a daughter's rejection, a son-in-law's resentment, Halston's greed? Which motive led to murder? Two pages of notes flew from my hand, all neatly written, but what was most significant? Was I still missing the one detail making sense of everything?

I looked at motivational forces again: love, lust, power, prestige, making or protecting money, making a good reputation or keeping one. These were the drama that could motivate eradicating another human life. For whom was the existence of Al Windemere unbearable?

The phone stabbed my unformed, random thoughts and brought me to the present.

"Jennifer?"

I recognized Rich Nichols' voice.

"Hi. What's up?"

"Decision time. The family made their furniture selections. Now you get to choose. I have pictures of the Eastlake pieces and wood samples if you want anything refinished. Some items definitely need it. I'd like to drop by with the pictures and descriptions. I'm eager to get this settled."

"Can't the pictures be e-mailed?"

"Sure but not the wood pieces."

"OK. If you can make it in the next hour; I'm turning in early." I gave him my address.

"I'll be right over."

I circled Rich's name on my list. He flitted about, always nearby. He and Aaron appeared quite different, although they apparently worked well together.

I made doodles with my lead pencil as though robotic while my mind hovered elsewhere. After a few minutes I looked down at a picture of a man with a smiley face. I crossed it out and penciled an ugly frown in its place.

Thirty minutes after Rich's call, the doorbell rang

"You made good time," I said to defuse the tension on Rich's sweat-covered face. He was gripping a manila envelope tightly in his right hand and walked past me into the living room. "Terrible traffic, and a car almost ran into me," he mumbled. "I admit I'm not the world's fastest driver, but this guy was hanging on my bumper."

"I'm sorry for your trouble." I immediately rejected the paranoid thought that someone followed him to my place.

Rich held up his hand. "Not your fault. I'm not used to stress. Aaron and I work with non-speaking objects like flowers and furniture. No complexity, little travel involved, and they don't hassle you."

I chuckled. Despite his overall slimness, his fingers were stumpy like carrots left in the ground too long.

"I understand you and Aaron are also involved in real estate investments? That must be a stressor at times."

"Our condos? Fortunately, they pretty much manage themselves. We keep everything simple."

"Nice."

Rich handed me the envelope. "Here's the antique list and pictures. I included some stain samples for the furniture pieces needing it. Everything is labeled. These shots don't do the furniture justice but you'll get the idea. The size specs are listed, which should help with your choices."

"Thanks. I've never received a gift of antique furniture before, but then my entire involvement with Al Windemere's family and associates has been unusual." I waited to see if he'd comment on the family, but Rich was all business.

"I'd appreciate it if you'd make your selections and e-mail me your choices as soon as possible. I'll have the actual pieces out at the storage warehouse for your final approval." As he spoke, Rich's gaze glanced around the house. He whistled. "Very nice. Who's your decorator?"

"Me."

"Impressive." I showed him around the living are, before heading him toward the front door.

I stood on the porch and watched Rich drape his long legs into a black sports car. *Another piece of the preppy image, Rich?*

He hadn't been gone more than ten minutes when the phone rang.

I went into the kitchen and checked the caller ID. I didn't recognize the number. I picked up anyway, still nervous since the car incident.

The voice was muffled, but cold and hard. "You don't listen well. This is the last time I'm going to tell you. End your involvement with the Windemere affair."

Click.

I froze. The same fuzzy sounding voice as before! "Cowards call or send notes," I said aloud, "and think they're brave. It's the ones who show up with a gun I have to watch out for." I considered calling Nick, but I didn't want to worry him. What could he do?

I prayed for the Lord's protection and told myself to stop thinking about the call. My brain disobeyed.

By the time I'd cleaned the kitchen, it was bedtime. I undressed quickly and locked the bedroom door.

Being used to a bed buddy, I find it hard to fall asleep alone.

The furnace *whooshed* on. How many hundreds of times had I not even noticed the familiar noise?

I couldn't shake my heebie-jeebies. Burying myself under my comforter, I finally drifted off.

49

What charm did morning hold to make even the previous night's scare seem a distant memory?

I zipped my minivan into the reserved parking space kept safe for me by my landlord. A sign threatened a towing violation for any other car. Without this protected spot, I'd have to park blocks away. The huge tourist epidemic had subsided, but enough visitors still crawled the streets of Lake Geneva to gobble up the sidewalks, parking spaces and end-of-season buys.

I moved through my entire day efficiently, feeling like a mistress of the universe. A day of routine gives me the illusion of a tranquil life.

Nick returned from Atlanta around 7:00 PM. I was on the phone, finishing a chat with my friend, Pat, when I heard the garage door open.

Nick strode into the house and headed in

the direction of my voice. My nose caught the scent of my favorite men's cologne. Nick's thick hair had been rearranged by a gust of wind. His arms shot around me as our lips connected.

He pulled back and looked at me. "Missed you."

I buried my face on his neck for a second. "Me, too, hon."

"How about a real welcome home on a blanket in front of the fireplace?"

"Your every wish is my desire," I whispered.

"Could I have that in writing?"

"That's lawyer talk. Now remind me; why did I marry one?"

Much later, Nick suggested we have dinner at Ye Old Hotel in Lyons. "We're supposed to be living like two honeymooners until the kids return next week. C'mon, good food and no cleanup."

"You persuaded me."

Outside, the night air held a late summer chill. I pulled my velour jacket closer.

On the way, I told Nick about the phone call. "I'm through with my complicated counseling after this week and promise to never get into this position again."

"Great and how exactly are you going to

get through it now?"

His tone made me bristle. "I'm done talking about this."

"I'm not. Did you have any trouble other than the phone call?"

"No, I would have told you."

"Sure. Like with the note?" Nick rubbed in his annoyance.

I put a pained expression on my face as we walked into the nearly empty restaurant. "I promised you I wouldn't hold anything back again, remember?"

"OK. Let's forget about it for now and enjoy tonight. Soon our munchkins return."

"You miss them as much as I do," I teased.

We ordered steak and mashed potatoes. Every now and then, I love a piece of beef. During dinner we probed for safe issues to discuss.

Nick filled me in about his trip.

"I received pictures of the antiques Rich is disbursing for Al. I'm selecting a beautiful Eastlake bedroom set."

"Nice that he knew you shared his fondness for antiques."

I smiled. "He admired the eighteenth-century bureau in my office and kept eyeing my desk chair."

We drove home in the comfortable silence married people enjoy when together, needing nothing more.

Before undressing, I went into my study to check my answering machine. The red light blinked repeatedly. When I clicked play, Lorraine's voice came on in a whispered tone.

"Jennifer, Aaron didn't show up at work today or come home for dinner. It's never like him not to call. This is so strange. Please contact me when you return, no matter how late because . . ."

The recorder cut her last words off.

I glanced at the wall clock, ten to ten, and punched in her number.

Lorraine answered after one ring. "I worried he'd been killed like Al." Hearing this sweet, bewildered lady's fear and frustration, compassion flooded through me.

"I didn't know who to call," she continued breathlessly. "No way do I want to involve the police. He came home fifteen minutes ago and won't say where he's been. He's upstairs now. Said he's going to see you tomorrow. Please try to find out what's happened and let me know?"

"I can't promise anything."

"I know but try."

I hung up and sank back against my upholstered chair shaking my head.

Nick entered the study. "Here you are.

What's up?"

"Aaron was missing all day. Nobody at work knew where he was. He's never acted irresponsibly before. Lorraine feared he might have been killed. He's back but won't talk about it."

"A drinking binge?" Nick pulled a chair up next to me, leaned back and lifted his arms behind him to form a triangle over his head.

"Maybe, although he claimed he doesn't drink on his intake form. Lorraine says it's totally unlike him to be out of touch. She's stretched tighter than a rubber band."

"Maybe you got Aaron thinking after your last counseling session, and he needed time alone to sort things out."

"Right. I fear thinking so much that he spent the day holed up contemplating an affair or divorce." I rubbed my forehead with my palms before looking up. "I hope he's not fooling around on her."

"The unknown's worse than the truth. She possibly also fears her husband is Al's murderer and that's why he ran off. Maybe he changed his mind and came back because running could be interpreted as an admission of guilt if he is the killer."

"She's a loyal wife who would try to protect him whatever. Hopefully, I can discover what's going on at our appointment tomorrow if he shows up."

"Aaron could be dangerous. Make sure you keep Ellen within earshot during counseling."

"I will. Don't worry. Relationships can be battlefields with more emotional casualties than all the wars."

"And the pain inflicted may be greater. I'm sorry our evening ended like this." Nick's took my hands and his tender look conveyed concern.

"One more appointment with Aaron, and I'm through. I see Paul Jacobsen tomorrow to give my final report. The family sessions have gone well overall although failing to solve Al's murder frustrates me."

Nick patted my shoulder. "Don't be hard on yourself. You weren't trained for detective work."

I felt my face flush. "You sound like Inspector Jarston. Don't rub it in. I so wanted to discover who killed Al. You know I hate not accomplishing what I set out to do."

"Better for your safety." I knew Nick was trying to console me. "While counseling Al's family, you could uncover information making you a target. I pray Psalm 91 — God's wisdom and protection for you daily." His eyes glistened. "I don't want to lose you."

I squeezed his hand, stood, and stretched my arms overhead. "It's good I'm about to close these Windemere files. I won't endanger any of us further." I wiggled my feet into mules and plodded into our bedroom.

Twenty minutes later, I climbed into our queen size four-poster and slipped under the cloud of quilts. I picked up the mystery on my nightstand to distract myself. Poor choice! I fell asleep with the Windemere clues swirling through my mind. I couldn't grab hold of one to examine it in depth, but I kept trying.

50

At 7:00 AM, I felt as if I'd slept five hours. Clad in my robe, I ducked my head out our sliding glass bedroom doors to breathe in the fresh morning air. The chill mocked the lush grass still smelling deceptively summerish. A parade of yellow leaves fluttered across our deck in need of another coat of stain. "Thank You, Lord, for finances to own and maintain this house. I take nothing for granted. Let Your praise be always on my lips."

I made my way into the kitchen and poured oatmeal, milk, and a handful of raisins in a bowl to microwave. During the two-minute wait, I did leg lifts using the kitchen counter for support. I dislike wasting time, minutes become lost hours. Reading *Cheaper by the Dozen* as a child helped me latch onto the importance of effective time management. I know Jesus loved both Martha and Mary, the doer and the sitter. I set my cereal on the coffee table to cool and pushed play on my favorite devotional music.

I praised God because this ordeal was almost over. Anyone could request continued future counseling with me, but this wasn't prerequisite to my signature on their discharge forms. I finished breakfast and dressed quickly. Before starting the car, I checked my messages. Ellen needed to take the morning off for an emergency dental appointment. So much for being there during Aaron's session.

The Jacobsen, Shearson & Reingold legal offices were located in a renovated 1920's historic home joined to houses on either side through covered porticos with courtyards.

A scripted brass plate on the center building announced the lawyers' names. I skimmed the list until I found Jacobsen's in the second building.

I gave a hefty push to the outer door of glove-smooth mahogany with an intricate wood grain that resembled a map of lake depths. Coppery red tiles separated by natural-colored grout covered the reception area dominated by a dark walnut desk and chair and four round-backed leather chairs. Two-story cathedral-type windows flooded the area with sunlight. The receptionist finished assisting an elderly gray-haired gentleman leaning on a cane then turned to me with a warm greeting.

"Mr. Jacobsen is expecting you, Dr. Trevor." Her twenty-something voice matched her perky smile as she directed me to his office halfway down the hall on the right.

Paul immediately rose and extended his hand.

"Jennifer, sit down, please. I've heard good reports from the family. They claim to have benefited from your time with them.

"I hope so."

"Crystal claims she was especially helped."

I chuckled. "I can guess what she said, 'Dr. Trevor's great, a regular miracle-worker. I've met the counseling requirement. Give me my inheritance.' "

"How did you know?" His eyes twinkled. "Anyway, I'm sure you were a blessing. Thanks for all you've done on behalf of Al."

At the mention of his name I lowered my eyelids as a flash of sadness surged through me. *Tend to business Jennifer, you're a professional.* "I do believe things are better, generally speaking. Anyway, we're reaching closure."

Paul pulled a legal pad over.

"I'll be sending you copies of each signed discharge form. I have one appointment left. Aaron's third session is today. He also has issues not directly related to Al needing follow up. If he wants to see me in the future, we can continue, or I'll make a referral. It's his call, but I hope he pursues more help."

"Either way, he'll have completed the minimum required." Paul's felt-tip pen skimmed his pad.

"Crystal is past extreme bitterness, but her residual hurts will take time to heal. She and her ex-husband John have a chance at reconciliation if they'll work at it."

Paul jotted another note on his yellow pad. "Any contact with Al's wife?"

I waited until he looked up. "Yes. She continues to see me although it's not mandated in Al's will. Rose appears fine emotionally despite another scare when Lorraine and Aaron's dog was shot. She's disturbed there's no closure regarding her husband's murderer, but that's another story. She's had to deal with a lot of pain from Al's previous behavior but worked through most of it after her cancer diagnosis."

"Good."

"Summing up, I can say Crystal, John, Aaron, and Lorraine have rooted out most of their extreme bitterness toward Al and have a clear understanding of what's needed for complete forgiveness."

I paused for breath.

Paul sat back.

"You did a nice job with Debold and Tuler. They were surprised but receptive to cashing their checks. Each claims no hard feelings, which is huge. Debold was plenty angry before he knew the money was coming. Al's partner objected but then owning all of American Realty Investment is a nice bone for Halston to lick," Paul pointed out.

"Despite legitimate gripes, I think Halston honestly liked Al."

Jacobsen added, "Anything else?"

"Did I mention Rich, Aaron's investment partner, and friend had hate issues that he claims aren't a big deal? Rich disliked Al personally but hadn't suffered any losses from Al's advice."

"That's it, then. Your counseling has been impeccable. You've helped clear suicide from Al's name and initiated healing in his family."

"I hope so."

Paul closed his folder. "You haven't had any more threats, have you?"

"No. I expect after today the murderer won't consider me a danger. I'll still make discreet inquiries regarding Albert's killing, but nothing overt."

"Good."

"I do notice my voice no longer trembles when I speak about the threats. Thank the Lord."

"Anything else, off the record?"

"Truly the consequences of Al's behavior may continue to impact his family. Emotional healing can be a lifetime process. But in each person, I can identify solid signs of progress. One more session with Aaron this afternoon and I'm done. I wish I could feel more excited. On a personal note, I'm disappointed, I was hoping to find a clue to Al's murderer."

Paul became momentarily pensive. "I understand. OK. It's a wrap up."

I collected my progress notes and stuck them into their folder "Seriously, I'd be totally happy, except there's still a killer on the loose."

"Be careful." Paul's gaze radiated concern.

51

Experiencing a huge wave of release, I hurried from the parking lot to my temporary office. *Al, I tried my best. I hope it was good enough.*

My relaxed attitude lasted as far as my office, where I did a double take. Rose Windemere sat primly in the common reception hall outside my office suite.

What was she doing here? Had I forgotten an appointment?

"Hello, Rose," I said. "Give me a minute to unlock the door." I flicked on the lights while combing my brain. Had she scheduled a crisis visit? Ellen had taken the morning off. Rose couldn't have reached her to schedule it.

I hadn't talked with Rose since the incident with Ann Tylore. I'd e-mailed her what I hoped was a note of explanation. This raced through my head in the seconds it took me to escort Rose in.

She must have seen my perplexed look. "No, Jennifer, I'm not scheduled. This won't take much time. Are you free?"

"It's my prep time before my next clients, but I can spare a few minutes."

Rose looked lovely in a navy cardigan atop a green and black pleated skirt, clutching a navy purse and notebook tucked under her arm.

"Thank you." She perched on the sofa and extended a spiral bound notebook toward me. "I want to show you what I found last night." Her eyes lit up as if she were transferring a first edition off Gutenberg's press.

The words Prayer Journal were handwritten in black marker on the front cover.

"Where did this come from?"

"Tucked in a bookcase in our den. It's Al's handwriting."

I flipped through pages while Rose eyed me. "You're sure it's his?"

"Absolutely." She nodded and pointed to the top of a turned-back page. "See the entry dated the day before his death."

I read aloud: "Dear Lord, I wish Crystal could believe I love her. I know I've hurt her emotionally. Jesus, please make her whole. Nothing is impossible with you." Verses about faith followed. A little further down I read, "Lord, I'm not afraid of the future. Events are happening just as your Word says."

"Certainly, these aren't the words of a man planning suicide." I looked up. "Not that you or I had any doubt."

"Right. Rose sounded almost jubilant. She pointed to the bottom of the last page. "Look at this."

I read Al's sprawling, felt-tipped script with a sense of reverence. "Tomorrow, I'm going to settle with him. He insists on seeing me alone. I agreed to the golf course. I'd prefer having this out in the open, but if privacy will help him, I'm willing. Lord, help me do the right thing."

My excitement mounted. "Rose, it appears the killer may have been this man Al was meeting."

Rose leaned back and nodded. "It has to be Harold Halston. He was at Pine Mountain. Al must have agreed to a private settlement severing their business relationship."

"It does seem to point to Halston and fits with the torn note found in Al's pocket. Al could have sent it referring to their business relationship no longer going on. Halston tore off the bottom and planted it on Al to make the death look like suicide. Have you looked through the journal and found other references to Halston?"

"I haven't gone through all of it yet. I'm on my way to the police station but popped in. Your office is on the way, and I wanted you to see it."

"I'm glad you did. May I make a copy of this page?"

"Certainly." Rose followed me to the copy machine. "I can't tell you how relieved I am. Now, surely, the police can't suspect Crystal, and she won't be so tense and harsh. This murder investigation has had us both on edge."

"I can only imagine." I returned the notebook to her waiting hands. I wasn't confident Crystal's sweetness could ever be 100 percent, but I understood a mother's love.

Rose clapped her hands solemnly. "Now, finally, we know."

The message in the journal haunted me through the day and was forefront in my mind as I prepared for Aaron's 3:00 PM appointment.

52

Aaron sauntered in a few minutes early for our session. I inhaled a draft of his after-shave, diffused through the air by my over-head fan. With a nonchalant air better than the rage of his previous visit, he situated himself in a wingback chair.

I noticed he'd jelled the sides of his sandy-colored hair that had outgrown its banker's cut. Puffy eyelids dominated his face. Not enough sleep lately?

I leaned against my padded chair cushion. Might as well be physically comfortable at least. Thus far our sessions only penetrated his emotions at surface level. *Give me wisdom, Lord, to help him go deeper where healing happens.*

"Aaron, thanks for coming. I pray our time will be productive today. Let's get started."

He lifted his hands then turned them over in an empty gesture. "We already discussed the primary concern — bitterness toward Al. That was improving even before he died."

"Tell me more about it."

Aaron lifted his shoulders. "Al started treating me differently. When we were kids he was a super athlete, and my father and mother fussed over him non-stop. Al teased me mercilessly. Plus, I was made fun of by Dad for my interests. I disliked sports, so Dad shut me out."

"What are some of your earliest memories?"

"For starters, wanting to go to the art museum and my dad ridiculing me. He also hated that I enjoyed working in the garden with my mom."

"That must have been hurtful."

"I didn't mind the mocking as much as being ignored."

Aaron's left eye twitched whenever he mentioned his dad. I forced myself not to stare. "How painful."

"Every night, the dinner conversation was about sports. My dad and Al replayed every game, all that crap." Aaron's voice grew louder. "We weren't well off, but Al always got whatever he wanted: uniforms, lessons, and equipment. When I asked for music CDs or art supplies, we couldn't afford it. I got nothing. Al never missed a chance to shove the favoritism in my face."

"I'm sorry. Often parents don't realize they can create deep animosity in siblings."

Mental threads of emotional neglect from my self-focused, alcoholic parents dangled before me and made me hurt even more for Aaron. I flicked them away.

Aaron exhaled deeply. "As adults, Al and I kept our distance. He ordered flowers from my business, and I bought some investments from him. That was the extent of our contact."

"But you said your relationship had begun to improve. How?"

The air in my office seemed to hush.

"When Al had a change of heart, some kind of religious conversion. I told him, 'Good, you needed it.' He'd drop by the shop from time to time to visit. I expected this change would be short-lived, but Al kept it up. Eventually we talked about the possibility of my changing, too." Aaron made eye contact briefly.

"For example?"

Aaron fixated on a point behind me, as if seeing images on a screen. "Al said as a kid he never noticed how hurt I was. Said I should have spoken up instead of turning inward. I knew he was right, but I hate confrontation. He thought maybe I was doing this now with Lorraine. Hey, he used jargon he probably learned from you."

"Specifically?"

"I shut down if Lorraine did something I didn't like rather than dealing with it. Al meant well. I got that he cared about me."

Aaron spoke softly; I could barely hear and leaned forward.

"Fact is, I liked his concern." He paused and smiled. "I lost some of the anger I had for years. That felt good."

I caught a glimpse of this. It lasted a split second, flickering through memories.

"And the bitterness?"

"We were working on that. If Al hadn't gotten killed, maybe we . . . well, things could have been different."

"With Al's peace as a new Christian, why did you think Al could have committed suicide?"

"I didn't really. Rich suggested I agree with that, so I wouldn't be a suspect since a lot of people knew about our past animosity." Aaron drummed his fingertips on his chair. As a florist, the man probably rarely kept his hands still.

"Interesting, your relationship with Rich. Do you always take his advice?"

"He's the best friend I've ever had."

"Moving on, Aaron. It sounds like you reconciled a lot of your anger. How about your wife? Was she angry with Al, too, because of your past? Did she encourage your forgiveness?"

"This session between us needn't involve Lorraine," Aaron sputtered. A white string of saliva formed in the corner of his mouth.

I'd touched a nerve. Was he trying to keep Lorraine safe because he believed she'd arranged Al's murder?

"Your marriage relationship is important also. One bad relationship can affect others. You said Al noticed a problem?"

He glared at me. "What goes on between me and my wife had nothing to do with Al!"

Aaron shot me a look I bet he'd never show the garden club ladies. "We had struggles. Al knew."

"Perhaps I can be of help. Communication difficulties, sexual problems? Had you shut her out from emotional and physical intimacy? Al arranged this counseling so you could have the opportunity to be emotionally healthy in every way."

Aaron didn't respond.

"Whatever the problem, together perhaps we can figure out a treatment plan. Whether you move forward with future counseling will be up to you."

His shoulders slumped. "OK, you're a counselor. You should understand." Aaron looked around the room, as if checking for an eavesdropper. "What I tell you stays here?"

"Totally confidential unless it's relevant to Al's murder."

"It isn't." Aaron crossed his legs. "I care about my wife and don't want her hurt, but she's not . . . I mean . . . well she hasn't satisfied me sexually for some time, since . . ." He floundered and sighed loudly.

"Go on."

"One night, after she and I had a blowup, a friend — I'm not going to name him — well, he and I went drinking. I had a few more than I could handle." Aaron stared at his hands averting his eyes from mine. "Instead of going home, I went to my buddy's place to sleep it off. He started fooling around sexually." Aaron looked up self-consciously.

"Go on."

"I was two sheets to the wind, but I liked how I felt until the next day when I was ashamed and embarrassed. I told him no more. Next thing I knew, well, being together became a habit." Aaron paused and looked down at his loafers. "Maybe it's how I was born. I always felt a bit different."

"Actually, research has never identified a genetic basis, although many studies have tried to find one. It is true some people have more male or female physical characteristics than others." I held my gaze steady, as if I discussed this sort of thing daily. I didn't.

"Anyway, after every incident I'd say, 'That's it.' Yet when the opportunity came up, I didn't refuse. I felt an attraction to him and concluded maybe I'm bisexual. Truth is, I've never been totally comfortable. Inside I have this sense of guilt but it's becoming less. Am I being old-fashioned? Is this stuff OK now?" Aaron squirmed in his chair. "I call myself a Christian, but I'm not a regular churchgoer. I don't read the Bible. I'm not sure."

"It's possible to deaden your conscience even though subconsciously you still believe this isn't right. Christians know that homosexual behavior is morally wrong based on biblical teaching — the practice, not the temptations — but committed Christians reject these temptations, no matter how often they recur, and discipline themselves with God's grace not to act out.

"Often underlying psychological issues must be resolved also."

"That's what I don't get. If it's not genetics, why are men attractive to me?"

"There's no single answer to that, but I can explain some possibilities. Stop me if I'm giving you more information than you want."

"No, I'd like to hear all sides on this. I only know what I experienced."

"For some, the homosexual lifestyle may be an easy out. In your case, you don't have to deal with feelings of inadequacy and the shame your father made you feel because of your artistic interests or because your brother was so popular and successful in school. Feelings of inferiority and insecurity get buried when acting out feelings of lust."

"That's all?"

"No. Actually a lot of other factors can impact this. Most common cause is confusion of sexual identity, stemming from a poor relationship with the same sex parent. Emotional abandonment, lack of attachment at a critical stage of sexual identity development, extensive physical absence of the same-sex parent, exposure to pornography. Also when a heterosexual relationship doesn't work out, it's easy to get caught up in homosexuality while seeking a sense of worth."

"Guess I'm a perfect candidate then?"

"Unfortunately, yes. Studies have confirmed other causes — some more traumatizing. Like being sexually violated during childhood."

"I didn't experience that, but I sure had rejection from my dad." Aaron smacked his fist into his palm. "Until this stuff happened with" — he caught himself before saying the name — "I thought I was OK in my marriage. Now I'm conflicted. I don't know what to do."

"I'm sorry that this is creating such confusion and anxiety for you. It's helpful to remember you have a perfect Father in heaven Who loves you unconditionally and always has. You can invite Jesus through the power of the Holy Spirit to heal any damaged emotions from your past. He can clear up your confusion and ease your anxiety. Your homosexual leanings can be dealt with openly and honestly. With counseling and prayer, a life of abstinence or a heterosexual God-honoring lifestyle is possible. The choice is yours."

Aaron stared at his hands several seconds before looking up. "Al knew about my homosexuality."

"You told him?"

"Of course not. Maybe my brother saw this person and me out somewhere. He bugged me all the time to stop. On the other hand, my partner wants me to 'come out.' I worry this could hurt business, but mostly, I don't want my wife hurt. Still, I hate being deceptive. I don't want to lose her or him either."

"Just so you know, male friendship can be a deep, healthy bond. An attraction to a person of the same sex is fine, without acting out sexually. It's possible to maintain a non-sexual close friendship. Living a homosexual lifestyle isn't inevitable. Back to Al. How did you respond?"

"Told him it was none of his business. He wouldn't let up, though. Bought me books, got me pamphlets, support group info, you name it. Mostly, I threw the stuff away. My buddy saw some and was furious with Al's interference."

My heart skipped a beat. "So that's what Al meant when he said you were involved in something dangerous. He'd be worried for you physically and morally. That makes sense. I'm hearing you say this is enormously difficult emotionally. How about physically? Have you been tested for HIV? What about hepatitis?"

"I'm careful. No worries."

I sighed. "There's no such thing as 100 percent safety, Aaron, no matter how careful you are. I suggest you get checked."

"You sound like Al trying to scare me."

421

"I want you to be fully informed. That's all."

"To me, it seemed like Al wanted to wreck the life I'd built for myself." Aaron's tone hardened. "He suggested I seek counseling and get my buddy out of the business. Bossing me like when we were kids."

Business? Rich Nichols? Did Aaron realize he'd let this slip?

Aaron's hands flailed in the air. "Why, all of a sudden, did Al care? You don't know what a rat Al used to be growing up. Often times, I wished him dead." Aaron reddened, popped off his chair, and paced around the room.

I shuddered. Logic told me this emotional outburst meant Aaron still had deep anger and hurt. Had he killed Al? I exhaled heavily. Or had Rich killed Al to protect the anonymity of his and Aaron's relationship?

Aaron slumped onto the chair. "The literature got me thinking maybe homosexuality wasn't right. Plus, I never wanted to hurt Lorraine." Aaron lifted his head and looked at me. "She's a good person, sweet. I truly care for her. Sometimes I feel sliced in two." He fiddled nervously with a button on his shirt.

"Because you still have feelings for her," I said softly, "and she for you. Your marriage could be renewed. You'd have to be honest with her. Sadly, when you were young, your manhood wasn't affirmed in your relationship with the important people in your life, your mom, dad, brother. Working through that will improve your relationship with Lorraine."

"She has no clue. I always gave a reasonable excuse for every absence." He sighed.

"Except yesterday?"

"How'd you know?"

"She called me."

"It's the first time I went off without covering myself with a solid excuse. I knew I was coming here today, and I needed to think."

"At some level, maybe you wished she'd find out. Why not discuss this with her?"

Aaron shook his head. "I doubt she'd want me if she knew." He looked forlorn.

"You can't know Lorraine's reaction. I've seen amazing things happen when secrets are out. People get free, really free, Aaron."

He gave me a quick sideways glance, shifted his legs, and managed a weak smile.

"Please consider what I've said, and pray for wisdom. I'll pray for you, also. If you decide you're interested, I can refer you to a homosexual support group and to a counselor who specializes in this area.

People leave this lifestyle all the time. You can, too, if you truly want to."

"Don't count on it."

"I leave outcomes to God. Remember I'm available after our sessions to help you work on your marriage or this if you choose, or I can make a referral."

"I'll think about."

"Good. As for the estate counseling requirements, we're finished. You said you no longer harbor ill will toward Al. Your discharge papers have been given to Al's lawyer."

"Thanks." He held out his hand. I prayed for him as I looked into his troubled eyes.

After Aaron left, I swiveled to my desk and closed my eyes. This man had emotions like a yo-yo. He could be capable of murder. So why did I believe he was innocent?

Halston was the man with the most to gain, and Al's journal seemed to indicate Halston was Al's murderer.

53

The minute Aaron left, Ellen strode into my office, her cheeks red. "Rose Windemere called for you. I told her you were with a client, and she gave me a message. The police picked up Halston and charged him." Ellen dropped her notepad on my desk and pressed her hands together. "I can't believe I was wrong about Aaron. I was sure he did it."

Ellen picked up her pad and read from her notes. "Rose said Halston admitted he was at the Dells the morning of Al Windemere's murder, and he may have exaggerated the story about John Vandley's death threat to Al. He got scared when he learned he was a prime suspect but is denying the murder. The police say it's just a matter of time until Halston confesses. Since he lied about John Vandley, it's a sure sign of guilt."

"Rose must be relieved. I'm sad for Halston's assistant, Angela. She's lost the two men she respected and, in her way, loved. Any other messages?"

Ellen picked up her pad. "Rich Nichols telephoned. He'd like a callback ASAP." She handed me a yellow message slip with his number.

I dismissed her and returned Rich's call.

"Jennifer, I'm sure you're busy. Me, too. I'll get right to the point. The furniture you chose is pulled out on the floor, refinished and ready. You need to approve it before delivery. One dresser didn't turn out as well as I'd hoped. I want to make a substitution. Can you stop by tonight to approve it? The warehouse is on your route home."

I pulled up my calendar. "How late will you be there?"

"Until nine thirty at least. I'm buried in paperwork."

My last appointment was at seven. Nick had a meeting and wouldn't miss me. "OK, I'll be there depending on the time I finish, maybe around eight-thirty. I can't say exactly. What's the address?"

"We're located at 701 Sand Mount, building's last one on the right."

Only a few minutes. I could manage that.

At eight twenty I was on my way.

The smell of rain hung in the air like a

piñata awaiting one last strike to send its innards plummeting. I hoped it stayed in suspension until I got home. Driving through a downpour wasn't one of my favorite things.

A block later the sky turned totally black. Torrents of rain started a drumbeat on my windshield. My car crept like a turtle, and I struggled to see the road. The overworked windshield wipers kept a steady beat.

I located 701 Sand Mount at the end of the industrial park. An enormous metal building loomed in front of deep woods edging the entire rear of the property. A lone car in the lot, a Ford Bronco, must be the alternative to Rich's sports car.

I pulled my fold-up plastic rain poncho from the glove compartment, ready for any emergency like a good Girl Scout. I squirmed around in the driver seat to pull my head through the neck opening and draped the thin plastic over my shoulders. With the hood up, I probably resembled a plastic-covered crow.

Steeling myself, I made a run for the entrance about twenty feet away and reached the front door arched with a line of fluorescent light.

To my dismay, it was locked. I pounded, but no one came.

Peering quickly left and right from under my floppy hood, I noticed a side door, waddled over through quickly forming puddles, and gave a frantic tug. It swung open to reveal total darkness except for a slight illumination at the far end of a long corridor.

"Rich?" I entered.

I waited. The only answer being the sound of rain hammering the metal roof.

I slid my hand along the wall and hunted for a light switch. Nothing. Must be a central control panel. Rich could at least have left lights on. I called his name again and yet again, louder each time.

My dripping, rustling poncho sounded like a rampaging buffalo in the echoing hall. I used the flashlight on my phone and inched my way to the end of the corridor. It led not to an office as I expected, but the huge main storage building. Rich must be back there.

I finally found a light switch on my right. Nothing happened when I flicked it. Had the storm caused a power outage in the area? Unless Rich had a secondary power source or good flashlights this would be a wasted trip.

My vision gradually adjusted to the semi-darkness. The exit signs, probably on a generator, provided dim light. "Rich!" I yelled again.

Still no answer. Had he left? If so, he'd forgotten to lock the side door. I checked the time on my phone; he'd said he'd stay until nine thirty. Someone should be here with the Bronco outside.

Squinting, I made out two doors about fifty feet from where I stood.

Rows of furniture stood between the back wall and me. Individual pieces draped with green upholstery covers and dingy looking thick white cloths formed uneven rows like an army of ill-clad, untrained recruits. Dresser legs, armoires, chests, and library tables produced ghost-like forms. Each piece, probably beautiful in the daylight, seemed an eerie shrouded hulk.

I wished I'd never come.

54

I heard a muffled voice come from the far end of the cavernous space. "Jennifer, in the back."

"Rich?" I plunged ahead through rows of furniture, wooden fireplace mantels, and arches twice as tall as me. A memory surfaced of when I was six. Our family had stopped at a roadside farm to pick raspberries. I wandered into an adjacent cornfield, became disoriented, and lost. I could hear people calling me in the distance. I kept trying to find my way out but couldn't. Winding through row after row of giant corn stalks, I panicked. Surely, I'd be lost forever. Finally, a stranger found me, lifted me up, and carried me out.

I shivered. Raindrops splattered off my poncho to the floor. "Stop spooking yourself," I scolded myself aloud. "You're not afraid of the dark. Settle your business and leave."

I wove snakelike in and out among the narrow aisles in the direction of Rich's voice. The building extended for what seemed a mile. I intended to check this furniture fast.

The muffled voice called my name again. Now I was deep into the warehouse. I walked boldly forward.

Suddenly, Rich emerged from behind a huge armoire.

I jumped. Fear exploded through my body. "Rich, if you wanted to scare me, you succeeded."

He grinned. "I'm glad the weather didn't keep you away." His voice chilled me. In his right hand, he held a liquor flask. Almost six feet tall, Rich loomed over me like a giant monster, and he reeked of alcohol. He slowly drew a gun from his pocket.

"What's with the gun?" What a dumb question. I was unnerved. How many times had I been face-to-face with a revolver? "Put that away before you hurt someone."

"I've waited a long time for you."

"I'm leaving." My voice shook. I thought of the gun in my glove compartment. Who would have expected to need a gun to select furniture? Dare I turn my back on him?

Rich stepped in front of me, blocking my way. His voice was without inflection. "Jennifer, you shouldn't have gotten involved. You ignored my messages."

I froze. "Your messages. The notes and call were from you!" My knees turned to rubber.

"Yes. I'd hoped to scare you off. I hated your snooping around. Checking into the family affairs. Unfortunately, you're a stubborn woman." He waved the gun in the air.

"You made the attack on Rose?"

"I never did anything to her or the dog." Rich eyed me through a stupor. "I slipped around behind you and locked the door you came in. Clever, aren't I?"

"More like diabolical." I mustered all the indignation I could through quivering lips. I had no idea where another exit was. My legs wobbled. I could scarcely make them move.

I inched backward along the row in which I stood.

"I turned off the only light in the entrance area to have a private conversation, just like I had with Al on the golf course."

All breath left my body. Queasiness spread through my stomach. I reached for the edge of a tabletop to steady myself. He'd killed Al and was having this conversation with me because he never intended for me to live to repeat it.

My hands trembled violently. One primordial goal surfaced: to prolong my life. I visualized my children mourning me, sobbing. I wanted to grow old with my husband. *Lord, I love him so much.* I gasped involuntarily. "Why?"

"Al kept wanting Aaron to end our relationship. Just when I'd almost convinced Aaron to be comfortable with our relationship, his brother waltzed into his life with religious propaganda about God's best plan, sin, and redemption. He wouldn't stop badgering Aaron who already questioned our ties."

I willed my mind to think of questions to ask while my gaze darted about, seeking a way to escape.

"And the fire?"

"Not me."

"My children's accident?"

"I didn't even know you had children. It was probably just road rage."

"But you killed Al to end his influence?" I heard the fear in my voice.

"Kill Al? No way! I admit I didn't like him trying to draw Aaron's affections away from me, but I'm not a murderer."

I gasped and pointed at the gun. "That suggests otherwise."

"Listen; that's all I ask. I owned several profitable real estate investments. I was having financial problems and needed money fast to pay gambling debts that I didn't want Aaron to know about. I asked Al to buy me out. We discussed a settlement. Al was willing to help. One less connection between me and his brother.

"How did you end up at the golf course? Why there?"

"My idea. I wanted a private cash transaction and didn't want it done at the florist or Al's office. I knew the family was going to the Dells, and Al would play golf. I insisted this had to be done privately because Aaron would have been upset with me."

"You truly cared about Aaron?"

"Very much. Still do."

"What made Al willing to go along?"

"He'd always been kind to me. He offered a chunk of cash, more than what they were worth, and brought an addendum paper for me to sign, hoping I'd be willing to end my relationship with his brother. "No more contact . . ." Rich smiled. "I knew Al wanted to see the last of me." Rich used the barrel of the gun to scratch his cheek. "No way would I sign that. I understood his trying though."

I widened my eyes. "You took his money and then shot him so you could continue your relationship with Aaron and have the cash and condo investment, too?"

"No!" Rich's menacing tone made shivers crawl up my arms. "You're not listening. I took the money because I had gambling debts to pay off. I didn't want to jeopardize my relationship with Aaron. He thought I'd quit gambling."

I continued to inch forward. "If you didn't kill Al, who did?"

"When I walked off the course, Al was alive. I was devastated. The only explanation was Aaron had followed me and killed his brother. I knew how much he hated Al. I was scared to death you'd figure it out."

"You're saying I became a problem because I might connect the dots through counseling Aaron and find out he killed his brother?"

"That's why I tried to frighten you off." Rich's body radiated coldness. He wiggled the gun in my face to accentuate his words.

"You still think Aaron killed Al?"

"I started to wonder if I was wrong when Aaron seemed genuinely upset about losing his brother."

"Then who killed Al? Was another person with him the morning he died?"

"Someone could have been hiding near the green or on the cart with him. I never saw the golf cart. Al parked at the green and walked into the woods behind the green. At one point, I even wondered if you killed Al when I found out you were at the resort at the time, but I couldn't come up with a motive for you unless he'd had an affair with you and dropped you, and you were getting even. The more I knew about you the unlikelier that seemed."

I pointed to the gun. "Why do this to me now?"

"When Aaron came back to the shop today after your session I saw more literature about joining a recovery group. I'm sick of your interference in the whole business. I want you to stop for good. If Al hadn't made that stupid will provision, you wouldn't be messing with Aaron and me."

I thought of Nick. Would he check on me? It would be hours because he'd assume a crisis with a client had come up, and I'd been delayed.

"I admit I'm a lousy drunk — this was an impulsive idea. I came here, started drinking and then got angrier and decided to teach you a lesson you'd never forget."

We were close to an exit sign now. Perhaps pressing on the door would set off an alarm.

"I'm no longer a threat. I'm through counseling Aaron."

"You'll always be in the picture, available

whenever his doubts pop up."

"So you intend to kill me?"

He twirled the gun. "Isn't it cozy being here just the two of us inside locked doors so we can really talk. I have you all alone. Can I trust you not to tell the police any of this? I don't want them to think I shot Al."

I took a deep breath. Lord, please help me. Rich is going to kill me and no one will know. "How did you get onto the course?"

"Easy." Rich drained the flask and shoved it in his pocket. "I parked my car two blocks away and entered through a yard that backed onto the course. I knew no one would be around early on a Sunday. I waited behind the green as prearranged."

"Go on," I urged.

"Al had the document for me to sign, handwritten so his secretary didn't see it. The last sentence read, 'The terms for this buy-out are that the business and personal relationship between Rich Nichols and Aaron Windemere will no longer continue. He'd already signed it, but as I said, I refused to sign. I don't think he was surprised. I knew he'd still honor the financial agreement regarding the property sale."

Rich laughed, not the folksy, wholesome laugh I'd heard in the store, but a sinister drunken sound.

"Then what?"

"That's all I know. I left first. He said he'd wait a few minutes behind the green like he was looking for lost golf balls to give me a head start. I didn't want us to be seen together. Then he'd play his round of golf. I think someone shot him and ripped off the rest of the note."

The sound of a door opening gave me hope until I saw by the dim light of the exit signs who entered. All hope evaporated.

I willed myself not to pass out.

55

Aaron had entered the building.

A chill shot down my spine. Aaron's in on this, too! They're going to kill me together!

"Rich, where are you?" he called out.

Lord, help me. Was I about to experience my own murder? Or was Rich just toying with me to finally frighten me off?

Rich jerked me backward toward the direction we'd come. Then, with a surge of strength, he shoved me to the concrete floor. I scraped my knee on something sharp and cried out, but Rich clamped his fingers vise-like over my mouth and squeezed my cheek-bones.

I tried to squirm away, but Rich pressed his entire body over mine. Rolling my head sideways, I saw his wide, drunken eyes before he pinned me.

I thrashed, trying to make noise but couldn't get free. I tried to think. Why was Rich hiding me? Evidently, Aaron's arrival wasn't part of his plan.

Aaron's footsteps drew closer. A flashlight beam began its search. Maybe Aaron had heard my muffled scream.

My arms were useless, but I could move my fingers. I wiggled and stretched them to reach the corner of a fabric dragging on the floor covering a piece of furniture. Pinching one edge in my fingers, I worked it between my thumb and forefinger then wiggled my fingers to push the fabric back into my palm.

When I had a secure grip, I tugged as hard as I could. A metal pitcher atop clattered to the concrete floor and rolled along noisily until it hit a dresser. Aaron raced toward the noise. Rich scuffled with me pulling me back along the row of furniture.

"Rich!" Aaron yelled.

"Leave, Aaron. Now!" Rich insisted.

"No, Rich. Listen."

Rich tightened his grip on my arms.

I twisted my head despite the pain searing my neck. "Help me. He's got a gun."

"Don't hurt her, Rich." Aaron's voice was shaky but insistent as he eyed the gun. He edged closer. "Al's murder was enough." His voice was begging now.

"What are you talking about? I didn't kill your brother. I thought you did. I'd never do that." Rich laced his words with anger.

Aaron inched slowly, steadily, toward us. "It's over, Rich. I'm calling the police. I'll get you the best lawyer I can. I promise. I suspected you from the start. I realized you did it for me."

"Did what? I only tried to keep Jennifer off your trail by scaring her off with a little fire." Rich turned toward me, "I'm sorry, I never intended for that to do so much harm."

Rich sobered up fast. He pushed me out in front of him and approached Aaron. "I'm just messing with Jennifer to get her to stay out of my life and yours. I didn't kill anyone. This is an antique gun. It can't fire, and it's not loaded."

"Then what's going on?" Aaron looked from one to the other of us, clearly bewildered.

I jumped to my feet, scowled, and brushed myself off. "If you don't want me to press charges, tell him everything," I ordered Rich. "Right now."

Rich summarized his meeting with Al.

Aaron listened in silence. His face turned white. "How could you think I'd kill my brother? What do you take me for?"

To his credit, Rich told the truth. He'd had drunken frustration and poor judgment in threatening me, but he wasn't a murderer. The fear and revulsion I felt turned to pity.

My stalker was Rich, and the threats from him were so I wouldn't discover his relationship with Aaron and identify Aaron as Al's killer. I doubted their relationship would survive this.

"Rich," I said, "I won't press charges about the gun with certain conditions: you'll join support groups like AA and encourage Aaron in whatever decision he chooses about his future."

We talked it through for another half hour. Rich became more and more chagrined and extremely apologetic as he sobered.

Afterward, I sat in my car too exhausted to move. If not Rich, who killed Al?

What other person could have been there the morning Al died? Someone he trusted implicitly not to reveal his secret rendezvous with Rich.

Yes!

I pounded the steering wheel. *I think I know who killed Al.* I started my car reenergized.

56

Impulsively, I sped into town. Before I got out of my car, I stuck my gun in my waistband and pulled my sweater over it.

Rose opened her door on my second knock. "Jennifer, what a surprise." She held the door half-open but didn't invite me in.

I brushed past her into the foyer and turned to face her.

"Humor me, Rose. I've been wondering about something. What time did you wake up the morning Al was shot?"

She stared at me with amazing composure. "Why?" Coldness edged her voice.

"Al told you he was going to the golf course, didn't he?" My attention riveted on her face. "Maybe even invited you to ride along?"

"What if he did?"

"You knew about Rich and the buy-out arrangement, didn't you?"

"How ridiculous. You're distressing me. I

need my pills." Rose reached for her purse hanging on a hook next to the door. Instead of medicine, she pulled out a gun and aimed it steadily at me. "Your murder, Jennifer, will be unfortunate but not unexpected. We can settle this tonight."

"You killed Al. Why?" I was stunned and had to know.

"Finally it comes out. I wondered if this day would ever come. I put up with his self-centeredness and the humiliation of his affairs all during our marriage. He treated me terribly and then thought he could just wave it away with religious hocus-pocus. Well, it wasn't that easy. I refused to forgive the pain and embarrassment he caused me. I pretended rather well, don't you think? Finally, my chance came to even the score."

Her hatred pierced my heart. "Why not simply divorce him?"

She waved her hand around the lovely living room of her estate home. "I paid a high price for this. I wasn't about to give up the lifestyle I enjoyed as his wife. I've seen enough divorcées living in near poverty."

"But murder?"

"You may have liked the change in Al. I didn't. He began giving our money away to every charity that asked. He told me he wanted to die poor and dispose of our fortune. After all I put up with, he expected me to change my lifestyle, live like a pauper, so he could do good deeds, be a generous benefactor, and make amends to soothe his conscience." Her eyes glinted.

I avoided looking at the gun. I had no doubt it was real. Could I overpower her before she shot me? Very unlikely. I needed to stall, to think. "You managed to get on the golf course. How?"

"I asked Al if I could come with him on the golf cart for a ride. I knew he was meeting with Rich Nichols. I promised to remain out of sight. Al agreed."

"Rich never saw you?"

"No. After Rich left, I approached Al on foot." Her lips formed a diabolical twist. "I said, 'Al, it's time to make things right.' I pointed the gun I'd taken from our nightstand. You should have seen his face. He couldn't believe I'd ever take revenge. Not me, gentle, passive Rose. I enjoyed watching his reaction — one of the sweetest moments of my life. He deserved to die for destroying my life and Crystal and Ken's — he drove our only son away forever. For years I dreamed about that moment. Now I had a perfect opportunity. In case you'd like to know, Albert's last word was, 'Jesus.' "

"How cruel." I tasted bile.

Rose's tone sparked with hate. "He's silent forever. No more lies."

"And the note?" I asked.

"I tore off the bottom, and left '. . . no longer continue.' Still using a handkerchief, I placed the gun in Al's hand and stuck the torn note in his pants pocket, carefully avoiding the blood. I liked playing around with the suicide theory and confusing issues by asking you to investigate Halston and telling the inspector I was afraid for my life. That way, no one would suspect me."

"Clever," I said, sick to my stomach with disgust. "How did you get back from the course?"

"Simple. I walked."

All the time she talked, I thought of my gun. How could I pull it out before she got a shot off? "No one saw you return?"

"Who would notice a woman out for a morning stroll? If they had, it wouldn't matter. I committed the perfect crime until you got too involved. I had no idea about those stupid stipulations in Al's will. I hated your counseling to remove the perpetual bitterness Al deserved. Now you must die."

"Wait! What about the dog?"

"Extremely clever, wasn't it? What better way to avert suspicion from me and implicate Aaron? I rather enjoyed the dramatic acting opportunities this afforded me. There was no man in a baseball cap at Lorraine's house. I made that up from your arson story. I shot the dog. It's been too long since I performed for an audience."

My heart raced. I opened my mouth to speak, but nothing came out. *Oh, Lord!*

Hate had poisoned Rose's personality and turned her into a killer. She actually boasted about using her theatrical skill to deceive.

Before me stood a self-centered woman, a pathological liar, and an excellent actress. I sensed my grave closing in on me. Where were the cute words that people in movies toss out glibly as they gaze into death? *Dear God, help me,* I prayed. *Don't let my life end like this.*

Rose moved closer.

"Getting away with killing me won't be easy, Rose."

We heard the sound at the same time — car tires rolling up the driveway. Through the foyer window, I saw Crystal's auto pull into the parking space next to my car. Rose moved closer to the door. I glanced downward. She stood on a small throw rug on the ceramic foyer tile, inches from me.

Rose tried to hide the gun in her hand behind her purse while keeping it aimed at me.

"Don't say a word, Jennifer, or I'll kill you, and after that your husband and children. I swear I will."

Rose looked deranged. I didn't for a minute doubt she'd try. Anxiety charged through my veins. I heard Crystal knock and then use her key to open the door. "Jennifer, I thought that was your car. Mom, what's wrong?"

"Jennifer killed your father and came here to shoot me. I've just managed to get this gun away from her."

"No, Crystal," I shouted. "Your mom was about to shoot me. Don't believe her."

Rose turned slightly to face Crystal. I dropped to the floor, grabbed the edges of the throw rug, and pulled with all my might causing Rose to lose balance and stumble backward to the floor. Her purse slid across the tile but her fingers still clutched the gun.

Crystal ran outside. Through the open door, I heard her yelling into her cell phone.

Rose raised the gun and swung her arm in my direction to take aim. I kicked at the gun catching only her wrist. A second kick knocked it from Rose's hand.

The gun slid across the tile floor. I lunged for it while reaching into my waistband for my revolver. Rose tackled my feet. For her age, she was remarkably strong. We struggled and rolled over straining to reach a gun first.

Rose's proximity gave her the advantage. Seconds later, she came to a sitting position and faced me with the gun pointed at my chest. Gasping for breath, eyes black, a frantic look across her face.

She had a clear shot. "You ruined everything. I never wanted Crystal or anyone else to know!" Suddenly she turned the gun away from me and toward herself.

"No, Rose!" I screamed. "It doesn't have to end like this."

Sirens sounded. Rose placed the barrel in her mouth and squeezed the trigger. The gunshot reverberated as her body went limp.

Stunned, afraid I'd vomit if I tried to stand, I laid my head on the floor and wept.

Lord, have mercy on her soul.

EPILOGUE

The next morning, I completed the police report with Nick's help. I wasn't completely coherent until then. Having a woman die within three feet of me does not contribute to an orderly state of mind.

I returned to work two days later. Ellen bombarded me with questions I answered as best I could.

"The poor woman driven by pride and bitterness, couldn't forgive her husband. She'd successfully fooled everyone about Al's murder, but could never have explained away my death. Her reputation would have been ruined. Plus, Rose truly cared for Crystal and didn't want to put another emotional burden on her daughter. Foolishly, she thought her suicide wouldn't."

"How sad."

I nodded. "Rose had allowed her mind and soul to be poisoned by resentment and self-pity. She'd fully expected to get away with murder and maintain her lifestyle as long as she lived. When Rose saw Crystal arrive at her house, she knew avoiding exposure was hopeless."

Ellen shook her head. "Was Rose really physically ill?"

"Rose's oncologist said she'd blamed her cancer on Al. Her first bout was real, the second a sham she used to arouse more sympathy and draw suspicion away."

"The same reason she killed Lorraine's dog?"

"Yes, conveniently with no witnesses."

Ellen looked aghast. She owned two collies. "How could anyone shoot a dog?"

"According to Lorraine, Rose never liked animals."

Aaron looked ten pounds lighter the next time I saw him. He and Lorraine scheduled marital therapy with me. Al's former pastor offered a six-week marriage seminar at his church, which they also attended. Fine by me, whatever works. Last I heard, Aaron had joined a homosexual support group and helped several other men switch to a heterosexual lifestyle.

Rich moved to Miami and started his own floral business with his investment payout from Al.

Crystal and John are dating seriously. Crystal's not making any commitment. She's calling this a test, but I'd say their remarriage is a given. If I'm right, John says that they'll marry in six months and be off to see the world with her inheritance financing the trip, to Al's heavenly delight, I'm sure.

Al's son Ken was located living a secluded life in Grand Bay, Canouan, a teeny Caribbean island in the archipelago of St. Vincent and the Grenadines. Working as a scuba diving instructor, and loving his simple life, he refused to be burdened by wealth. He declined counseling and instead donated his inheritance to a foundation for saving the whales.

If only Rose had been able to find her way to Christ instead of allowing all the hurt and resentment to dominate her.

As for me, I'm still playing catch-up with my schedule. Another vacation would be awesome, but our children are home. I'm a full-time mom, wife and counselor again and loving every minute.

ABOUT THE AUTHOR

Dr. Judith Rolfs is a licensed professional counselor who initially wrote "How-To" non-fiction books to help people heal broken relationships and get healthy. She discovered clients could be helped effectively by "Mysteries with a Message" based on real life which she says are a lot more fun to write.

Judith lives with her husband Wayne, also a writer, in Wisconsin and Florida.

The employees of Thorndike Press hope you have enjoyed this Large Print book. All our Thorndike, Wheeler, and Kennebec Large Print titles are designed for easy reading, and all our books are made to last. Other Thorndike Press Large Print books are available at your library, through selected bookstores, or directly from us.

For information about titles, please call:
  (800) 223-1244

or visit our website at:
  gale.com/thorndike

To share your comments, please write:
  Publisher
  Thorndike Press
  10 Water St., Suite 310
  Waterville, ME 04901